OZARK DOGS

ELI CRANOR

HEADLINE

First published in 2023 by
Soho Press, Inc.

First published in Great Britain in 2023 by
HEADLINE PUBLISHING GROUP

1

Cataloguing in Publication Data is available from the British Library

Hardback ISBN 978 1 0354 0172 7
Trade paperback ISBN 978 1 0354 0173 4

Offset in 13.11/18.25pt Sabon LT Pro by Jouve (UK), Milton Keynes

Printed and bound in Great Britain by Clays Ltd, Elcograf S.p.A.

Headline's policy is to use papers that are natural, renewable and recyclable
products and made from wood grown in well-managed forests and other
controlled sources. The logging and manufacturing processes are expected
to conform to the environmental regulations of the country of origin.

HEADLINE PUBLISHING GROUP
An Hachette UK Company
Carmelite House
50 Victoria Embankment
London EC4Y 0DZ

www.headline.co.uk
www.hachette.co.uk

*for Dad, who taught me how to write
with a bucketful of baseballs*

This was how sudden things happened that haunted forever.

—Daniel Woodrell, *Winter's Bone*

Inmate: 06-2140
Cummins Unit
P.O. Box 500
Highway 65
Grady, AR, 71644

All these letters I keep writing but I still ain't got the guts to send them. All these questions in my head. Did you think about me before you pulled the trigger? Maybe so. Maybe that's why you did what you did.

I'll never know.

I'll never know you, either. Not really. Don't matter how many letters I write, I still got to walk around this town with everybody talking about what you done. I live in the wake of your storm. Can't tell you how many people I heard around ▮▮▮▮▮▮▮▮ *say they would've done the same damn thing. But talking about it's one thing, and pulling the trigger's something different altogether. Them bullets you shot tore a hole in my life too. Ain't a day goes by I don't feel the weight of what you done.*

That little red dot's still blinking above the junkyard office door. Sometimes, when I get in real late, I close my eyes and I can see through the lens of that rickety-ass security camera, the kind that swivels side to side but only catches half the story.

I can see what it saw that night.

The tower of cars where you sat and waited, rifle in your hands, rifle to your shoulder, and then you pulled the trigger. I blink and the camera moves on, creaking as it turns to the north where the bullet found its mark and the boy fell. Eighteen years old. And that other boy, who'd just turned fifteen, ran.

Fast.

The camera don't linger. It don't remember. It just keeps going, pointing toward the jagged gash in the tree line up Highway ██. All that's left from that night. The twister that tore its way across ████████████, tossing Baptist churches and redbrick banks aside. Dollhouses in the hands of God. The funnel cloud was headed straight for the junkyard, like God knew what you were about to do, but then it stopped.

And that's the part I'll never understand. God knew. He knows everything. So why the hell did he turn that twister up Highway ██ just as the shots rang out and the one boy fell and the other ran?

Don't answer that.

And don't think about it too much, okay? If I ever decide to send this letter and it makes it past the prison mailroom and they don't black out all the good stuff, then just think on this: that camera's still out there, turning on its tracks, watching me like it watched you.

Jo

1.

The sun sank behind the ruins in ribbons of red, long
shadows running the length of the junkyard. Cars
stood in towers above the old man. He steered the front
loader as two prongs pressed down on the hood of a rusted
Crown Vic. A claw emerged and the engine block came
out clean. In the distance, a hydraulic slab crunched a Ford
truck like a beer can.

The last of the day's light caught and gleamed on a
small glass bottle in the man's breast pocket. Tucked neatly
behind the bottle was an envelope. Sounds of destruction
crackled as the man guided the Crown Vic into the crusher
atop the flattened Ford. He reached for the pocket, letting
his finger slide across the bottle's plastic lid, rough at the
edges. He took the envelope instead, black fingerprints on
white paper, eyes scanning the words:

> *Dear Joanna Fitzjurls,*
> *We are delighted to inform you that the Com-*
> *mittee on Admissions has admitted you to the*
> *University of Arkansas's class of . . .*

The letter crumpled in the old man's hands. He stood in the cab, stretched, then exited. His steps stirred small clouds from the dried red dirt. He walked up close to the crusher. Close enough to see the dark splotches marring the giant slabs. In the dying light, the oil stains reminded him of blood. With a flick of his wrist, the letter disappeared inside the deconstructed Crown Vic.

Junkyards were good for that.

Still, the old man knew nothing was ever buried in the junkyard, only lessened, reduced, then stacked high to the sky, pyramids built block by block, secrets hidden deep within their tombs.

The crusher descended again and the old man limped away. He was thick around the waist. More square than round. Thick all the way through, from his ankles to his neck with skin the color of natural leather, pale but tan. The oval nameplate on his Carhartt work shirt read, "Jeremiah."

The sun disappeared over the heap as he made it back to the office, a sheet-metal structure with concrete walls. No windows. A small patch of thorny roses grew up through the cracked earth beside the front door. Jeremiah steadied himself, the bottle quivering in his fingers.

"Drink up, Hattie," he said, pouring the brown liquid around the base of the stems, a ritual he performed every evening.

Jeremiah tucked the bottle back in a pocket of his camouflage cargo pants and opened the door. The office was more than an office but not quite a home. A fireplace. A hearth. Two chairs around a table in what could be considered a kitchen. Cellar shadows shrouded the expanse, darkening a largemouth bass that hung above the doorway. Jeremiah closed the door, tapping at an electronic keypad welded to the wall. A red light, a green light, and then a heavy clunk—the office doors locking behind him.

Music came from the depths of the office house. The trebly tenor out of place. The walls reflected the sound in eerie echoes, the thick concrete erected for protection, not acoustics. Jeremiah tiptoed his way through the living room, glancing toward the melody. In the corner, back behind the threadbare sofa, there stood another door, this one small, barely reaching his shoulders, but thick. Six inches of steel. Jeremiah ducked as he entered the vault.

Inside there were enough guns to start a war, or end one. The room was an armory, the walls lined with friends from his past: sawed-off shotguns, Glocks hanging from their trigger guards, assault rifles with bump stocks, infrared scopes, and banana clips. An M72 LAW, an anti-tank weapon, lay atop a table in the back of the room as if it were a rusty lawnmower blade, some broken part the old man had put off fixing.

Jeremiah dug in his pocket for the bottle, then placed it on a shelf. The handgun went up next. He hung the belt and the holster from a hook up high. Dangling beside the gun was a Bronze Star, a thing Uncle Sam had given Jeremiah once he'd taken everything else away. In rows beside the star stood books, shelves of them: Hemingway, Faulkner, Flannery O'Connor, even some John Grisham and Stephen King. Then there were the ancient tomes, books that held the answers: Plato's *Republic*, a few thicker volumes of Schopenhauer, a skinny paperback edition of the *Tao Te Ching*, and of course, the Bible, its spine loose and bendy—leathery—like the old man's skin. There were more books than guns. Jeremiah learned long ago a book was a weapon, and like always, he'd gone about arming himself.

There was a single picture tacked to the wall: an old man and a child, the sun setting over the tip of a distant Ozark hill. Jeremiah lingered there, eyes falling to the lone rusty rifle in the vault. The rest of the guns were clean, spotless, even the old rocket launcher. Jeremiah closed the door on his way out.

He walked briskly through the house now, free of burden, the music growing louder the deeper he went. He stopped outside the bedroom door, peering through the crack, and watched as his granddaughter mouthed the words to a song he did not know. Her room was dull despite the pinks and paisleys, the only light coming from a fluorescent tube flickering above her head. She wore shorts and a Razorback T-shirt, the University of Arkansas mascot snorting across her chest. A full-length, fancy blue dress hung long and sequined from the closet door. It had cost more than the junkyard brought in over the last two weeks. The dress sparkled as Joanna brushed layer after layer of thick pale powder onto her cheeks.

"Can't hide it, Jo," Jeremiah said, standing outside the door. "You are what you are."

Joanna glanced over her shoulder. "And what's that?"

"My granddaughter."

She smiled.

"Just think you might be overdoing it."

"Go get dressed," Jo said, leaning into the mirror. "You got to be presentable, too."

"You sure about this?"

"Who else is gonna walk me?"

Jo turned and looked at her grandfather, her face a mix-ture of everything good from both her parents: steel-blue eyes, full lips, high cheek bones, and the cutest little nose that turned up at the tip when she smiled. But try getting the good people of Taggard, Arkansas, to see beyond the girl's history, her father, or worse—her mother. Maybe tonight, Jeremiah thought, lost in those dark-blue eyes. Maybe just for tonight, they'll forget.

"You hear me?" Jo said.

Jeremiah blinked.

"You think we could call him?"

"Already running late."

"Shit, Pop."

To look at her, you'd think Jo was a saint, but the girl already had a mouth on her, and Jeremiah knew right where she'd gotten it.

"Cost an arm and a leg to make that call," Jeremiah said. "Hell, there's no guaranteeing he'll call back."

"*Pop.*"

That was all she had to say: that one word, those three letters, and Jeremiah would do just about anything. He pro-duced a blocky flip phone out of his cargo pants. He dialed the number, pressed the ancient device to his ear, and waited. Jo eyed only the phone. There was a silence behind the music. They were closer now, back to where it had all begun. The junkyard felt it too, despite the four-foot-thick weatherproof walls, despite the armory in the living room vault. These hallowed grounds had not for-gotten the storm.

"Need to leave a message for an inmate," Jeremiah said, breaking the silence. "Yeah, Thomas Fitzjurls. Tell him to call his daughter in the next thirty minutes. She's about to win Homecoming Queen."

Jo beamed and turned back to the mirror. Her hair was woven in tight braids around her head, an attempt to control her thick mane. Jeremiah knew she'd done the braids herself. A girl raised by a grandfather had to learn to do things herself: hair and makeup, cook and clean.

"You heard anything else from Tech?" Jeremiah said, sliding the phone back in his pocket.

"*Tech?*"

"I'd sure like to keep you close."

"You know I'm going to *the* University, Pop. Going up to Fayetteville," she said, pointing at the snarling tusker on her shirt. "They got the best pre-veterinary program in the state."

"I could still use some help around here. And money, we ain't even talked about the money."

He studied her reflection in the mirror. Her eyes gave nothing away, steady and focused. He knew the school would email her—he could only crush so many letters—and then summer would come and she'd be gone.

"Jo?" Jeremiah said, tugging at his lapels. "I's thinking tonight, me and you could climb up Babel and watch the stars."

"But we got the dan—" Jo cut the word short, eyeing her grandfather. "Yeah, Pop. Sure. That sounds good."

Jeremiah grinned.

"But now I got to try and squeeze my ass in that dress."

"Right," Jeremiah said and turned.

"Let me know when Dad calls."

Jeremiah closed the door behind him. He waited until he heard the security chain on the other side slide across the groove, a sturdy, secure sound, and then he limped back down the hall.

It took Jeremiah less than five minutes to shave and change into his suit. His pants were black, the blazer blue. Dangly buttons lined his cuffs like golden cicada shells. Jeremiah was unaware of anything other than his old phone, waiting for something he knew better than to wait for.

"Damn it, Jake. Call the girl back." The old man's voice hissed against the silent walls. "It's the least you could do."

He tossed the phone up, caught it, then walked back to Jo's room.

Three knocks.

Nothing.

Jeremiah knocked again and then he heard talking, low hushed tones. He knocked twice more before the security chain slid away. Jo stood before him, the dress erasing any misconceptions he'd had of her still being his little girl: tight in the hips, the curves of a woman above and below.

"Talking to somebody?" Jeremiah said.

"Humane Society. They want me to work tomorrow."

"The Saturday after Homecoming?"

"Said it's the least I could do, since you're always crunching up their strays."

Jeremiah nodded, but his eyes were trained only on the phone in her hand. "You didn't call her, did you?"

"Who?"

"You know who."

"Pop, come *on*. I don't even have her number."

Jo held the cell phone at an angle where Jeremiah couldn't see the screen. She'd heard this speech before. She turned to face the mirror, smiling at her reflection as she said, "This'll do."

Jeremiah had never been good with words, especially when Jo and sparkly dresses were involved.

"You hear from Dad?"

Jeremiah considered lying, telling her the prison had called back and said the phones were down, but it was too late. Jo was staring at him now. Jeremiah looked away, down at the nightstand. The stationery he'd gotten her last Christmas—and every Christmas since she'd first learned to read and write—burned holes into the old man's memory. The fountain pen she'd bought herself with the money she'd earned from the Humane Society rested neatly on the stationery, a half-written letter to a man she barely knew.

"I'm sure something came up," Jo said and turned from the mirror, snatching her purse as she started past him. Jeremiah caught her arm before she made it to the door.

"You check your gun?"

Jo flashed him a look.

Jeremiah wasn't letting this one go.

"It's in the nightstand drawer, Pop. Right where it's supposed to be. Safety's on and everything."

"One in the chamber?"

Jo leaned forward on her toes, pecked his cheek, and whispered, "There's always one in the chamber."

And then she was gone, down the hall, halfway across the living room when Jeremiah called out for her.

"Yeah?" she said, already at work unlocking the series of bolts and chains attached to the front door.

"I's thinking maybe tonight you should take The Judge."

Jo stopped and turned to face him, eyes wide because she knew the reverence her grandfather held for his truck: a jacked-up, 1984 Chevy Silverado 4x4 with KC lights, a brush guard, and ribbed mud tires so thick they made short work of the Ozark hills.

"You mean it?"

"Figured you might need something mean to go with that dress."

"What're you gonna drive?"

"Thought maybe we could ride in together."

Jo looked down. "But I'm already late."

"I'm ready," Jeremiah said, lifting his keys from the kitchen table.

"*No*," she said, then caught herself. "I mean . . . All the other girls won't be riding to the game with their parents."

"Neither would you," Jeremiah said, a look on his face like *I'm just Pop*.

"You know what I mean."

Jeremiah tossed the keys across the living room. Jo caught them with one hand.

"But I *will* be the only girl rolling up in a souped-up Chevy."

Jeremiah watched his granddaughter turn and start working the locks again. Beyond that door were bloodlines and violence that ran deeper than the limestone caves burrowing their way through the Ozarks. He'd tried to explain it all to her before, tried to drudge up their history and put what had happened into words, but it never came out right. There were no words for the past.

The old man was so lost in his memories he didn't realize the door was open now, revealing the junkyard and all that came with it. Jo's voice brought him back, though, just like it always did.

"See you at the game, Pop. Don't be late."

2.

Evail Ledford watched his cousin Dime Ray Belly scribble the slogan onto another wrinkled poster board. Dime was a short round man with a scrunched face that gathered near his jowls and puckered like the protruding ass of a monkey. Evail, on the other hand, was wholly unremarkable. Average height. Bald and skinny. Beyond that, he held no identifying marks. No tattoos or scars like so many others who'd done time inside. Evail had stayed away from the skinheads and their homemade tattoo guns. The process was disgusting. The needles were mostly just springs from mechanical pencils, and the ink was melted-down Styrofoam. Tattoos weren't free, either. Everything on the inside had a price. Evail had passed his time at Cummins *thinking*. Hour after hour, day by day, Evail had paced the confines of his cell and plotted his revenge.

The television flickered behind Dime, the reception fuzzy at best, Andy Griffith and Barney Fife talking about Otis, the town drunk, trying to decide what to do with him.

"Can you explain to me," Evail said, "what exactly it is you're doing?"

The marker squawked to a stop. Dime looked up. "Getting ready, man."

"For what?"

"The rally. What you think?"

Evail rocked forward in a shabby recliner, his lithe, clean frame standing in stark contrast to the rest of Dime's singlewide trailer. There was one bathroom, one bedroom, and this room, with the television and the flags covering the windows like curtains. Confederate flags: red, white, and blue, the stars cutting diagonally across the middle like crosshairs slightly askew. Gadsden flags: yellow, with the coiled rattlesnake and DON'T TREAD ON ME printed in loud black letters. So much history crammed into such a small place. So much hate.

"Do you even know what it means?" Evail said.

Dime stared blankly at the TV, lost in Mayberry, awash in the black and mostly white sitcom from days gone past. The signal scrambled just as Barney was about to shoot himself in the foot. Dime laughed anyway.

"What *what* means?" Dime tossed the marker on the table and slapped at the television.

"Those words: 'Blood and Soil.' Do you understand their importance?"

"Sure," Dime said as the screen flickered and Barney reappeared, handing his gun reluctantly over to Andy, a disappointed look on the sheriff's face. "It means what it says. Blood and—"

"*Boden*," Evail snapped, his German coming out a little stiff. "*Blut* and *Boden*, Dime. That is what it means."

"Butt and what?"

"A catchphrase, popularized by Richard Walter Darré.

Hitler liked it so much, he stole it for the Lebensraum program."

Dime turned back to Mayberry, Andy lecturing Barney while Otis burped in the holding cell. "Why're you telling me all this?"

"That slogan," Evail said, at the window now, peeling back the rebel flag and peeking outside, "was a rallying cry for the native Germans. The Aryan race. It spoke to them, to their hearts. Some even say it led to the Holocaust." Evail let go of the flag and turned to Dime. "Are you ready for that? Are you prepared for the ramifications of tonight?"

"Shit," Dime said, standing now too, the remote dangling from his fingers. "I just like the way it sounds. It's kinda badass."

Evail pointed to the remote in his cousin's hand and curled his fingers.

"Let me at least watch it through to the end," Dime pleaded. "This the one where Andy lets Otis stay in the drunk tank and Barney throws a fit."

"If you already know how it's going to end," Evail said, snatching the remote and pointing it at the screen, "then what's the point?"

Dime's eyes tightened. "It's just nice. It's a nice show to watch."

"It's a lie. There is no truth in it."

"You know Andy and Barney was cousins?" Dime said, arching his eyebrows and nodding back to the sheriff and his deputy.

Evail almost pushed the button anyway but hesitated when Opie Taylor entered the scene. Try as he might, Evail couldn't ignore the boy's freckles and curious twinkling eyes.

"Always thought Opie kinda looked like Rud." Dime's voice was quiet across the tiny trailer. "You know, back when he was little."

"Do not," Evail said, pointing the remote at Dime now, "speak of my brother."

The screen went black.

"Come on, man!" Dime wailed. "It was just getting—"

"Your slogan," Evail said, stepping on the poster boards Dime had strewn about the room, "it's perfect."

"Really?"

Evail took another marker from the coffee table, fingers foraging through the cigarette butts, weathered *Hustler* magazines, and folded tracts outlining the steps toward pure white hate. The marker ran smooth and neat across the poster's glossy surface, an almost feminine scrawl. Evail stepped back and surveyed his work.

"Sangre—y—Suelo?" Dime said, sounding it out. "The hell?"

Evail slid the marker into the front pocket of Dime's crusty jeans, his fingers lingering a little on the way down. "Your message was right, cousin. You've just been speaking the wrong language."

Dime's hand went to the marker in his pocket. "I can handle a little German, but now you're talking Mexican?"

"I need you to do something for me," Evail said, turning toward the door.

"I'm all in, cousin. You know that. Me and you, we been working on this since high school, since—"

"I've secured an all-terrain vehicle for tonight," Evail

said, cutting his cousin off. "I simply need you to pick it up."

Dime's hand was still pressed to his thigh. He lifted the marker, holding it carefully, like a loaded gun. "What you need a rig like that for?"

Evail ran a hand across his slick, shaved head, staring back at his tattooed cousin. "I'm going hunting."

"Want me to come with you?"

"Meet me at the rally," Evail said, "after you pick up the ATV."

"My car's got a tow hitch and all, but it ain't no truck," Dime said, his face scrunching up in thought. "I still drive that old Impala."

Evail turned before opening the door, a small grin on his threadbare face.

"Perfecto."

3.

Before he left the junkyard, Jeremiah checked every camera across the lot. Checked them twice, and then decided it was time to go. He was halfway out the door when he remembered he needed Jo's keys.

Jeremiah crept back into her bedroom and rummaged through the nightstand. The keys were sitting next to the snub-nosed pink handgun he'd bought her when she'd first turned thirteen. A revolver that fired .410 shotgun shells. A gun she wouldn't have to aim. Checking the firearm for bullets, Jeremiah almost missed the faded photograph sticking out from under Jo's pillow.

The picture reminded him of the college acceptance letter—another heavy, weightless thing. Much of the color had drained from it, but there they stood: Jake in his football pads and Lacey in a blue dress similar to Jo's. The dress wasn't the end of their likenesses, though. They had the same high cheekbones, the same eyes, even the same slight upturn at the tip of their noses. The only difference between Jo and her mother was something that couldn't be seen, a darkness that clouded the woman's heart, spilling out like ink and staining Jeremiah's only son—his family—forever.

The old man studied the picture, letting his mind drift back to the beginning of the end. He fought the urge to destroy it, take it out to the crusher and dispose of the past. But then he noticed the flower pinned neatly to Lacey's dress and realized Jo had forgotten all about a corsage. There wouldn't be some boy waiting to pin one on her when she arrived. Jo didn't have time for the pencil dicks running around Taggard, not with basketball and work and the junkyard. Jo was Jeremiah's, and Jeremiah's alone. The thought led the old man outside, to the only flowers he knew.

The floodlights cast the rose garden in a harsh light. They didn't look great to begin with, not after all the whiskey he'd dumped on them over the years, but somehow, they remained. Hattie's flowers. Her final attempt to make the junkyard a home and bring some color into their rusted, crumbling world. His wife had always been impatient, wanting the flowers to blossom, just like she'd wanted everything to go back to normal after Jake was gone. Hattie never saw a single red rose bloom. She never even saw Jo take her first step.

Jeremiah clipped the tallest one, the rose with the thickest petals, and stuck a safety pin through the stem. A few minutes later, he was driving fast down Highway 7. He was late. If Jo was left standing there alone when it was time to take that picture, she'd never forgive him.

In the school parking lot, Jeremiah squeezed his way up and out of Jo's tiny Ford Fiesta. The old man was much too large for the compact car, big boned with fingers like sausages and scars on every knuckle. He held the flower as if it were a baby bird, cupping it in both of his gnarly paws. The football field glowed in the distance. Jeremiah took a deep breath and stepped toward the light. His limp turned to a hobble as he made for the field. Already the rose was wilted, like it needed that whiskey-dry dirt. Jeremiah knew the feeling. Knew it well. He'd been thirsty for nearly eighteen years. Not a single drink since it was just him—only him—and that little baby girl.

The handgun slapped his ribs beneath the blazer. He clamped his elbow down, steadying the piece, and scanned the crowd for Jo. She was ahead of him, looking lost within the throng of fathers and daughters.

Standing outside the ring of the well dressed and fashionable, Jeremiah took note of his own suit for the first time. These men were the same boys who had whispered across church pews and over tailgates for the last twenty years. Jeremiah knew they talked. Everyone talked, especially the rich: doctors and lawyers, men with daughters who made Homecoming Court. Men with money and time to burn. This was the upper crust of Taggard, the ones who'd somehow avoided the fall of Nuclear One, when the plant went broke and took most of the town with it. Not these boys, though. They were the sons of the men who'd convicted Jake all those years before. An all-male jury—in Arkansas—nonetheless, a red state that believed wholeheartedly in the Second Amendment and all that came with it. But still, they'd convicted Jeremiah's only son of murder. Not manslaughter, not some lesser sentence. *Capital* murder. Life without parole.

"Jeremiah Fitzjurls?"

Jeremiah took a deep breath, peered through the crowd to Jo, and swallowed. He could withstand what was coming because it was for her. Tonight, after the scoreboard flickered and the stadium went dark, they'd climb to the top of the tallest tower in the junkyard, sit on the hood of the original Judge, a rusted Chevy—Jake's first truck—and look at the stars. Jeremiah thought ahead to time with his granddaughter, stuck out his hand, and said, "George Junior."

"God, Mr. Fitzjurls, haven't seen you out in a coon's age."

"Special occasion."

"Reckon so. What I hear, Jo's got Queen in the bag."

George Barker Junior's suit was tight, his shirt buttons bulging across his midsection. George's father was the longtime Bulldog Athletic Director. George Senior had also served as a juror in Jake's trial.

"That's usually how it goes, ain't it?" George Junior said.

Jeremiah turned a cold stare to the man, eyes tight and dark like bullet holes.

"What're you talking about?"

"Shoot," George Junior said, loose fat bulging beneath his chin. "You know, when a girl starts going with the—"

"*Pop?*"

Jeremiah turned his cloudy blue eyes.

"Come on," Jo said. "It's time to take our picture."

Jeremiah tried to turn back to George Junior, but Jo yanked him past the chain-link fence and onto the field. There was a lightness to her touch. Jeremiah felt it in her hand, saw it in the loll of her head, as if she were experiencing everything for the first time, like she had no idea about all the history in this place, the whispers following her wherever she went. *That's Jake Fitzjurls's girl.* Jeremiah could almost hear them. *You remember when he shot that boy in the back?*

Most had sided with Jake early on, but then there were the pictures. The court case where the whole damn town of Taggard showed up, ready for the show. Nobody likes seeing a gunshot up close. And a hole in a boy's chest big enough to fit a fist through tends to change people's minds real quick. It's one thing to own a gun—get a concealed-carry license, strap it tight to the ankle—it's another thing to shoot a man.

Jeremiah's mind drifted to the war, to the jungle, a place where long hot days melted into long hot nights, back before he had the limp and that Bronze Star.

"Your jacket don't match your pants."

Jo's voice brought him back.

"Blue jacket. Black pants? You look like a bruise or something."

Jeremiah had kept the makeshift corsage concealed in his palm. He wanted to surprise her. Right before the pictures, right when she realized she'd forgotten such an important trinket—Pop would swoop in and save the day.

"You're the one forgetting something," he said.

Jo's nose crinkled.

Jeremiah raised his arm and opened his palm. The rose, the tallest in the junkyard—a flower planted nearly eighteen years before—looked pitiful in the bright stadium lights, wilted and slicked with sweat.

"What's that?" Jo said.

Jeremiah's eyes crawled up the rose to his granddaughter. He was about to say her name when she looked away, rising up on her tiptoes, waving over his head. Before Jeremiah turned, he could feel what was coming way down in his gut somewhere.

"I'd like you to meet Colt Dillard." Jo reached back, taking hold of her grandfather's hand, the one that held the rose. "He's kinda like my boyfriend."

4.

In the deep woods, miles from the stadium and the throbbing crowd, the Ledfords' eyes were aflame in the glow of a burning cross.

"Jesus Christ, the light of the world . . ." Bunn Ledford's voice was ancient, the voice of tent revivals from a time gone past. "These brothers and sisters are here to take Your light and burn away the darkness."

Bunn continued the prayer as he studied the new recruits, their hooded hatred burning against the night, more new members than they'd had in years, but still a small number compared to what once was.

"It's a time of reckoning, Jesus. We will be Your shield, Your sword."

He paused, cutting his eyes to his son. Though the hood covered his face, Bunn knew Evail's eyes were open. That was the problem with the boy, always looking, always searching, no reverence for the cross, burning or not.

"Lord, most of all, we want—"

"Didn't come out here for no church."

Bunn scanned the hoods for the voice.

"Came for that Ledford Lightning."

Bunn's eyes twitched above the melted scars on his face, working hard to pinpoint the source of dissent when Depeche Mode's "Enjoy the Silence" blared electric-blue from his son's cell phone, echoing across the crackling fire and the calls of the whip-poor-wills cooing across the night. Evail said nothing, offering his father no help against the burgeoning rebellion. He simply broke the circle and headed toward the tree line, digging for the phone in the depths of his white robe.

The hooded heads rose, all of them with the same question in their eyes, no longer bowed in the presence of the cross or the Holy White Spirit. Bunn's throat went dry as he watched his son—the only one he had left—pull the phone from the depths of his robe and press it to his cheek.

"*Bunn*," whispered Belladonna.

Her voice shook him back to action. "Forgive us, Lord," Bunn said. "In the end, that is all we can ask."

"How about some crank, man?" It was a different voice this time, but the question was the same. "What I heard, you Ledfords got the best crank in Craven County."

"There aren't any drugs," Bunn said. "Not no more."

The crowd murmured as their hoods lifted, eyes peering out into the darkness for a light other than the cross. "Ain't you gonna say amen?" whispered Belladonna, but Bunn knew better. The prayers of the fallen had no end.

The Ledfords were the last to leave. Bunn took the cross down, extinguished the flame, and went about loading it in the bed of his ragged Ford Ranger. The melted scars on his face were slick with sweat, as if they remembered the fire. Belladonna picked up the discarded tracts. She'd printed nearly two hundred flyers on the backside of the paper she'd salvaged from trashcans at the school where she mopped the floors and cleaned the toilets, even after the boys came out grinning like they'd pissed on the rim on purpose.

Evail lingered in the woods, phone pressed tight to his ear.

"Belladonna, I swear," Bunn said.

"Don't."

"That boy gonna buck me every chance he gets?"

"It's different now, Bunn. Everything's different. He's doing the Lord's work, just like you. See how many new recruits we had tonight?"

Bunn grunted.

"How many we have before Evail started working that cell phone?"

"Yeah, but how many here for the right reason? Tell me that," Bunn said. "You heard what they was after."

The stack of papers had grown thick in Belladonna's hands. "Can't judge a man's heart, Bunn. Not all that long ago, you weren't doing it for the right reasons either."

"That was different."

She cocked an eyebrow.

"We was cooking. It's one thing to cook it and serve it. That's God's work," Bunn said, hood off now, exposing what little hair the fire had left him. He turned to the tree line. "Evail, son, I swear if you don't get your ass over here and help me lift this crossbeam . . ." Bunn's voice trailed off.

The whip-poor-wills went quiet, like the still before a storm.

"Boy?"

A roar came from the tree line, unnatural against the sounds of the night like the shrill cry of the phone had been. Evail emerged, hunkered down in a gnarly four-wheel-drive ATV, the white robe wadded up in the passenger seat. The night was cool, but he was sweating. A glistening like gold dust speckled his scalp.

"Where the hell you get that?"

"Father," Evail said, his voice calm and steady. "Please."

"I wanna know."

"Cousin Dime just dropped it off."

"*Dime?* Where'd Dime Ray Belly get money to pay for a thing like that?"

Evail stared straight ahead and said, "Mexicans."

Bunn stumbled, staggering under the weight of his son's confession.

"*Evail.*" Belladonna kneaded the fabric of her white robe. "Ain't no reason to do your daddy like that."

"Like what, Mother?"

"Talking of Mexicans right after a rally. They're what started this mess in the first place."

"In Mexico, pseudoephedrine has never been banned."

"So?" Bunn said. "We ain't got no money to pay for none of that either."

"Who said anything of money?"

"You just said—"

"There are different forms of currency, Father."

Bunn stiffened.

"How much would you pay for a life? Warm skin, red blood?"

"What the hell kinda question is that?"

"The kind the men from Juarez are asking."

The crossbeam still glowed in Bunn's hands, embers lighting his face in ghost-story orange. "Son, I ain't got a damn clue what you're talking about. But I swear—"

"Promises," interjected Evail. "You keep making these promises, but I'm the only one who delivers."

The cross fell heavy from Bunn's hands, sparks popping like fireflies in the still of night. "I don't give a damn what you think you're doing, I'm about to put an end to it."

Bunn reached out, his hands almost to the ATV's roll bars, when the engine snarled and the headlights flashed, casting Bunn in stark white light. He shielded his mangled face with the crook of his arm, small dark eyes narrowing like some giant lunker catfish brought to the surface.

The vehicle lurched forward.

"*Wait*," Belladonna said.

The ATV stalled, taillights burning red and impatient.

"Where you going, baby?"

Evail's face was hidden behind the light. "After tonight, we won't have to gather in the woods with a horde of toothless degenerates. After tonight they will flock to us. Just like before."

Bunn muttered something as Evail revved the engine and tore off through the woods. After a time, the whip-poor-wills went back to their calls.

"*Mexicans*," mumbled Bunn, grunting as he lifted the crossbeam into his truck bed.

"You blame him?" Belladonna said, stuffing the pamphlets into a fold in her robe.

"Blame him?"

"He looked up to his brother in a holy, reverent sort a way."

"*Rudnick*," Bunn said, his late son's name rolling easy off his tongue. "That boy was right as rain. Wish I could say the same for Evail."

Belladonna huffed and pulled herself into the Ford truck. The cab shook a little from her weight. When the door slammed shut behind her, Bunn closed his eyes. He knew his wife was slow to anger, steady and consistent like the seasons and the storms, but this last tussle had made her stir. Eyes still closed, head bowed now, Bunn whispered the only word that made any sense, his voice blending in with the songs of the night.

"*Amen.*"

5.

Jeremiah closed his eyes and thought only of prayer, or lack of it. He had known sooner or later this day would come, but he'd hoped—he'd prayed—for later. It was upon him now.

"Say something," Jo said.

Jeremiah felt a twitch in his eye, like the lines were clamping down tight. The boy held a corsage in his hand. A real one. Healthy flowers grown in a garden, or a greenhouse, somewhere other than the junkyard.

"*Boy*friend?"

A bright flash popped across the field. Another member of the Court stepped down from the homemade stage and made her way to the sideline where the girls would sit and wait until the Queen was announced at halftime.

"Okay, Jo," said Mrs. Franks, an English teacher at Taggard High. "You're up."

Jo smiled and went to the woman, the dress glittering and glowing as she moved toward the stage.

"Your corsage," Mrs. Franks said. "Don't you want to wear your corsage for the picture?"

Jo's eyes went to Colt. She gave him a quick wink then turned back to her grandfather. "Looks like I got more corsages than I know what to do with," she said. "Pop, that one of Granny's roses?"

"Yeah," Jeremiah said, turning his palm over. "It is."

"Well, come on. You still got to pin it on me."

Jeremiah's world lifted. The football field, the photographer, the crowd already gathering in the bleachers, that boy—boy*friend*—gone; all that was left was Jo. That's how it'd been for some time now. A whiskey cure if there ever was one. Eighteen years flew by and landed on this moment. Jo had chosen his flower. She'd picked her Pop. Jeremiah hitched his pants leg and stepped onto the stage.

"Be my honor," he said, unclasping the safety pin's needle. Jeremiah's sausage fingers fumbled as he went to work pinning the single flower onto her dress.

The rose looked like a dried scab—a red stain— against Jo's bright blue dress. Jeremiah reached forward, adjusted the flower, and took Jo's hand. They stood together, both of them smiling, waiting to be positioned for their picture.

Jeremiah's mind raced back to the photograph he'd found earlier. Jake and Lacey. They'd stood right here, in this exact spot, on this same stage, but where were they now? He knew where Jake was; the same place he'd be on through to the end. But Lacey? He'd heard rumblings the woman had never left Taggard, drifting in and out of the shadows, staying close enough to find her next fix.

The flash popped. Jeremiah blinked, and Mrs. Franks said, "Looks good."

Still wearing her grandfather's pitiful little rose, Jo looked straight into Jeremiah's eyes. "I'd like to get a picture with Colt, if it's all right?"

A pressure filled the old man's chest. His hands went to it, trembling, but found instead the sharp, foreign bulge of his handgun.

"Sure," Jeremiah said. "Y'all go ahead."

The boy walked past him. Jeremiah couldn't look him in the eyes, but he watched him close. His hair was light brown like Jo's, but his hands were huge like Jeremiah's, a good size for the gridiron. Jeremiah watched those hands, making sure they stayed far away from the sparkle and curve of that blue dress.

"Aren't y'all cute," Mrs. Franks said and adjusted her camera.

Jeremiah watched with death-grip eyes as the boy lifted his corsage. It was different from Jeremiah's, not only fresher and prettier—it didn't pin on. Colt stretched the elastic band in his fingers and slid the small bouquet over her wrist. It was a hard image for Jeremiah to swallow, sensual in a way, like a garter belt. But still Jo wore his rose—Hattie's rose—and somehow that was enough.

Another flash, and then it was over.

The boy helped Jo down off the stage then turned to Jeremiah, extending his paw. "Nice meeting you, Mr. Fitzjurls."

The boy's thick hand hung in the space between them. Jeremiah watched it for a moment, but then Jo huffed. There was enough disappointment in her breath to push Jeremiah to action. He took the boy's hand in his, hoping to swallow it whole, show him what years upon years of metal and junk, lifting and crushing, really felt like. But the boy's grip was stout, their hands equal in ways beyond size or strength. Jeremiah finally looked the boy in the eyes, and what he saw there shocked him:

Jake.

The picture from before resurfaced, all those letters stuffed in Jo's nightstand drawer, that fountain pen. Jeremiah closed his eyes, willing the past away. When his eyes opened, he was no longer shaking the boy's hand. Colt was gone, jogging back toward the field house and the rest of his team.

"Sorry, Pop."

Jeremiah turned. "For what?"

"Should've told you. It ain't nothing serious. Not really. He's young anyway. A sophomore, just moved in. But he is the starting quarterback."

"Quarterback?"

"Yeah, just like—"

"*Yeah,*" Jeremiah said before she could mention her father. "It's fine, Jo. Fine."

"You sure?"

Jeremiah turned from her to the crowd, the bleachers already writhing behind him. "Where we supposed to sit?"

"We?" Jo said.

"Yeah, me and you."

Jo pointed across the field and laughed. "*I'm* gonna sit over there with the rest of the girls." Jeremiah followed her finger to a semi-circle of white foldout chairs arranged neatly on the track. "*You're* gonna sit up there," Jo said and nodded to the stands.

"Naw," Jeremiah grumbled, his hands starting to quiver again.

"Families sit in the bleachers during football games. You'd know that if you ever left the yard."

In the stands, Jeremiah already saw too many faces he recognized. He could almost feel their eyes from up high looking down on him, on her.

"Shit, Pop," Jo said. "Want me to hold your hand?"

This was how they'd survived the bad years, sarcasm and laughter in the face of all that pain. He'd uttered that same line many times throughout her childhood: the first day of school, birthday parties, doctors' visits—all the places Jo did not want to go.

Jeremiah grunted, but he didn't move. He was still staring up into those bleachers when he heard someone call his name.

"Jeremiah? *Jeremiah* Fitzjurls?"

He turned, peering slowly over his shoulder. The voice belonged to a good-looking blonde, as well built a woman as there was in Taggard. Jeremiah almost didn't recognize her out of uniform: curly locks bouncing loose over her shoulders, thick in the thighs but carrying it well. As she got closer, Jeremiah saw the flash of her badge and knew exactly who she was.

"Not now, Mona."

"Aw, come on."

"Ain't you got more important places to be," Jeremiah said, "than a high school football game?"

"Comes with the badge."

"That ain't all that *comes with the badge*."

"Sheriff McNabb," Jo said, cutting in. "Would you be so kind as to escort my grandfather to his seat?"

Mona McNabb grinned, hand on her hip. "This man giving you trouble?"

"Has been for some time."

"All right then, that does it," Mona said. "You're gonna have to come with me."

"I ain't never," Jeremiah said, frowning as the sheriff took him by the elbow and began leading him off the field. Her fingers were cool and smooth, so different from the junkyard. A woman's touch.

"Is this really necessary?" Jeremiah said through clenched teeth.

"Ain't letting you ruin Jo's big day. What I hear, she's got Queen in the bag."

Jeremiah looked back over his shoulder to his granddaughter, but already she was gone, hurrying across the field to the foldout chairs, the other girls taking selfies and smiling as they waved her over.

"Where the hell you think you're taking me?"

"To your seat."

"I don't aim to sit in them stands."

"You gonna stand down by the fence and miss the show?"

Jeremiah hadn't thought about it like that. There's no way he'd be able to see from ground level, not with all the people milling around. They were to the fence now, the bleachers rising beside them, every row packed except for the very top.

"How about up there where nobody's sitting?" Mona said, letting go of his arm and pointing. "You think you can make it?"

Jeremiah looked past the buzzing mass of people filling

the lower two-thirds of the stands. He could almost hear the whispers. That far back row looked better by the second. He took the first step and a red-hot pain shot through his bad knee. Again, Mona took him by the elbow.

"I can make it," Jeremiah said, jerking free of her hold. "And I sure as hell don't need the damn *sheriff* to help me."

6.

The ATV's tires grumbled across the asphalt. Evail wore no glasses, no coat, despite the crisp, cool air of early October. It was illegal to drive a rig like this on the road, but there would be no cops out tonight, not on—

"*Homecoming*," hissed Evail, his words lost in the low growl of the engine.

The stadium lights burned in the distance. Evail jerked the mud buggy to a stop, tires squealing against the long black road. His cell phone glowed blue against his cheek.

"I'm watching the Homecoming ceremonies, Dime. Where are you?"

"Still hunting up your Mexicans."

"I told you where to meet them."

"I ain't there yet."

"Dime?"

Silence on the other line.

"Do you understand the gravitas of our situation?"

"The *what*?"

From the stadium, a sound like waves rushing to the shore. The opening kickoff. The game had begun. Evail remembered his older brother out on that field: Rudnick Ledford, God of the gridiron, a man amongst boys, and then fire and blood and a heavy, gaping hole nothing would ever fill. Not until tonight.

"The weight," Evail said, and the engine thundered to life again, bellowing in concert with the clamor of the crowd. There were whistles and chants, shouting up ahead, sounds like chaos as the crowd stomped their feet and clapped their hands. Evail held tight to the wheel and pressed the pedal to the floor.

7.

Jeremiah and Mona made it up the stands, to the very back row, as the ball exploded off the kicker's foot and the crowd went wild.

The metal seat was icy through the thin fabric of Jeremiah's dress pants. He was an old man, older than he looked, and things like the cold affected him differently after seventy years. He could feel the end coming when his hands started to shake, could see it when he checked the books at the junkyard. The Agent Orange money—another government attempt at recompense—was nice. It helped during months when the junkyard failed to provide. But those checks were just like that Bronze Star hanging in the vault: Band-Aids to cover the wounds, a way to stop the bleeding.

Mona turned, eyeing the old man's trembling fingers. "You still drinking?"

"Who told you I's drinking?"

"Nobody *told* me nothing, Jeremiah."

"I ain't drank a drop since—"

Even now he couldn't say it, couldn't bring the past

to light, not up in the stands where he'd watched Jake throw touchdown pass after touchdown pass all those years before. And he especially couldn't say it to Mona McNabb. Sure, she'd done her part over the years, keeping a close watch on Jo, making it to most of her basketball games, taking her out to eat about once a month, probably thinking the girl needed a woman around, and for that, Jeremiah was thankful. But it didn't change the past. The McNabb name still carried a pain all its own.

"I know," Mona said. "You done a good thing for that girl down there."

Jeremiah looked to Jo sitting pretty with the other girls. From this far away she looked just like them, a regular high school girl with regular worries. Jeremiah knew better, though. Jo carried the sins of her parents with her wherever she went.

"You really think she's got a shot?" Jeremiah said.

"At what?"

"Queen. You know, after what—"

"Times have changed," Mona said.

On the field, Colt Dillard scrambled free of the pocket, the Denton defense in hot pursuit. Jeremiah watched, trying not to remember Jake running for his life.

"There's always something to worry about," Jeremiah said. "Any sheriff worth a damn knows that much."

"Don't start in on Daddy, Jerry. I'm serious."

A whistle blast cut across the field and the boys trotted to the sideline. A timeout had been called, but things were heating up now, getting closer to the truth, the pain. Chuck McNabb was the sheriff back when Jake got sent away. He was the man who'd looked Jeremiah straight in his eyes and laughed, like there wasn't anything for either of them to worry about—and then there was.

Jeremiah readjusted his weight on the cold metal. "You're one to talk about your daddy. Look what he done to you."

"What'd he do to me?"

"Never married, no kids, and now you're wearing his damn badge."

Mona sucked in loud enough for Jeremiah to regret saying what he'd said. Colt Dillard dove across the goal line and the Taggard faithful stood like a congregation rising for the opening hymn, stomping, clapping, hands raised high toward heaven.

"Just thought you'd done been married, had a whole houseful of kids by now."

"You see any eligible bachelors on the premises?"

Jeremiah scanned the crowd: potbellied men with wads of tobacco bulging from their bottom lips, camouflage hats, fingers wrapped tight around cow bells, arms jerking and swaying, drawing wavy S shapes against the night as they clomped and howled.

"Always figured you were bigger than Taggard."

"Roots are hard to pull free of, Jeremiah."

The Taggard kickoff team raced down the field and demolished Denton's diminutive kick returner. The crowd thrummed with excitement.

"Maybe I's born just a little too late," Mona said and elbowed him. When she did, her arm grazed the hard steel strapped tight to Jeremiah's ribs.

Mona gave him her *sheriff* eyes.

Jeremiah stared right back at her. "Ain't no telling when they're gonna show up again."

"Who?"

"You know *who*."

"The Ledfords?"

Jeremiah winced at the name. "Yeah, them meth-dealing, white supremacist sons of bitches."

"They're gone. Long gone. We ain't seen hide nor hair of them since after"—Mona paused—"the incident."

"You can call it what it is, Sheriff. Ain't no use dancing around it."

"All right, then," Mona said. "Since after the *murder*."

Already, Denton had to punt. The ball shot back between the snapper's legs. The little kicker caught it, but before he could send the pigskin spiraling, the Taggard Bulldogs piled on him. The ball squirted free. Number thirteen for the home team scooped it up and trotted into the end zone.

"Who's number thirteen?" Jeremiah asked.

"Don't recognize him? He just scored our last touchdown."

"That's Colt? Jo's boy—"

"You can call it what it is," Mona said, grinning. "No use dancing around it."

Jeremiah licked his lips, trying to keep his mouth from going dry. He was on the cusp of saying it, just admitting the truth, when the scoreboard buzzed and the first half came to a close. The announcer's voice crackled over the loudspeaker:

> *"If the families of the Court would please make their way down to the field, we'll be getting ready to crown the Queen here shortly."*

Jeremiah stiffened, forgetting instantly the pain of that new boyfriend.

"Best start heading that way," Mona said.

The steps were already filled with the Taggard faithful, fat men like George Junior, whispering women with questions and Sunday-morning stares. Jeremiah stood, wishing for time, a couple more minutes on that scoreboard, but he knew better.

"You want some help making it down through all that?" Mona said.

"How many times I got to tell you," Jeremiah said, standing and surveying the milling crowd, "I don't need your damn help."

George Barker Junior waddled onto the football field, his bleach-blond daughter prancing along beside him. The announcer's voice echoed across the bleachers, relaying a laundry list of Brynn Barker's achievements: cheer captain, National Honor Society, an active member of the First Baptist Church, on and on to small-town high school celebrity.

"You got a list like that?" Jeremiah whispered.

Jo's lips pursed. "Only thing Brynn Barker ever 'achieved' was sucking more dick than any other girl in school."

"*Joanna.*" Jeremiah nearly choked. "Where'd you learn to talk like that?"

"Everything I ever learned," she said, the corners of her eyes crinkling, "I learned from you."

Jeremiah swallowed.

"Taught me not to be scared of nothing. Fancy people

included. Don't let this sparkly dress fool you, Pop. It's still me under here."

The sweat cooled on Jeremiah's forehead. He was about to respond, about to tell her how proud he was, when the announcer said, "*Joanna Fitzjurls, Senior, class of . . .*"

Jo took the first step, dragging her grandfather along. Everything was on autopilot, their steps slow and measured. Jeremiah couldn't help but feel it: this was something her father was supposed to do, not her Pop. The announcer continued down Jo's list:

"*Ms. Fitzjurls is employed at the Humane Society, a three-year letterman for the Lady Bulldogs basketball team . . .*"

Jeremiah fought his limp, but it was as if his bones felt the power in the moment and pushed back against the blood. When people asked, he told them the bad knee came from the war, but the truth was found in the junkyard. All his secrets were buried there. The memory made the pain grow hotter, sizzling as the townsfolks' eyes stared down on him from the stands. Two steps later, Jeremiah's bad knee buckled.

Before he hit the ground, Jo caught him, forcing a grin as she worked to keep him steady. Jo was strong, stronger than any girl Jeremiah had ever known. She'd been through more heartache, more hardship, than most women his age. The thought was enough to cool the flame in his heart.

The announcer moved on to the next girl, and the Fitzjurls made it to their place in line with the rest of the Court. Jeremiah could feel Jo breathing, her chest rising in quick gasps against the tight blue dress.

"*And now, if the crowd would please stand,*" the voice

from the loudspeaker boomed. *"We're ready to announce your Bulldog Homecoming Queen."*

Jeremiah's hands went wild, shaking so hard he couldn't control them. It didn't matter that he'd quit drinking all those years before; his old bitching liver worked hard to make sure he'd never forget. He pushed both hands inside his coat, his pinky finger sliding over the gun strapped tight to his chest.

"Everyone please give a round of applause," crooned the announcer, holding out every word, every syllable, *"for your Homecoming Queen—"*

Jo's hand barely rose, reaching out for Jeremiah.

"—Brynn Barker."

Jo's hand slapped back against her waist. Both Jeremiah's paws were still quivering against the gun as the Barker girl bounced out to the middle of the field, head so small, so pointy, the crown looked like a bedazzled toy sitting askew in her thin yellow hair. George Barker Junior carried the wry smile of a man who knew the score. Hell, Jeremiah thought, George Junior had known the score his whole damn life. When your daddy's the Athletic Director, votes tend to come your way. Homecoming votes. All Conference, All State votes. But old George Senior didn't cast a vote for Jake. Not back then. Not when it mattered. It was enough to make Jeremiah hold tight to the gun, squeeze it. He took a step toward the Barkers, but again, Jo caught him.

"Pop."

"Slimy sumbitch, George Junior rigged the goddamn—"

Jo squeezed his arm hard enough Jeremiah turned to her. What he saw was far from anger, far from sadness. Jo was smiling.

"And you wonder where I got my mouth?"

Jeremiah swallowed. "I'm telling you, Jo, the Barkers rigged the whole damn thing. They probably been—"

"Shit happens," Jo said as the Bulldogs trotted back onto the field, their red and black jerseys pulled tight over their pads. Jeremiah's eyes were on Jo when she looked past him—through him—for the second time that night. He didn't turn his head. Didn't have to. Jo's smile made small lines in her makeup. Jeremiah could see she was happy, and that was enough.

"Proud of you, Jo."

"For what?" she said as she waved over Jeremiah's shoulder.

"Don't think many girls could handle all this."

"All what?"

Jeremiah glanced behind him, following Jo's gaze. Colt beamed from the sideline, already warming up his throwing arm, tossing spiral after spiral to a lanky receiver twenty yards away.

"All what, Pop?" Jo said, finally turning to her grandfather, but when she did, he was gone.

By the time Jeremiah made it back to the bleachers, the Bulldogs had scored again, extending their lead to three touchdowns over the Denton Pirates. Jeremiah couldn't bring himself to walk back up those steps. It wasn't the knee; it was everything else. They'd be talking now, *really* talking. With the victory secured, he knew the home crowd would be rolling thick in the rumor mill, whispering about Jo and why she hadn't won Queen.

Jeremiah hung his arms over the chain-link fence, trying

his best to get his mind off Brynn Barker and that crown. He watched as Colt Dillard single-handedly dismantled the pitiful boys from Denton. Just a few years back, the Denton Pirates were one of the best teams in the state. They had a run of brothers—the Lowe boys—as mean and nasty as junkyard dogs. But Denton, like all small towns throughout the Ozarks, was prone to tragedy in the rawest form, the human kind.

The crowd was all murmurs now, a dull roar compared to the stomping and hollering from before. Jeremiah kept glancing back up in the stands, searching for Mona, but she was nowhere to be found. By the start of the fourth quarter, the mercy rule was in effect, the clock running without pause, trying to keep the score from getting any uglier. Jeremiah watched the minutes tick away until finally the scoreboard buzzed and the game was over.

As soon as the players finished shaking hands, Jo trotted onto the field. Colt caught her midstride, lifted her up, spun her around, then planted a wet, salty kiss on her cheek. She was still huddled up with the boy when Jeremiah reached them.

"Jo?" he croaked, trying to steady his tone. "About time to get going."

Jo jerked free and turned to her grandfather. "Hey, Pop," she said, stalling. "How about that game, huh? Four touchdowns? Not bad for a sophomore."

Jeremiah said nothing. The thought of that kiss—only a peck on the cheek—grew thick and hard to swallow.

"Doesn't Dad still have the record? Seven touchdowns in one game?"

"That's all he's got," Jeremiah said.

Jo cocked a hip. "Well, I don't think you got any football records."

"Don't need no records."

"Why's that?"

"I got you."

Jo blushed through her makeup.

"Good game, Colt," Jeremiah said without looking at the boy. "I've seen better, but that was good enough."

"Yes sir."

"Need to work on your feet, though." Jeremiah turned to him now. "Y'all get in the playoffs, you won't always be the fastest, strongest kid on the field."

"Yes sir," said the boy again. "Appreciate it, Mr. Fitzjurls."

Just when Jeremiah was softening to him, Jo said: "Colt asked me to be his date to the Homecoming Dance." She paused and forced a smile. "You care if I go?"

The knee, the hands, even the dried-up liver—all of Jeremiah's pains coiled together in his gut. "I *care*?"

"Yeah, you know—"

"Thought we had a date with Babel. You know, look at the stars?"

Jo closed her eyes, the bust of her dress rising and falling in one long breath. "I know, Pop, but it's my senior year, and it's Homecoming, and I just thought it'd be . . ."

The hand on his neck was cool and smooth, like a good skipping-stone still wet from the water. "Awful impressed by how your granddaughter handled herself tonight. How about you, Jeremiah?"

The old man turned. Mona McNabb beamed back at him, her blond hair glowing like a halo in the towering stadium lights. "Didn't complain or nothing when Brynn Barker got that crown."

It'd been a long time since Jeremiah was caught between two women. And that's just what Jo was—a woman—and *that* was the problem.

"Yeah, she's good at handling bullshit. Been handling it all her life."

"That's one way to put it," Mona said.

Jo and Colt stood silent, an arm's length apart. Jeremiah studied his granddaughter, his eyes drifting to the little wilted rose pinned awkwardly to her dress.

"Midnight."

Jo's mouth fell open, and then she yipped, a short, happy sound like women make when they finally get their way. "Are you serious? Pop? *Pop!*"

She was in his arms before he had time to respond, the weight of her more than he could handle. His knee quaked, but then she pulled back, smiled, and kissed him on the cheek. Jeremiah couldn't help but smell the salty tinge of sour boy still clinging tight to her dress.

"I'll be home by twelve. I swear."

"Go on," Jeremiah said. "Before I change my mind."

Jo took Colt's hand and they were gone, bounding off the field toward the darkened cafeteria where loud music and the thick heat of a hundred teenagers awaited them.

"Proud of you, *Pop*."

"God, woman, ain't you got something better to do than gigging old men?"

Mona slid her arm around him and they started for the parking lot. She smelled young, like the first daffodils of spring.

"This is Taggard, Jerry. All I got to worry about is a couple speeding tickets and making sure Ms. Barclay don't get her lawnmower stuck in the ditch." Mona paused, grinning. Her confidence reminded him of Jo, innocence behind every word. "And, hey, don't call me 'woman.' It's *Sheriff* McNabb' to you."

8.

They'd had it planned for weeks: drive over to the dance, park in the back lot—Jo knew her grandfather would be stalking the school like a man possessed—and then walk to Coach Turner's house. What came after, well, they'd been planning that too.

"Can't believe he let you take his truck," Colt said.

"She's got a name."

"She?"

"The truck. We call her The Judge."

"The *Judge*?"

"This was the truck Pop had waiting for Daddy when he went off to college, up to the U of A to play ball for the Hogs. There was another Judge, the one before this one, a red Chevy Daddy drove back in high school."

"Where's that truck now?"

"Where you think?"

Colt nodded. "Why y'all call it The Judge?"

"It's what they called Pop back in the jungle. He was a sniper in Vietnam. From the way Daddy tells it, he was a badass. Something like thirty confirmed kills."

"Holy shit."

"Yeah."

Jo put the truck in park. Lights flashed through the windows of the cafeteria like lightning bugs trapped in a jar. A low boom bounced rhythmic across the parking lot, beating in time with the young couple's hearts.

"You sure you don't wanna go in and dance a little?"

Jo smirked. "You scared now?"

"Maybe we should just go in for a little bit." Colt's Adam's apple bobbed up then down. "Make sure some people see us."

Jo slipped out of the truck without another word, head on a swivel, scanning the parking lot. All the other kids, the teachers, the chaperones, were inside. Nothing stirred across the smooth black asphalt. The moon hung low in the sky, only a sliver hooked into the top of a distant hill. She started walking toward Highway 7, the road that led back to Coach Turner's house.

"Hey," Colt said. "You hear me?"

Jo's steps grew quicker, almost a trot. She reached back for his hand.

"Just wanna make sure you're sure. You know? This being your first time and all."

Jo stopped. "You trying to say something?"

"Just weird you ain't done it yet."

"You keep talking, you're gonna make me lose interest real fast."

Colt said, "Yes ma'am," and fought back a smile.

"Ain't funny."

"What else you want me to say?"

Jo looked straight at him and bit her bottom lip. "A thank you would be nice."

"*Thank you?*" Colt said. "What I got to say thank you for?"

"You'll see."

Colt's eyes widened as Jo took his hand, squeezed, and started to run. She laughed, head back, revealing a pale line where the makeup met the underside of her jaw. They dashed across Highway 7. Cars zoomed past, their headlights casting the young lovers in a light brighter than the moon.

The ATV's headlights were off, growling on idle as Evail peered through a heavy set of binoculars. All thoughts of his cousin and the Mexicans were gone now, diminished by the thrill of the hunt. The parking lot was cloaked in darkness, but he didn't see the girl's car anywhere.

Evail was at least a quarter mile away from the school, sitting on a rise in the distance. He'd done his homework: Joanna Fitzjurls drove a white 1994 Ford Fiesta. But through the lens of the binoculars, he saw no such vehicle.

The binoculars were something Evail had used, years ago, when he and Rudnick sat in the night and waited for the coyotes. Evail was always on lookout, always the one with the binoculars instead of the gun. He'd never been much of a hunter, but he went because Rudnick had asked him to, and Rud didn't ask his little brother to do much. Evail remembered how the coyotes' howls had scared him, a harrowing sound in the thick dark, a scavenger's song.

The beasts were attracted with a "predator call." Rudnick would blare the old tape over his truck's loudspeakers, the cries of wounded baby rabbits echoing across the night. The kits' calls were too much for the coyotes. They always came, one at a time, their long tails swishing as they trotted almost sideways into the field behind the Ledfords' house. The coyotes hunted alone, never getting within a hundred yards before seeing the truck, but by then it was already too late. Rudnick had always been good with a rifle.

As Evail scanned the parking lot for the girl's car, he knew he could rely on no such call. He thought, maybe, the girl would be brought to him, but he was beginning to have his doubts.

Evail loved his big brother, a bond that went even deeper than blood. In a way, Rudnick was the start of everything, all those nights in the field, the kits' calls playing out scared and lonely. It was just like the hunting. Rudnick had simply asked if Evail would do it, and then he did. Again and again. For a while, the brothers went hunting almost every night. It was the summer before Rudnick's senior year in high school. Evail on the cusp of sixteen.

And then Rudnick was gone, Evail went to prison, and everything changed. The darkness shifted and the calls howled from the inside out. When Evail returned, he took to the field alone, no longer using the recordings, opting instead for the darkness, working along the tree lines and stalking his prey. He wore the hides of the creatures he'd taken. A mass of fur and bone death-still in the shadows, Evail crouching, waiting, the gun barrel blue in the night. Coyotes were loyal and thick as thieves. When one went down, the others came running. It wasn't until there was a pile of blood-warm bodies that the big boy would finally come sauntering up from the shadows. The alpha. Rudnick had always been the alpha. He wasn't anything anymore.

"Where are you hiding?" Evail whispered, the binoculars by his side.

Cars zipped past across Highway 7, running north and south. A school bus eased out onto the road. The Denton Pirates, a busload of bruised and hurting boys, turned north. The blinking light of the yellow dog lit the tree line on the far side of the road, like a lightning flash, and that was when Evail finally saw his prey.

Instead of binoculars, Evail looked upon the girl through the scope of a rifle, the same rifle he'd used to slaughter countless coyotes, a Smith and Wesson MP15-22 with a banana clip and an infrared scope. A good gun for dogs.

Colt promised there wouldn't be anyone at the Turners' house on Friday night; Mrs. Turner went to see her parents, and Coach Turner stayed down at the field house, doing laundry, watching film, getting ready for the next game. It seemed too good to be true. Jo knew the real problem would be escaping Jeremiah's watchful eye. That's why they'd waited until Homecoming. With the dance as an excuse, they would sneak off and do the thing all teenagers dream about doing until it is finally done.

As they scampered through the Turners' front door, Jo couldn't help but notice the difference in this house and the junkyard's living quarters. The ceilings were so tall Jo couldn't have touched them even if she jumped, and she could almost grab a basketball rim. There were so many rooms, so much space, too much house for a family of two. The Turners didn't have kids of their own. They were young. Coach Turner couldn't have been over thirty, and that was why he'd taken Colt in. That and the fact that Colt was the best quarterback in Craven County.

The townsfolk hadn't been sure what to make of Coach Turner's generosity. The donut shops and hardware stores were ablaze, old men hunched over their coffees, recalling the tragic tale of another nearby coach—a Californian, if Jo was remembering correctly—who'd brought a boy into his home.

From what Jo could recall, it had all gone down in Denton and the boy was a running back, by far the most talented player on his team, but he had one crazy-ass family. Colt never talked much about his family, but Jo knew he lived with his grandparents before he came to stay with Coach Turner. They lived way up in the hills, so far out Colt had to get up at five every morning and walk two miles just to make it to the nearest bus stop.

Jo was thinking about that other boy, about how some people said his family was the reason that Denton coach had gone missing, when Colt pushed open his bedroom door.

"This, uh . . ." he said, the quiver in his voice easing Jo's mind a little. "This is it."

Behind him, the room was cast in shadows. Jo could just make out the bare walls and the freshly made-up bed. It didn't look anything at all like what she'd been expecting. Much too neat and clean to house a teenage boy. It reminded her of a hotel room, which, for whatever reason, Jo found comforting.

Colt reached out and took her hand. "You ready?"

His fingertips were cold, the rest of his hand warm,

almost hot. He wasn't pulling her along, wasn't forcing her to do anything, and that was nice. Jo squeezed his hand, reminding herself that Colt Dillard was the one, the boy she'd chosen above all the others, and followed him toward the bed.

9.

In the vault, Jeremiah plucked the picture of him and Jo off the wall. A brass tack skittered and fell to the floor. The picture had been taken at his wife's funeral, Jo smiling, barely one year old. She smiled because she didn't know. Jeremiah feared she was out there learning real fast. He bent for the tack. It'd fallen by the butt of his favorite rifle, the rusty M21.

Five minutes later, he was climbing the highest tower in the junkyard, the place where he and Jo had spent so many nights together. His bad knee quivered and fought his every step. His mismatched suit was damp with sweat when he made it to the top and lay back on the hood of The Judge. The *first* Judge. It was a good truck. He'd bought it used for Jake nearly twenty years before. Jeremiah only bought used trucks. Period. Too many computer chips and parts he didn't understand in the newer models. Besides, there was something about an old truck, something about all that steel and rubber, heavy rigs worth fixing. Trucks these days had too much plastic.

He wasn't watching the stars, but instead his mangy

pack of junkyard dogs trotting around the lot. The dogs came out only at night. Nobody stole from a junkyard in the daytime. Over the years they had slowly but surely regressed to their natural state: nocturnal beasts, hunters of the dark.

Jeremiah had gone no longer than three minutes without checking the time, and that was after he'd driven through the high school parking lot for an hour, making sure The Judge was right where she was supposed to be, parked nice and neat near the back. Jo knew if she came back with a dent in the door, a single scrape of the paint—there'd be hell to pay.

Jo knew.

Jeremiah had been tempted to go inside the cafeteria and lay eyes on his granddaughter, but the fear of actually seeing her pressed up against that boy, dancing while the music drummed on, was enough to send him back to the junkyard, back to wait on the hood of the truck he'd saved for his son.

There were no stars. Without Jo, what could he expect? The sky was oil-spill black, greasy and swirling. The moon fought the clouds, revealing its hooks occasionally. Jeremiah's mind rumbled back to when the first Judge was still in operation, the night he lost his son.

He could almost taste the rain. It hadn't rained since August, maybe before, but it'd been raining that night. The tornado sirens wailed, the air charged, electric. He'd told Jake to leave it be; a few bucks' worth of stolen parts weren't nothing to worry about. Later he'd learn that there was more to it than that, so much more to the story than he'd known at the time. And Hattie was right—she was always right—if he hadn't been drinking, Jeremiah would have seen it coming, or at least had a better idea. But instead, his vision was cloudy like the night, and it wasn't until a year later, when three quiet knocks came at his office door, that he'd finally been able to lay the bottle down.

The sound of low growls and claws scraping rose beneath him. The dogs bored and fighting now. Jeremiah checked the time again. 11:37 P.M. glowed up through the green screen on his digital watch.

"Almost time, Jo."

He took the picture from his pocket, placed it face up on his belly. He was high, at least thirty feet off the ground, six different vehicles stacked one after another.

"Babel," Jeremiah sighed, wondering if Jo had ever recognized the significance. Maybe she had. Maybe he didn't give her Sunday School teacher enough credit. Jeremiah always liked how Jo gave names to his ruins, just like her father had done years before. Jake had named his first truck after Jeremiah, but the boy never knew exactly how many men had to die in order for a bunch of dope-head soldiers to start calling a man "The Judge." He'd never told his boy about the girl with the broken-heart birthmark. He'd never told him the truth.

Jeremiah hit the button on his Timex watch: 11:59 P.M. shined bright, unwavering. He could see down Highway 7 for miles. The road ran long and slick in the grease of the night. No headlights. No cars. Nothing.

Jeremiah grumbled and rubbed his face. His thick fingers worked at the doughy meat of his cheeks and eyebrows, trying to force the image of his granddaughter into a reality.

A dog barked from below.

Jeremiah's vision was still blurred, but the dogs were swarming now. He had planned to surprise the couple, watch how they exited the truck, see if that kiss on the cheek turned into something more, but when his eyes finally focused, he did not see his granddaughter. Instead, pacing along the edge of the chain-link fence was the largest coyote the old man had ever seen.

The dogs howled.

Jeremiah checked his watch: 12:04 A.M.

The stock fit perfectly into his shoulder, the same spot Hattie used to lay her head at night until Jo came along. The trigger was cool against his finger. The fur on the nape of the coyote's neck stood on end. Through the scope, Jeremiah noticed scars, places where the beast's coat had been torn away. It'd been the same in Nam. Jeremiah couldn't help but notice birthmarks, moles, a pendant dangling around some poor Viet Cong's neck, a sign of a religion far from Jeremiah's, a look in the man's eyes like no one was watching—but Jeremiah was always watching—and the result was always the same.

Jeremiah whispered, "Forgive us our trespasses, as we forgive those who trespass against us," and then he pulled the trigger.

10.

It was a sharp pain, nothing like Jo had imagined.

She'd never been naked in front of a boy before, much less let one touch her like Colt was touching her now. But she was a senior, and the only girl on the basketball team who hadn't been touched by a boy, or a girl. So she'd made up her mind weeks ago. Tonight she'd let Colt do more than touch—she'd let him go all the way.

The bed sheets were cold against Jo's bare skin. Colt's breath warm and ragged in her ear, smelling faintly of ketchup. He'd worked hard, moving his fingers up and down, in and out. But so far, nothing had happened. Jo thought something would've happened by now. Maybe it was the pill. She'd been unsure how the pill actually worked. Mona just said, "Make sure you take the pill." So Jo swallowed it while Colt wasn't watching on the walk over.

He was watching her now.

When she'd first crawled into Colt's bed, a warm bubbly feeling had blossomed out from her heart through her hips. But as soon as he touched her down there, Jo lost it. His fingers were ice. All the warmth she'd felt from before, gone.

Colt stroked harder now and licked her ear. "You like that?" His voice was not his own, words Jo guessed he'd gathered watching porn stars whisper to each other in their perfectly staged, clinical throes of passion.

"You like *that*?" he said again, louder.

"No."

Colt stopped and stared down at his hands a moment before whispering, "What's wrong?"

"I don't know."

He sat up in the bed. Jo jerked at the sheet, covering herself. It felt good to be warm again, felt good not to have his icy fingers plunging away at her.

"I, uh . . ." Colt said. "I got to tell you something."

Jo stayed quiet, pulling the sheet up to her chin.

"I ain't what you think."

"You don't know what I think."

"Don't help that you're a senior, and I'm just a sophomore."

Jo glanced over at Colt, studying the lines of muscle running down his back.

"I mean, hell. I bet I looked over at you sitting there in that sparkly blue dress between every other play. Coach even asked me what I's looking at."

"What'd you tell him?"

"You never looked back. Not once."

Jo grinned beneath the covers. "What you got to tell me, Colt Dillard? What's your big secret?"

He turned his head, keeping his eyes downcast, locked somewhere on the floor beside the bed. "I ain't never done this either," he said, finally, then looked straight at her, sad eyes, soft and brown like the pups' at the animal shelter.

"Done what?"

"*This.*" Colt's arms waved across the bed, across her. "None of this."

Jo smiled, glad she wasn't alone.

Colt took his head in both hands and slumped forward. Jo watched the two ridges on either side of his spine go hard and tight, a valley in between. There was something about his vulnerability that sparked the flame again. Her hand slid down, the backs of her fingernails tracing the smooth, firm line where her hip met her thigh. She followed the crease until her fingers found the final line, the line that opened to form all lines in the world. Her hand was warm, so much different than Colt's. She watched Colt's back, only his back, as her fingers found their rhythm.

A few heartbeats later, Jo lifted the sheet, peeling her eyes away from Colt's toned back to her pale body hidden beneath the covers. This was how it worked in the junk-yard. There were no images of boys that danced through her head, only the soft peaks and valleys of her own flesh, the small swell of smooth skin around her belly button, the rise and fall of her breath. She curled a finger, lifted it, and realized she'd achieved what Colt had been working so hard for earlier.

Jo moaned at the sight of her own arousal.

Colt shook his head. "You just gonna keep laughing at me all night?"

Jo offered a small whimper in reply.

Colt turned. Only Jo's face was exposed, eyes closed, biting her bottom lip.

"Jo?"

She opened her eyes. Her hand slid from under the covers and took hold of his, fingers glistening at the tips. "Here," she said, and now it was her voice that was breathy and hot, "let me show you how to make it feel good."

Colt wiped himself clean in the bathroom, studied his face in the mirror, and knew he was in love. He wasn't supposed to fall in love. That wasn't part of the plan. Football: that was the plan. Living with Coach Turner, beating Denton, dating Joanna Fitzjurls—those were all steps along the road that had been paved for him. But what he'd just felt? No. That was far, *far* from the plan.

He looked to the mirror again. His chest was speckled and red. There were bright red lines on both of his pectorals where Jo had clamped down during their final, heaving moment together.

Colt remembered how they'd lain in silence, simply trying to breathe. How the world had come back to him in stages. The old country music he'd put on before taking off his clothes and getting into bed. Willie Nelson singing "Always on My Mind." Then his vision, and finally, his sense of smell—a saline mixture of the lower latitudes. He'd felt suspended, hovering there above the bed as if raised up on some pedestal. It felt kind of like scoring a touchdown. Hell, it felt better than scoring a touchdown. He'd wondered if he'd ever be able to feel anything again.

When Jo returned from the bathroom and slid back into bed, Colt felt her warmth and was thankful all his senses had finally returned.

"Was it," Jo paused, looking up at the ceiling, "good?"

"Better than good."

A small wet sound followed, Jo's lips peeling back from her gums before she said, "It was good for me, too."

"What time is it?"

Jo leaned over, giving Colt a peek at her backside as she reached for her phone on the floor. "It's only ten thirty."

It was Colt's turn to smile. "Guess I didn't last as long as I thought."

"It was good, Colt. Don't matter how long it lasted."

He'd almost completely forgotten about the bottle hidden under the bed, but the talk of duration, and the buzz still whirring about his head, reminded him of one thing, and one thing only—whiskey.

"*Hey*," Colt said and reached over his side of the bed. "Maybe we could take another whack at it. I've got something that might help me last a little longer."

When Colt pulled the plastic bottle of Early Times out from under the bed, the blissful look on Jo's face melted.

"The hell is that?"

Colt inspected the bottle. "It's the cheap stuff, but it's all—"

"No way," Jo said. "You so much as open that bottle, swear to God, I'll walk home."

Colt held the bottle like a football, cradled in the crook of his arm. "But I heard the guys talking in the locker room. Said if you drink a little it'll make you last longer. You know, *whiskey dick*, or whatever."

Jo shook her head. "You can drink it. But you'll be drinking alone."

"Come on. It's just—"

"*No.*"

"Jesus," he'd said, cracking the bottle as he stood. "Now I see how a woman can drive a man to drinking." He laughed as he sauntered into the bathroom, shut the door, and began to wipe the last of Jo from his skin.

Still gazing into the mirror, Colt touched the red marks on his chest, smiled, then turned the bottle up. The liquor burned his throat and he liked it.

"Just wait," Colt hollered from the bathroom. "I'm gonna be fired up for round two."

There was no response.

His eyes were red. Water lined his lids like he'd been crying, but he hadn't. Colt had been through some shit—some tough shit—and he'd go through it again to feel what he felt tonight.

His phone vibrated across the bathroom counter. He'd almost forgotten about the plan, about Coach Turner, about any repercussions that could come from this night. The buzz from the whiskey and the sex went flat. Colt reached for the phone, felt the vibrations like whoever was on the other line was trying to rattle him. The phone finally quit shaking, but then it started again. This time Colt silenced the call.

"No sir," Colt said, bubbling the whiskey bottle again. "Need just a little while longer."

Colt's feelings of love from before morphed as the whiskey settled in his belly. Gone were the memories of Jo's gentle touch, her guiding hand. His mind went back to the only sex he'd ever known, all the videos he'd watched over the years, naked women on a screen, hips bent at lusty angles, propped and waiting.

"You're gonna really like it this time," Colt said, as he exited the bathroom, bottle in hand. "I've got just enough whiskey in me to—"

The plastic bottle hit the carpet. A dull gong echoed across the room, a single note underscoring the fear in Colt's voice as he whispered:

"*Jo?*"

11.

When a heart beats for the final time there is a reverberation, a signal to the rest of the muscles and
organs that their shift is over, they can finally clock out.
Through the scope, Jeremiah thought he could see such
palpitations under the coyote's thick fur, but then guessed
he was just imagining it. He hoped he was imagining other
things as well, like the time—well past midnight—and the
fact that Jo still wasn't home.

Jeremiah lowered the rifle from his shoulder. The dogs
snarled and whined below, begging for a chance at the car-
cass. They'd eat that beast, dead or alive. Jeremiah made
a point to feed them only once a week. There was nothing
more vicious than a hungry dog.

Jeremiah worked his way down Babel, fighting
against his bad knee, finding footholds in the crunched
windows, hands clasping onto crushed door handles,
and then, finally, he was back on solid ground. The dogs
paced the fence line. They parted as Jeremiah made his
way through, knowing better than to bite the old man.
He kept them all together in one cage near the back of

the lot. They were all related. Jeremiah took to calling them "the Royals," in honor of their incestuous ways. Litter after litter, he kept all the pups. Only the strong survived.

Jeremiah pressed the button on the rusted wrought iron gate leading out to the highway. It creaked as it opened. The dogs swarmed the dead coyote. Sometimes, when Brother Frank got to preaching about Hell on Sunday morning, Jeremiah's mind went to the sound of his dogs eating, a gnashing of teeth if ever there was.

He'd decided to give Jo and Colt until one before he went out looking. He'd also decided when that boy stepped foot in the junkyard, he'd let the Royals come at him like an all-out blitz.

Jeremiah paced, holding the rifle butt in the palm of his hand, the barrel resting on his shoulder as the dogs ate and time ticked on. His mind rushed backwards, churning up the past. As painful as those memories were, they were better than the present. Better than the pain of waiting. Finally, the beasts looked up, their mouths Kool-Aid red, and Jeremiah knew there was nothing left of the coyote.

He checked the time: 1:07 A.M.

"That's it."

Jeremiah dug into his pocket for his keys, but when he got his hand on them they didn't feel right. The idea of cruising around town in the Ford Fiesta with a rifle dangling out the window was enough to give Jeremiah pause. He reached into the other pocket and pulled out his brick-sized phone.

Mona McNabb answered on the fourth ring.

"She still ain't home."

"What if I told you where she's at? Would you let it ride till morning, if I could give you something like that?"

"*Ride till morning?*" Jeremiah barked. "The hell are you talking about?"

"Just call it a woman's intuition," Mona said. "And, Jerry?"

The old man stood silent, barely breathing into the phone.

"Please, don't do anything stupid before I get there."

Mona arrived in four minutes and thirty-seven seconds. Jeremiah timed her. The headlights of her '67 Mustang bounced as she drove through the gate, illuminating the eyes of the dogs hunkered down amidst the jumble.

"Where's your cruiser?"

Mona shut the Mustang's door. "Sit down, Jeremiah."

"Sit down?" he said, looking at the hard clay dirt around him, the car debris littering the yard.

"You're gonna wanna sit down."

Jeremiah clutched the old rifle tight to his chest.

"And it ain't a good idea for you to be toting that elephant gun around, either. Not tonight."

"What you got to tell me?"

Mona chewed her bottom lip, scanning the stretch of the yard. "She ain't a little girl anymore, Jerry. You saw that tonight. Didn't you?"

"Guess that dress fit her like a woman."

"Ain't talking about the dress. Talking about how she handled herself out there in front of the whole town, knowing the Barkers done rigged the vote so skinny-ass Brynn could wear the same crown her skinny-ass momma wore twenty years ago. You knew it, I knew it, and I guarantee you Jo knew it, but she didn't let it show." Mona waited until Jeremiah looked her in the eye. "And that's what being a woman's all about."

Now it was Jeremiah who gnawed at his lips. He was still wearing the bruise-colored suit, dust on his pant legs and shoes.

Mona let out a long rush of air and said, "She's with that boy, Jerry."

"I know, and she's late."

"You ain't listening to me. She's *with* that boy."

Silence now, a long burn of it. Even the dogs took notice, peeking out from their makeshift dens.

"With him?" Jeremiah said. "You ain't telling me nothing I don't know. They went to that dance together. Of course, she's *with* him."

"She's with him," Mona said, pausing to shake her head, "in a different sort of way."

All of Mona's clues finally coalesced in the old man's mind, the impact something like a hollow point entering the brain.

"I'll kill him."

"Can't be saying that around me, not with that rifle in your hand," Mona said as Jeremiah's knuckles went white around the stock. "Please, just let me handle this. I'll keep a watch on Coach Turner's house, and come morning, I'll bring her back myself."

Jeremiah wiped his face with the back of his hand then spit into the dirt. "Coach *Turner's* house?"

"You really don't get out much," Mona sighed. "Dale Turner took Colt in last summer. Was the talk of the town for a hot minute. Coach's got a big heart."

Jeremiah leveled his eyes on her now. "You knew what she was doing, where she was going, and you didn't tell me?" The rifle barrel danced crazy-eights through the night.

"Jo came to me, and we did what girls do—we talked," Mona pleaded. "Lord knows she wasn't gonna talk to you about it. You imagine how that would've gone?" She ran a hand through her hair, holding the bulk of it at the top. "Probably something like this right here."

Jeremiah stood his ground, resolute.

"She's almost eighteen, Jerry. It was bound to happen sometime. At least she was careful about it, took the proper precautions."

"Precautions?"

"You know what I'm talking about. You've got to know what I'm talking about."

Jeremiah's steel gaze showed no sign of recognition.

"Birth control," Mona said. "Jo's on birth control."

Jeremiah's hands quivered. He doubled over, trying to hide the pain.

"Lord," Mona said, coming to his side now, rubbing his back.

The old man looked up through the tears in his eyes. "She's all I got."

"I know, but if you don't cut her a little slack, you'll lose her." Mona paused, as if she were measuring the weight of her words. "Same way you lost Jake."

Jeremiah jerked upright, towering over Mona's five-foot-five frame.

"Remember you asking me about why I never got married?" Mona said. "Why I never had any babies?"

Jeremiah closed his eyes then opened them.

"The truth is something like this stunt you're pulling now. Try being the daughter of the sheriff—it ain't easy."

"Easy?" Jeremiah groaned.

"You've worked your ass off raising up a beautiful, strong young woman, but at some point, you got to let her go."

Babel teetered behind Mona McNabb. Jeremiah fought to find the words, fought against the pain of all his crushed memories.

"I hear you," he said, finally. "Goddammit, I hear you."

12.

Mona's words mushroomed in Jeremiah's skull, expanding against his brain. He thought sleep might ease the pain and tried getting some shuteye, falling longways across the bed where he and Hattie had slept through nearly three decades of marriage.

Jeremiah could feel the mattress sagging beneath him, the two indentions marking their places like shallow graves. He could feel Hattie now too, the place she'd been for so long but wasn't anymore. What would she say if she could see him? Lying there, staring up at the ceiling just like he'd done all those years before. Tossing and turning while their only son was out doing God knows what, with God knows who. Maybe Hattie knew what Jake was doing. Hell, maybe she knew who he was doing it with. Maybe that's why all that was left of her was a dent in their queen-sized mattress and a few wilted roses out front.

There was no use trying to sleep. Jeremiah went back to the junkyard, passing the time staring at the rifle, the bottle, and then his watch, in that order, until he couldn't stand it any longer. Ford Fiesta, womanhood—whatever the hell it was Mona was talking about—damn it all to hell. He knew he had to go check on Jo and was surprised it took him so long to work up the nerve.

Dale and Katie Turner lived on the west side of Taggard—Rolling Hills Estates—where all the uppity folks stayed. These were families that had somehow escaped the collapse of Nuclear One, a power plant owned by the Entergy Corporation.

Entergy Corps ran Taggard for nearly fifty years. Brought wealthy families in from all the bordering states: Mississippi, Tennessee, Missouri, Louisiana, Oklahoma, and Texas, even those Alamo-loving cowboys made the trek into the hills for a piece of the nuclear boom. Back in the sixties, Taggard was the fastest growing town in America. But then people started messing with their thermostats, started thinking about things like "energy consumption," not to mention the competition from natural gas, wind, and solar power. It wasn't long until Nuclear One and Taggard began their swift decline.

The final straw was the reactor scare back in 1999. The sirens had wailed, sending the entire town into the surrounding Ozark Mountains. Turns out, there wasn't a problem with the reactor, just a faulty alarm system. Nuclear One closed a year later, taking with it over half the town's population. As a result, Taggard became a ghost town with barely ten thousand residents. A chicken plant popped up in the aftermath, a sprawling compound similar to Nuclear One but filthier. What jobs the plant had to offer went to men and women who didn't mind getting their hands dirty, immigrants who'd work for pennies and didn't ask questions. Wasn't long before racially charged factions like the Ku Klux Klan, Aryan Steel, and the White Arkansas Resistance, or W.A.R. for short, started forming across the Ozarks, men like Bunn Ledford leading revivals way up in the hills, preaching the gospel of white supremacy to a meth-mouthed congregation. Times had most definitely changed in Taggard, but the cooling tower still stood ancient and imposing out on the edge of Lake Dardanelle, a totem of days gone past.

The arrival of immigrants hadn't bothered Jeremiah. In Vietnam, he'd served with guys from all over the country. His spotter had been a Mexican American boy went by the name of Carlos. Wanted to be a barber when he made it back to Houston.

Jeremiah put a hand to his face, rubbing his temples as a sign appeared ahead, a gaudy concrete structure with lush green trees, blue water, and sprawling hills painted across the front. Looked like something out of a brochure. Something fake. Was this why he'd gone to Khe Sanh? Was this what Carlos had fought and died for? It wasn't what had gotten Jeremiah through the war, that was for damn sure. Every soldier believed in something, some greater power, some sort of faith that what they were doing—all that killing and walking and crawling as napalm dripped from the jackfruit trees—it had to be for *something*. Jeremiah had fought for his country. The ideals of his youth had gotten him through it all, but they were shattered in the process. When he came home, the bottle was the only thing Jeremiah believed in.

The sign for Rolling Hills Estates came and went out past the passenger side window. Jeremiah turned onto

Museum Drive. The houses grew larger the farther back you went, fancier too, circle drives giving way to wrap-around porches and towering double doors. The little Fiesta scurried along like a beetle on the neatly paved road. Jeremiah's rifle lay sideways in the front seat, the barrel sticking out through the open window. He hadn't even thought to change his clothes. The small bottle was tucked neatly in his coat pocket, rattling against the Glock strapped tight to his chest.

A dim lamp glowed in the window above the garage. The only light on in the whole house. Jeremiah parked a block away, then started back toward the front door. The Turners' grass was thicker than carpet, mowed in perfect rows visible despite the dark. Jeremiah snuck up alongside the garage, pushed his back to the red brick, and tried to steady his breath.

He'd thought about just going to the front door and knocking. He had nothing to hide. He wasn't in the wrong. It was his granddaughter who'd been stolen. He couldn't keep Mona's words from rattling around in his head: ". . . *with him in a different sort of way.*"

Jeremiah shuddered.

The rifle was his only problem. He knew he couldn't just waltz up to the front door carrying a sniper rifle. He leaned the gun against the side of the house and made his way to the front door.

Jeremiah was standing in the driveway when the garage jerked to life. As it clanked along the tracks, a light shone from beneath the door, a long shadow cascading back out toward the street. Jeremiah ducked behind a column on the front porch.

The shadow turned to form as Colt Dillard trotted out from the garage, head going side to side as if he were surveying the field for a hole in the coverage.

Jeremiah watched the boy and wished for the Royals, cussing himself for leaving the rifle behind. His hand went instinctively to the bottle in his pocket but instead found the handgun. When he popped open the leather strap, the boy turned to the sound.

"Who's there?"

The silent neighborhood offered no response.

"*Hey*. Who's out there?"

Jeremiah emerged from behind the column, hand still tucked in his coat.

"Mr. Fitz—"

"Where is she?"

Colt turned back to the road.

"*Boy*."

"We was just hanging out, and then I went to the bathroom—"

"Just hanging out, huh?"

Colt's eyes stayed on the street.

"Where the hell's Dale?"

"Coach stays at the field house on game nights."

"And Mrs. Turner?"

Colt paused, wringing his hands. "She ain't here, either."

Despite Mona's clear indications, Jeremiah had somehow convinced himself it wasn't true. Not Jo. Not yet. He felt his cheeks begin to tingle in the face of the truth.

"It ain't like what you think," Colt said.

"You ain't got a damn clue what I think." Jeremiah's fingers gripped the gun's coarse handle under his coat.

"I got an idea," Colt said, teetering in the driveway, "but it ain't like that."

Jeremiah slid his finger over the trigger guard. "I'm gonna give you three seconds to tell me where my grand-daughter's at."

"Yes sir, but—"

"Three."

"I'm telling you, I don't—"

"Two."

"Holy shit, mister, is that a pistol?"

Before Jeremiah could finish his countdown, headlights appeared on the road and he slipped the gun back under his jacket. The car came on fast. Jeremiah thought he recognized the purr of the engine, and by the time it bounced into the driveway, there wasn't any doubt left in his mind.

"*Jeremiah Fitzjurls*," barked Sheriff McNabb as she exited the Mustang without shutting the engine off or closing the door. "Damn it, I warned you."

"He's got a gun!" Colt yipped, pointing back to the porch.

"That true, Jeremiah?"

"You know it is."

Mona pressed two fingers to her eyes. "Then I don't got no choice. I'm gonna have to take you in."

"Take *me* in? When Jo's missing and this little shit right here's the only one knows where she's at?"

"Missing?" Mona turned to the boy. "Where is she, Colt?"

"I-I don't know."

"You don't know?"

"No, ma'am. I went to the bathroom and—"

"Save it," Mona said, her tough facade cracking. "Come on. Both of you."

The gun had grown jungle-hot in Jeremiah's hands. The memories of Nam and Jake, the knowledge of what pulling the trigger really costs a man, afforded Jeremiah enough mind to slide it back into the holster.

"Take *me* in," mumbled Jeremiah as he approached the Mustang.

"Don't make this harder than it's got to be," Mona said, opening the passenger door for Colt. The boy crawled behind the seat and disappeared.

"Naw, wouldn't think of making it hard on you, Sheriff," snapped Jeremiah. "I know you McNabbs like everything nice and easy."

Jeremiah plopped down in the front seat and glared up at Mona.

"Jerry," she said. "I'm warning you."

"You and your old man more alike than I figured."

Jeremiah tried to slam the door, but Mona caught it with her left hand. He felt a strength he wasn't expecting, her eyes shining down on him through the night.

"Always thought better of you," Mona said.

Jeremiah's hand was still on the door, but he wasn't fighting her anymore. "Guess that's been your problem all along."

13.

The crotch of Jo's panties was wet, sagging and rubbing between her thighs as she walked. She'd been on the road a while, venturing out of the Turners' fancy neighborhood and back down Highway 7. There were no cars, not this time of night. Every once in a while she thought she heard the distant rumble of exhaust pipes, tire tread tearing away, and would glance over her shoulder. But there was only the road, long and black, a straight line that led back to Colt's bed.

Jo's pace quickened, but the faster she walked, the worse it became, sweat augmenting the already wet spot between her thighs. She was stuck in the sparkling blue dress, strapless and tight around her chest. She was uncomfortable as she turned off the highway's shoulder and squatted in the ditch, glancing up and down the road. There were still no cars. Jo rolled the panties down her thighs and stepped out of them.

She pitched the lacy red thong over her shoulder. It hung in a tall patch of milkweed like a flag left out in a storm.

She walked on.

Jo's thoughts drifted back to what she'd done with Colt. What he'd done to her. It was good enough. At least it *had* been good, for a moment, when there was nothing but the warmth rising in her belly, Colt finally hitting his stride, pushing his heat up through her. Jo could almost feel it again, getting brighter and brighter, the darkness peeling away in the light.

Headlights.

Jo blinked and realized a car was coming straight for her. Except it wasn't a car. Too small, too low to the ground, and it was coming fast. A cool breeze picked up and swept between her legs.

"Joanna?" said a voice from the vehicle, almost imperceptible over the engine's low growl.

It was some sort of ATV. Some redneck with a rifle, trying to be a hero. Jo guessed Jeremiah probably had the whole town out looking for her. She ran a hand along the front of her dress, trying to hide any evidence of what she'd done. Her voice came out sharp and impatient:

"*What?*"

For a moment, there was only silence. Jo squinted and could just make out the shine of the man's scalp.

"It's time to come home," he said, his voice monotone and steady.

"Homecoming's over, man."

The muzzle flash was bright, the light filling her again, but this time it was hot instead of warm. Jo looked down. A line of red leaked out from under her dress and over her knee. Jo watched as the blood dripped onto the blacktop. There was no pain, only worry, the fear of what was coming stronger than the wound for now. Jo bit down on her bottom lip and thought of her panties hanging in the weeds.

The man was on her before she looked up. In his arms, she felt like nothing. He was stronger, harder, and tighter than Colt had been. There were places where he felt like bone, a skeleton man with a bald head. He dropped her into the passenger seat, the plastic cold against her exposed legs. Tape ripped free of a roll. Prickly against her wrists, her ankles. It tasted of plastic.

The pain came in waves, rising up from her thigh, pulsing through her skull as she watched the man work the tape around her midsection, securing her to the seat. When he finished, he paused and looked directly into her eyes. She saw something she recognized there, something in the void. She made an attempt to name it, but the tape caught her lips.

"Please," said the man. "You cannot stop what's coming."

And then he hit her.

It was a hard blow, a single raised knuckle straight to her temple. All thoughts of Colt and panties and Homecoming shattered, a dizzying, numb feeling, not far removed from ecstasy.

14.

There were two holding cells in the Craven County Jail. One was empty. The other held Jeremiah Fitzjurls. Mona had taken the gun, but she hadn't found his bottle.

Jeremiah had the whiskey out now, studying the amber liquid in the dim light of the cell's single flickering bulb. It was small, just enough to get him started. He knew it would only take one drink, one taste, and all his pain would disappear. For so long he'd carried the hurt with him, his cross to bear. He'd never gone to an AA meeting. There were no plans for reformation, only a pause, a window in time where he would raise his granddaughter with a steady hand, and once she was gone, he'd wash it all away.

Still, he waited.

Jeremiah could hear the hushed tones of the boy's voice from the office beyond his cell. Mona questioning him, prodding for clues. Any minute now Jo could walk through those doors, smile, and then what? What would Jeremiah do if he'd already started what could not be stopped?

He slid the bottle back in his coat pocket and waited.

He checked his watch. Checked it again. Less than two

minutes had passed. Jeremiah took the watch and slapped it against the concrete bench, doing his best to speed time up, or stop it altogether, when Mona spoke his name.

"Jerry?" Her voice soft, low. "What are you doing?"

The wristwatch fell to the floor in pieces.

"Trying not to take a drink."

"You got a bottle in there?"

"Always got a bottle."

The key rattled in the lock. Mona stepped inside. "That's about half the damn problem."

"I didn't drink nothing."

"You've drank enough already," Mona said, taking a seat on the concrete bench.

"Drank enough to still be thirsty."

Mona patted the spot beside her. "Sit down, Jeremiah. I ain't asking."

There was something in her voice that reminded him of Jo. He sat.

"It weren't your drinking that got us into this little predicament. It was Colt's."

"That boy was drinking? Around Jo?"

"Yeah, Jerry. That's why she up and left."

"So they didn't—"

"Didn't ask."

Jeremiah's chest rose and fell.

"I called Coach Turner," Mona said. "He's coming to pick Colt up. I told both of them if they got a whiff of you to call me. And if they call me—"

"This some kind of threat?"

"I ain't gonna let this thing get out of hand like Daddy did. Ain't gonna let it get personal."

Jeremiah huffed. "*Personal?* That how your daddy explained it to you?"

"Jeremiah, please. I'm just trying to help."

His mind unspooled the eighteen years to Sheriff Chuck McNabb sauntering across the junkyard, thumbs hooked behind his belt. Jeremiah remembered his words exactly: "*What Jake done tonight ain't nothing you or I wouldn't do. Hell, any man worth a damn would stand his ground. Your boy ain't got nothing to worry about, Jerry. Not a damn thing.*"

"Bullshit," grumbled Jeremiah.

"Don't matter now," Mona said. "Don't nothing matter except the fact that Jo's out there. Walking back to the junkyard as we speak."

"Then why the hell ain't you out there looking for her?"

"I already called Officer Jenkins. He's headed up Highway 70."

"Randy?"

"Yeah, he's the only other deputy on duty."

"You think Randy Jenkins is capable of doing anything worth a damn?"

"I hope so."

"*Hope?*" Jeremiah said. "You pray, Mona. Get down on your hands and knees and—"

The crackle of Mona's police radio filled the small jail cell. "Sheriff?"

"Yeah, Randy. I'm here."

"I, uh, I found something."

"You got her?"

There was a pause, long enough for Jeremiah's eyes to drift down to the shattered remains of his wristwatch.

"Naw, I ain't got her. But I found some—"

The radio hissed like boiling water. Mona fumbled with the small black box, turning dials, pushing buttons. Finally, Officer Jenkins's voice came through loud and clear:

"—*panties.*"

Mona turned to Jeremiah, looking at him as she spoke. "Sound like you just said panties?"

"I mean, I don't know what kind of undergarments the girl was wearing, but from the looks of them, you might could ask that boy."

"The hell?" barked Jeremiah.

Mona yanked the radio close to her lips. "Not following you, Officer Jenkins."

"They're all wet and stuff, and I ain't talking about from the dew. Looks like—"

The radio clicked off with the swift turn of a knob. Mona turned to Jeremiah. He was standing now, bottle in hand. He wouldn't look at her, though. If he saw Mona's eyes, he'd know what she was thinking, and Jeremiah wouldn't allow himself to go that far. Not yet. The old man rotated his shoulders away from the sheriff. He didn't want her looking at him either. Didn't want Mona to see the fear rising inside him, or the tears gathering in the corners of his eyes.

"Been waiting a long time for this," Jeremiah said, lifting the bottle, turning the whiskey to his lips. It all came rushing back: the jungle, Nam, Jake atop the tower, the storm, the trial, capital murder, a single hole in Hattie's forehead, blossoming rose red as it sprouted up from the rubble.

The first drop touched the old man's tongue, and then he drank the bottle dry.

Inmate: 06-2140
Cummins Unit
P.O. Box 500
Highway 65
Grady, AR, 71644

The girls around town look at me funny. Always thought it was because I lived in a junkyard, but I know better now. It's because of you.

I mean, yeah, I know you got it tough in there. You're paying your time and all, but shit, I didn't do nothing.

Is what it is, I guess. That's what people like to say. All the time trying to tell me stuff like: "Everything happens for a reason." Or worse: "That's just part of God's plan."

Bullshit.

The older I get the more I know God don't give a damn about me. Maybe that ain't right. Maybe He cares, but He just ain't in a position to do something about it. Like, He ain't playing favorites. Know what I mean?

I'm rambling now, but this is how I make sense of things. ▆▆▆▆ says it's good to keep writing. She says it keeps me leveled out and shows you I still care.

God cares just like I care about them dogs over at the Humane Society. You know I love them dogs, but I can't save every single mutt that comes through. I just can't. Don't matter what I do, some of them just stupid. Or ugly. Or got a wild streak that make them want out that cage so bad they run across the highway and get caught up in the trunk of a Buick and get crunched.

Not a damn thing I can do about that kind of crazy. And God's the same way. Does that make sense? He love us all the same, but He ain't like Santa Claus. He ain't just sitting up there pulling a lever every time somebody says a prayer. A woman in Walmart prays for a parking space and gets it, but all them little African babies with the swoled-up bellies just got to starve to death?

Nah, that ain't the God I know. He ain't that cold-hearted. He doing what He can. Doing His best. God can't change the wild streak that send some dogs running. God can't change the blood.

Can he?

Jo

15.

"Tengo a la niña."

Jo didn't expect to hear the man speaking in Spanish. His voice was quiet behind the rush of air in the ATV's open cab. She didn't know what to make of it. Any of it. Her leg throbbed, a pressure building from the tape he'd wrapped tight around the gunshot wound.

"Qué?"

Jo wouldn't look at him. She couldn't. Instead, she kept her eyes on the road, the dotted white line blurring into one long run as she strained to listen, wishing she'd paid better attention in her sophomore Spanish class.

"Mi primo nunca vino a conocerte?"

The tires grumbled as the ATV hooked a hard left. Jo's head, the same spot where the man had hit her, thumped against the roll bars surrounding the rig. She winced from the pain, but didn't move. Ahead she could just make out the faint outline of a house, a front porch with a single bare bulb offering its light to the coming day.

The man slammed the phone into the dash.

"Now what am I supposed to do with you?"

He was looking at her, a funny stare she couldn't quite place.

"God." He paused, cocking his head to the side. "You look just like her."

Jo's eyes tightened around his words, wishing she had something to hide behind. When she was younger, she'd hidden behind her hair, letting it cover her face when she'd start a new school year or go back to church after summer. But now it was braided in thick knots behind her head, leaving her face exposed.

"I know one thing," the man said, his voice scratchy, far away. "I can't let Father see you. There is no telling what he'll do."

Even though she knew better, Jo shook her head, trying to free her locks from the knots and braids, trying to cover her face. She closed her eyes, squirming, and then she felt it: a little damp, a little cool, but thick and coarse, just like her hair. The world turned instantly black. Instead of hair, a feed sack covered her face. Jo recognized the stench from the time she'd spent in the animal shelter. She tried to scream but couldn't, not with the tape pressed tight over her mouth. The damp fabric caught and clung tight to her nostrils, fighting her every breath.

The man laughed and said, "Much better."

Evail cut the headlights as they neared his father's house. Even if the old man heard the engine, maybe he wouldn't see them. Maybe it was a good thing Dime had pissed off Guillermo Torres.

Guillermo was a strange bird, but that was fine by Evail. He knew it'd take a certain kind of man to agree to what he had in mind. To stomach it. Evail had been working on his plan since high school. Since Rudnick. His brother's death made Evail pick up a Bible and go searching for answers. The Book of Genesis. The fall of *man*, and the fact that a woman was to blame. That sounded about right. That's what had happened to Rud. He'd let a woman—a serpent—whisper in his ear and then he was gone, for good.

Evail kept thinking while he was in prison. Thinking about the money he could make, talking it over with some of his Mexican friends, explaining his plan in immaculate detail, how girls disappeared in the hills all the time. Pretty white girls with hollow-eyed mommas. Mommas who never called the police. That got their attention. Evail told them he would supply American girls in exchange for meth. No cash necessary. Nothing up front. Just the crystal. Evail knew the power those crystals held over men. He'd felt it back when Bunn was running things. Deep down, Evail wanted power most of all.

But nobody would bite. Barely even sniff. And the reason was simple: Evail was a skinhead, a white supremacist, offering his services to a bunch of brown-skinned men.

Guillermo was different.

Evail found him on a darknet forum under the heading, "Cholo 4 Hire." After a few messages, they'd set up a conference, agreeing to meet in the middle, just outside of Abilene at a Tex-Mex restaurant called La Ranchera.

"No tattoos?"

That was the first thing Guillermo said. Didn't seem to bother him one bit that Evail was a white guy with a slick shaved head. Turns out, the two men had much in common. They were both lone wolves, free thinkers, outsiders in their own rights. More than anything, though, they were outcasts: a vegan skinhead and a wild-eyed cholo with a serious distaste for authority.

Five minutes into their conversation, Evail felt connected to Guillermo in a way he hadn't been expecting. He liked the way the guy talked, the way he looked. Guillermo had a mouth full of gold teeth and wore a black leather jacket with a fur collar, a bold choice considering the Texas heat. The little man never took the jacket off. Didn't sweat either. He just sat there and gnawed on a Blow Pop, or maybe it was a Tootsie Pop. Evail wasn't sure, but he knew he liked Guillermo's quirks. His high-pitched laugh, the way he couldn't sit still—it reminded Evail of the Joker, his all-time favorite comic book character. The Joker didn't have superpowers—he didn't need them. He was crazy enough to make up for it. *Yes.* That was it. It was that crazy look in Guillermo's eyes that told Evail he'd found his man, yet the young cholo's story still surprised him.

Guillermo had been born in a tiny village on the out-skirts of Ciudad Juárez, where every member of his family worked at Mr. Truijilo's corn farm, sunup to sundown. Guillermo was the youngest of nine and smaller than other boys his age. Short but wiry. Always getting into fights. Getting his eyes blackened, his lips busted. His mother did her best to protect her baby boy, which is why Guillermo was allowed to sit and watch Westerns on her VCR—John Wayne and Clint Eastwood shooting bad guys again and again—while the rest of his family picked corn for Mr. Truijilo. At the ripe age of fourteen, Guillermo left the village for the bright lights of Juárez in search of a gun, a tool he would use to reap a harvest of his own.

There was just one problem: Guillermo had no affiliations. He was a farm boy with no connection to any major cartel. That didn't stop him, though. He took whatever work he could find. Drug trafficking, sex trafficking, trafficking of any sort—none of it bothered Guillermo, as long as he was the boss.

After a few years of this, the cartels sent messengers, men in expensive suits with offers for the son of a fieldhand, offers Guillermo did not accept. He would never work himself to the bone for another man like the rest of his family had done for so long. Guillermo's uncompromising attitude earned him a reputation along with a following. He formed his own faction based out of Juárez, which meant he was free to work with whomever he pleased.

Guillermo told his story as if he'd recited it many times before. Evail nodded when he was supposed to and made all the right listening noises. By the time the waitress at the Tex-Mex restaurant brought the ticket, the two men had reached an agreement: fifty pounds of crystal meth in exchange for one white girl, the first of many more to come.

But now the deal had been postponed. Maybe it was for the better, Evail thought. It would have been hard to deal with Guillermo knowing Bunn was just beyond that door. The old man slept like he was awaiting another fire, the eye on the melted side of his face never quite closing. Guillermo posed problems of his own. One cross word from Bunn and the little cholo was liable to call the whole deal off. Evail knew he had to be careful with his new friend. Guillermo had the worst Napoleon complex he'd ever encountered. Yes, Evail concluded, postponing the deal had been for the best.

On the front porch a bare bulb burned, lighting the bone-hard remains of the Ledford property. The house had been passed down through generations, all the way back to when Moses Ledford was running moonshine, before moonshine—or the equivalent—became what a family man drank on a Saturday night. Belladonna never could get over her boys doing Bunn's dirty work, but she knew better than to say as much.

Bunn had tried playing it straight, early on, back when the boys were still boys. He worked an honest job at the nuclear plant, fixing leaky pipes and patching rivets along the spine of the old cooling tower. Everything changed when Nuclear One went under and the chicken plant moved in. Bunn lost his job and the whole town of Taggard was overrun with Mexicans. The influx was enough for Bunn to start his own chapter of the KKK.

Didn't surprise Evail one bit. He knew what drove his father. It was the same thing that drove him. The same thing that drove all men who'd been helpless for too long.

Power.

Evail had done his homework. He'd read up on his family history, how the Ledford clan came from Ulster-Scot stock, an ethic group more commonly referred to as "Scotch-Irish" in the States. These people rose from the very bottom of the moldiest scotch barrel in Northern Ireland. They'd been stepped on, cast aside, and trampled all throughout history. These were the same folks who'd gone about trying to tame the Ozarks in the early 1800s, scraping and clawing their way up from nothing, searching for a land to call home.

Not much had changed in the two hundred years since they'd first arrived, and that's just how they wanted it. Which was why Bunn had zero trouble stirring up hate in the wake of the chicken plant and the steady stream of immigrant workers that came along with it. Everybody was pissed back then. The rallies were packed, and that's just what got Bunn thinking it was time to go back to the family business.

There were similarities between running meth and running moonshine. Both could be manufactured way up in the hills, even if it did require a shit ton of work. Evail and Rudnick became Bunn's delivery boys. "*Meth cooked right here in the hills, just like the old shine.*" That's how they sold it. That's what the hill folk wanted to hear. They'd never buy some drug from a place—a people—they didn't understand. So Bunn cooked it in the greenhouse out back, his boys delivered it, and Belladonna kept the porch light on while her boys were out.

It was a superstition of sorts, a way to keep her worries at bay. As long as she kept that light on, her boys would be okay. They'd come in late from a football game over in Denton, or get in after cutting up down at Snake and Earl's, and the light was always on. The night Evail ran home from the junkyard—blood speckling his shirt, the final breath of his brother still rasping in his ear—the greenhouse in the back caught fire and took half Bunn's face with it. A weaker woman's light would've burned out right then, but not Belladonna. She just couldn't bring herself to turn that bare bulb off. So what if Rudnick was gone and Bunn was done cooking? Evail was still out there. Even when he got sent away, even while he was locked up, Belladonna's light stayed on.

The ATV crept down the dirt road toward the front of the house. Beyond the porch light, the house was dark. Evail studied his home, a structure built by blood, the front porch mangled and tilted from years of going without power washing or proper stain. It looked like a meth house, but it wasn't. Not anymore.

Evail pulled around to the backyard, cut the engine, and turned to the girl. She was wound tight in a cocoon of gray tape. She didn't move. She'd been quiet the whole trip. He'd made sure to wrap her leg properly. It was only a .22 caliber bullet, a glancing shot through the thigh. She'd be all right, but still, he was surprised by her grit.

The tape ripped free of the passenger seat. Evail hefted the girl over his shoulder. She was heavier than he'd imagined, struggling a bit as he crept up the backside of the house. The warmth of the girl's breath pulsed through the feed sack, and for that, Evail was thankful. She was no good to him dead.

The root cellar took shape up ahead, the place where Belladonna had once kept all her carrots, beets, parsnips, and the like. It was just a hole in the ground lined with flat rocks Evail and Rudnick had brought up from Piney Creek. The hole had been there all the way back to Grandpa Moses's time and before. Inside, the walls were limestone, the floor soft from the water that had worn the earth away over the years. Back when they were cooking, the root cellar was where they stored the meth. Those little crystals kept better in the damp cool, just like the vegetables.

The door looked like that of some ancient vault, rusted iron with a thick beam laid sideways across the front. Evail lifted the beam and entered the cellar. During tornado season the cellar doubled as a shelter. There was no light. Evail remembered being locked down in that hole many seasons ago, thunder and lightning crackling around the door. Evail had always been afraid of the dark. He could stare evil straight in the face. What he couldn't see scared him.

The night Rudnick was killed the shooter had remained in the shadows. Evail remembered hearing the gunshot before seeing his brother thumped to the ground by the bullet. It had been raining, the bullet like a bolt sent down from the heavens.

Evail took the girl from his shoulder and placed her on the ground inside the cellar. She still didn't fight him. She barely even moved, board stiff with the gray tape all around her.

"Do you know the name of my brother?"

The musty feed sack pulsed in and out against her mouth.

"You should," Evail said, reaching down and petting the girl as if she were a downed calf. "You are the reason he died."

16.

Mona tried to keep Jeremiah in the holding cell. Said it'd give her time to do what she had to do without the old man getting in the way. Jeremiah didn't say anything. Just laughed, straight in Mona's face like she was his granddaughter instead of the Craven County sheriff.

"Twenty-four hours," Mona said, giving it right back to him with her arms crossed. "That's all I need, Jerry. Surely you can wait that long before you do something dumb."

The old man's liver-spotted hands took hold of the bars. "Earlier tonight you told me there weren't nothing to worry about in Taggard. Remember that?" Jeremiah flexed his jaw and nodded toward Mona's duty belt. "Bet you ain't never even fired that gun before."

Mona planted both hands on her hips. "No, I've never fired my sidearm, and I don't aim to start anytime soon."

"You say it like you got a choice."

"There's always a choice, Jerry."

"What if it's between pulling the trigger and getting Jo back?" Jeremiah said through gritted teeth. "That don't sound like no choice to me."

Mona lifted one hand from her hip and pointed through the bars, the coral-colored tip of her fingernail aimed directly at the empty bottle on the concrete bench. "Don't stand there lecturing me about choices," Mona said, a new sharpness added to her tone. "You already made yours."

Memories surged in the old man's blood, coursing through his veins like the whiskey. Flashes of fire and light. The pain that came after you pulled the trigger. A hurt he hoped Mona McNabb would never know.

Jeremiah said, "Fine," and let go of the bars. "I'll give you your twenty-four hours, Sheriff. But I ain't staying in here, and we both know you can't make me. Not unless Coach Turner plans to press charges."

Coach Turner didn't want to press charges. The young coach knew better than to get involved in whatever nastiness was brewing between the junkyard and the hills. Thirty minutes later, Jeremiah stumbled out of the jail, into the Fiesta, and his granddaughter's world engulfed him: gum wrappers, Diet Coke cans, tampons in the glove box.

It was too much.

Made him think of those panties they'd found on Highway 7. Jeremiah had somehow gone eighteen years without ever catching sight of Jo's undergarments. The girl did her own laundry. Came out of the bathroom fully dressed. She was careful with her Pop. So damn careful, and smart, and tough as bootstrap leather. That's why none of this made sense. Jo knew better. She knew what Jeremiah had told her. Even if he hadn't told her everything, she knew enough.

There was only one thing that could keep Jeremiah from thinking about those panties and what they meant. It was simple math, addition by subtraction. Jeremiah went straight for Red's Grocery and bought a case of Busch Light. Drank one hot in the parking lot, another on the drive home, bottle after bottle, until the smoldering embers of his addiction took to flame once more.

It was just as it had been, but worse. The drink consumed him. He made no motion for the cracked highway where blue lights lit the shadowy tree line. Jeremiah kept his promise to Mona McNabb and did his best to drown Jo in a sea of whiskey and beer. He did nothing but drink, and by morning he was simply a shell of his former self, a paragon of denial.

When the sun broke the horizon, Jeremiah was finally downed. He lay atop Babel, the rifle empty in his hands. Below, the dogs peeked out from their holes long enough to see that the shooting had stopped but still did not try their luck at the open range of the junkyard.

Three dogs lay dead in the dirt.

Light crept over Jeremiah's eyelids, bringing him to life. He licked his lips. His mouth was dry and tasted of rust. A dozen empty bottles stood on the roof of the truck. Two of the bottles fell from the tower. The crash echoed back up to the old man as he guzzled what remained of another.

In this state, Jeremiah was nothing more than a routine: pop a top, drain it dry, piss, and repeat. Motions repeated a thousand times. Auto-pilot fully engaged.

On Saturdays the Fitzjurls went to church. It was a small service at a small church with laser lights and a four-piece rock-and-roll band. Jeremiah liked it because it reminded him of nothing. So far away from the straight-back pews over at First United Methodist, the organ droning on through the years when Hattie and Jake were in his life. But Saturday church was nice; it was part of the routine.

Jeremiah climbed down from his tower, took the Bible from his vault, and headed for Christ *Zone*.

Christ *Zone* was an old Walmart. They'd yanked the cash registers out, painted Bible verses on the walls, and summoned forth the Holy Spirit. They kept it haunted-house dark on the inside and pumped fake fog into the sanctuary. A young boy named Zane banged away at an electric guitar slung low about his waist as lasers danced across the ceiling. The boy's voice sounded like something Jeremiah had heard down at the VFW on Karaoke Night. The whole place smelled of pancake syrup.

Eventually, the music died off and Brother Frank lumbered onto the stage. Jeremiah liked Brother Frank. He was the Bulldogs' old football coach, back before Dale Turner took the reins. In total, he'd lost four games over twenty-one seasons, but his record was shrouded in controversy.

Somewhere in the middle of his career Brother Frank was called to ministry. Just gave up coaching altogether and started Christ *Zone*. During his absence, the Bulldogs lost twice as many games as they won. Two years later, the Lord "led" Frank back to the gridiron. He didn't skip a beat. Took the Bulldogs all the way to a state championship then retired the next year. This was when the whispers started. Some said Frank only got into preaching because he saw the slow-footed, skinny-armed boys coming up through the junior high and didn't want to tarnish his record. In the end, the naysayers were heavily outnumbered by the true believers, townsfolk who thought of

Frank Rodgers as the Second Coming, a man who could win more football games and save more souls than maybe even Jesus Christ.

Jeremiah watched Frank take the microphone, wipe it clean, and get right to preaching. "Jesus is coming," bellowed the thick-necked preacher. "Don't matter what you've done, matters what you're doing. And I see you sitting out there. I see you, and so does He." Frank pointed toward the ceiling. Jeremiah followed the finger and saw a missing panel, darkness beyond it.

The missing ceiling tile made him think of Jake. He'd been an acolyte at First United Methodist. He'd walk down that aisle, dressed from head to toe in a white robe, and light the altar candles, bringing the Light to the congregation. Jeremiah always liked that.

"He's coming with eyes aflame and a fiery sword. Has a whole army of angels ready to descend upon the heathens. Y'all hear me out there?"

A chorus of "amens" echoed through the crowd. Jeremiah couldn't get his mind off Jake. He should've been thinking about Jo, but Jeremiah didn't want to consider the full ramifications of those panties. He wouldn't let himself look any farther down that highway. If he did, there'd be no turning back.

"Clouds and fire and trumpets and beasts like you can't imagine, coming down to clear it all out." Brother Frank paused, peering out over his people like he'd done a thousand times in locker rooms and on football fields across the state.

A man in the front row stomped. A woman near the middle raised both hands, waving her fingers like she was ready for the first fast drop on the Arkansas Twister, a roller coaster over in Hot Springs.

"Are you sure He ain't coming for you? This fiery-eyed Jesus and His army? You ain't got no guns that can protect you. He's coming, and you better watch out. There's only one thing that can save you . . ."

This was the part Jeremiah hated most. He liked everything about Christ *Zone* except the altar calls. There were no altar calls in the Methodist Church. You simply sat in silence with your sins, or stood when the droning organ clamored to life.

"Confess!" Brother Frank lifted his arms. Sweat stains oozed out from under both pits. "Come now and save yourself from damnation. Come on!"

Zane began plucking lightly on his guitar, a melody similar to Guns N' Roses' "Sweet Child O' Mine." Jeremiah stood because he couldn't watch it, not again, not even with the whiskey in him. As he exited through the back door, Brother Frank caught his eye. The gristly ball coach simply raised one bushy brow and nodded.

Back in the parking lot the whiskey was wearing off. Jeremiah tugged at his jacket but found only his clunky cell phone. The things he hadn't done in the last eight hours had begun to weigh on him.

Jo's out there, he thought, *and what've you done?*

He knew the answer. It was exactly what he'd done when Jake told him that the Ledford boys were stealing from the junkyard. Jeremiah drank, and when he finally sobered up, it was already too late.

Jeremiah jabbed at the phone, the buttons worn from

where he'd pressed them so many times over the years. He left a message for Jake and stood in the parking lot, doubting his son would return the call.

The music started up again from inside, Zane wailing away to the chorus of "Here I Am to Worship." The music grew louder, as if a veil had been lifted. When Jeremiah turned, Brother Frank was standing in the open door.

"Thought maybe you were coming down front today," Frank said.

"Thought you knew me better than that."

Frank nodded. Jeremiah stepped away from him, keeping his distance.

"How much you had to drink?"

"Guess you know me good enough."

"That can be forgiven, Jerry. All you got to do is ask."

"You think God ever gets tired of us asking?"

Frank frowned.

"I'm sure it gets old," Jeremiah said. "Bet He thinks, 'Damn, can't somebody down there just live a good life, stop all this lying and killing then coming around and asking me for forgiveness.'" Jeremiah shook his head. "That's what I'd be thinking."

"Already had somebody come live that life."

"I know how it works, Frank."

"Jesus paid the price, bought it with blood."

"What if just one Saturday, instead of you telling everybody they get a free pass as long as they love Jesus—you stood up there and told them to stop being so damn mean to each other? How you think that'd go over?"

Frank unbuttoned his shirt cuffs and began rolling up his sleeves. "We'd probably lose a few members."

"Lose a lot in that collection plate, too."

"Damn straight."

"I like you, Frank. Don't know nothing about them two years you took off from the Bulldogs, but hell, if that's the only thing you ever done—"

"Done a lot worse than that."

"I believe you."

The two men stood together in silence for some time, the sun hanging high above their heads, too hot for early October. The music inside grew softer. Frank put his hand on the door.

Jeremiah said, "I got a feeling my time is coming."

"You get back to drinking, it won't be long."

"Tried real hard for eighteen years."

"Know you did. Seen you trying." Frank pinched the loose skin dangling under his chin. "We held a prayer vigil this morning. Thought you should know."

"A what?"

"A prayer vigil," Frank said and swallowed. "You know, for Jo."

Jeremiah shook his head twice then made himself stop. Something like this was bound to happen. Word travels fast in a small town. He just hadn't expected it so soon.

"Can't blame you for skipping out," Frank said and popped his neck. "Hell, I's surprised to see you out in the congregation."

"Didn't have nothing better to do. Waiting on Mona." Jeremiah said. "She said she wanted to do it the 'right' way."

"You say that like you don't believe there's such a thing."

"There's only one way, Frank. You know that as well as I do." Jeremiah paused and ran a hand through his thin gray hair. "Jesus got an answer for such a thing?"

"I ain't Jesus."

"I was listening earlier." Jeremiah glanced back through the door. A little cloudy spot remained where the Walmart sticker had been peeled away. "Jesus with His burning eyes, fiery sword, and an army of angels bringing forth salvation . . . I liked that."

"You got it backwards, Jerry. Salvation ain't got nothing to do with that sword or that army. The believers, they're spared from the sword."

"I deal in salvage," Jeremiah said. "Made a life from it. The salvation I'm talking about, it ain't for the believers."

"What then?"

"I'm talking about *His* salvation."

"Who?"

"*Jesus.* That man lived thirty-three years of perfect life then died for it. Don't that sound like a bitch? Then, finally, His old gray-haired daddy says, 'Son, I'm gonna let you take a whack at 'em—go get your sword.' And Jesus's blue eyes turn to fire."

A wake of buzzards circled the church, feathering the thermals without moving their wings. The music died off, the parking lot Sunday-morning silent on a Saturday at noon.

"I got to go back in and give the benediction." Frank thumbed the crotch of his khaki pants, an old football tick. "But listen, I don't like the way you're talking. Starting to sound like you're thinking about doing something like what Jake done."

Jeremiah opened the door for the pastor. "I ain't talking about Jake. I'm talking about the same thing you just got done talking about."

"I ain't got a clue what you're talking about."

"I know," Jeremiah said. "Best keep it that way."

Brother Frank drug a hairy knuckle across his lips before he walked back through the glass door and into the dark shroud of Christ *Zone*.

Jeremiah's hand was still on the door when the shrill ring of his cell phone blasted out across the parking lot.

"Damn, son," Jeremiah said, studying the screen at arm's length, squinting. "About time you called your daddy back."

17.

Jake didn't say much. Jeremiah didn't either, mostly just grunts and mumbles, repeating the same mindless phrases as he drove Jo's Fiesta through the rust-colored town. Only reason he'd called his son was to tell him the news. Took him a while to get around to it. When he did, though, Jake was silent. A different silence than before.

Jeremiah steered the Fiesta down Highway 7, imagining his son behind the glass where they kept the phones, younger in his mind than he was now. Jake'd spent as many years on the inside as he had in Taggard, but still, everywhere Jeremiah looked reminded him of his boy. The Kum & Go on the corner of Sixth and Main. The gas station wasn't there anymore, but Jeremiah could still see his boy behind the wheel of The Judge, coasting into the pump on fumes. Dwight Elementary came and went. Seemed like yesterday Jeremiah was dropping Jake off at the front doors for the first time, trying like hell to keep from tearing up. The school reminded the old man of how Jake had taken a shine to his tags. A scrap of metal with Jeremiah's name, blood type, and other information stamped across the front.

Dog tags.

Jake wore his father's tags on through high school. Showed them off to his friends like they were something he'd gotten at the quarter machine outside of Kroger. Jeremiah couldn't bring himself to tell his only son what those tags meant. He thought maybe the boy would see it in his eyes as he grew older, but Jake spent most of his time looking in the mirror. A vain child, and that troubled Jeremiah more than anything.

Eventually, Jake said something about Jo. Something Jeremiah wouldn't remember. Something like, "Thanks for letting me know," and then he hung up.

Jeremiah pulled the Fiesta into the junkyard, the cell phone still hot in his hand. Stabbing at a different set of numbers before he pressed it to his ear.

"You heard anything else?"

Mona took a deep breath on the other line. "We're working on it, Jeremiah. These things take time."

"So you ain't heard nothing."

"No, but if you don't go get your truck off the high school parking lot, we're gonna have to tow it."

"That truck's about the farthest thing from my mind," Jeremiah growled. "Thought the same would've been true for you. Them twenty-four hours about up."

Mona's breath quickened across the line, but she said nothing. Jeremiah ended the call and surveyed the junkyard. The three dead dogs had begun to stink. The rest of the pack sulked about, keeping their distance as Jeremiah exited the Fiesta and started for the office.

"Best eat up," he said over his shoulder, unlocking the door. "Might be a while before I get back."

Once inside, Jeremiah went straight for the vault. His old ghillie suit lay crumpled on the floor. It looked like the hide of some long-forgotten beast, twigs and leaves and strips of camouflage sewn into the fabric. In the jungle he'd had Viet Cong walk damn near on top of him, just lying there, barely breathing.

He lifted the suit and held it out. It smelled of blood, even after fifty-some-odd years. But blood was hard to erase, hard to clean, even harder to forget. Jeremiah pulled the suit over his head and slid his arms through.

It still fit.

There was a half-pint of Jim Beam on the vault's top shelf. He drank the whole bottle, then took the Bronze Star from its hanger and draped it over his neck. It was another heavy thing, a weight the old man carried with him always. He closed his eyes and could still see their shapes in the hut. All six of them, including the girl. The walls were bamboo, just shadows through the slits. He did what he had to do, easing off on the trigger, and the M21 did the rest.

He fingered the medal around his neck, the cool run of smooth bronze bringing him out of the memory and into the vault. Jeremiah reached for his rifle, but the M21 wasn't in the gun safe. A cold streak ran down the old man's spine as he tried to remember where he'd left the gun. His memories were hazy brown, the color of whiskey.

In the kitchen, one of the camera monitors flashed. Jeremiah peeked around the vault door in time to see a truck turning in off the highway. "I'll be damned," Jeremiah said, stepping outside as Gus Ray's big red tow truck pulled through the front gate, The Judge rolling along behind it on the front tires. Gus maneuvered his truck with a grace and ease born of time and habit. Gus was like Brother Frank. Gus was all right.

"You lost?" Jeremiah said.

Gus grinned around the cigar clamped tight in his teeth.

"Sheriff told me my truck was getting impounded today," Jeremiah said. "This ain't the impound, G-Ray."

"Want me to take it back?"

Gus lowered The Judge down. In less than a minute, she was back on all fours.

"Why'd you do this for me?"

Gus gnawed at the unlit cigar. "Ain't many of us left."

"Old bastards?"

The tip of the cigar rose as Gus grinned. Jeremiah knew what he was getting at. G-Ray was in the club. He'd shed the same blood. Seen the same shit. War was still damn hard to talk about, though.

Gus flicked a match with his thumbnail and cupped his gnarled hands around the cigar. "Didn't start paying us that Agent Orange money," he said, a thin line of smoke rising between his eyes, "till they knew there weren't but a few old limp dicks left hobbling around."

"I ain't dying, G-Ray."

"After what I heard," Gus said and took the cigar from his mouth, picking at his tongue, "figured you might be speeding up the process."

The two men stood for a long while but said no more. The ghillie suit, the Bronze Star, the three dead dogs left out in the open—none of it brought another word to their mouths.

"Appreciate it."

G-Ray gave no indication of having heard Jeremiah. The tow truck shuttered to life, and with that, he was gone.

Jeremiah felt stuck as he watched the truck bounce off the lot and disappear. He wanted to get on with it, just start the chain of events that couldn't be stopped, just like the first drink led to the last. But he wasn't prepared. He knew that much. He needed his rifle and he needed to know where he was going.

The Judge glistened in the late afternoon light. She was beautiful, tires as big as a small tractor's, exhaust pipes the size of fire hydrants, and clean. Jeremiah kept his girl clean. Peace could be found just sitting in a clean truck, and if he remembered correctly, there was a fifth of Jack Daniel's locked in the glove box beside an old Ruger six-shooter that once belonged to his daddy.

Jeremiah pulled himself into the cab. It still smelled of Jo: perfume and a tinge of girl sweat. Jeremiah leaned over the console and went to unlocking the glove box. Before he opened it, he sat there, surveying his world through the front windshield. The car towers reached up, swaying slightly with the breeze. There might have been some beauty in the junkyard, but Jeremiah could not see it.

He popped open the glove box and took out the bottle. The whiskey burned like it always did. He paused to catch his breath, readying himself to turn the bottle up again, when he realized something was missing. Something was wrong. He capped the bottle and reached for the glove box, knocking insurance papers and the thick driver's manual to the floor.

The old revolver was gone.

Before Jeremiah could turn, he felt the cold steel press into his neck.

"Easy now." The voice was warm and smelled young like green wood. Jeremiah turned his ear toward the sound. "I don't want to hurt you."

18.

Evail slept like a child, curled in the single bed where he'd slumbered most all his life, except for the year he'd done after getting caught with ten grams of Ledford Lightning. Adjacent to him was another bed, a twin. It was made, sheets pulled so tight you could bounce a quarter a mile high. No one had slept in that bed for some time.

Evail opened his eyes. Light oozed through a crack in the blinds. He looked to the other bed, the empty one.

"Rud," he whispered and wiped his face.

Evail was shirtless, jeans slung low around his waist, revealing a hard V of muscle leading down toward his crotch. He was a skinny man, a vegan. Evail wanted to live a long life, so he'd given up red meat and milk, even whiskey, all the things his people were raised on. Grandpa Moses had lived well past a hundred. As big and strong as Rudnick was, there's no telling how many years he would've had ahead of him, but then he had one taste of the forbidden fruit and it led him to the junkyard. After that, Evail swore off everything but vegetables, grains, and water. Wouldn't even eat a deer if he'd watched Bunn shoot it himself. It was a tough way to live in prison. Even tougher when he got back home.

The smell of Belladonna's cooking drifted down the hall and into the room. One of Rudnick's tattered Taggard Bulldogs shirts was folded neatly in the top dresser drawer. Evail pulled it on and made for the door. He was reaching for the knob, the shirt hanging loose at his shoulders, stretched in the neck, when he noticed the man lying on the floor.

"Why are you in my bedroom, Dime?"

Evail could smell his cousin over the bacon grease.

"Got to sleep somewhere," Dime mumbled, stretched out on the floor like a dead man. "Them Mexicans wouldn't talk to me. That gold-toothed hombre said he could read my tats. Yeah, my ass. Said he only wanted to deal with you."

Evail said nothing.

"So I came back and slept on the floor. Didn't wanna mess up Rud's bed."

Evail nodded, watching as his cousin rolled to his feet. Evail knew Dime believed whole-heartedly in the Cause. They'd both grown up going to Bunn's KKK rallies, but Evail didn't want to hide behind a hood. He wanted the whole world to know his name. That's why, in high school, he started a band. The Occidental Observers. Dime was too dense to get it, but he played the hell out of the bass. They were in deep back then, reading all they could of *Hammerskin Press* and *Resistance Magazine*, listening to the Blue Eyed Devils and Berzerker, heavy white metal that sounded like a chainsaw massacre. Evail never knew the camaraderie of a locker room; football was Rudnick's sport. Evail believed in the Cause in those days, too. He liked being a part of something bigger than himself. But then Rudnick died, Evail went to prison, and Dime stayed home, carving swastikas in bathroom stalls, getting tattoos he didn't understand.

"You failed me last night, cousin."

"I told you, that boss beaner wouldn't even talk to me. Besides, it didn't feel right, conspiring with the likes of them."

"It's the only way."

"Won't sit right with W.A.R.," Dime said. "They'll string us up for a deal like this."

Evail had come face to face with the White Arkansas Resistance during his time on the inside. Like most things in his life, once Evail saw the W.A.R. boys up close, the mystery was gone. Even the acronym "W.A.R." was jacked from a tried-and-true gang out west. The boys in Arkansas seemed to lack the imagination necessary to create a formidable rebellion. Thus, gone were the ideals of Evail's youth—the Cause—those tracts they'd copied and placed in mailboxes and stapled to light poles all around Taggard. There was no philosophy, no greater purpose, only tattoos like the ones covering cousin Dime: letters from the Runic alphabet, a pre-Roman language of which his cousin couldn't read a word; the numbers 14, 23, and 88, all silly codes, veiled in secrecy; and of course confederate flags, swastikas, and a few Bible verses interspersed throughout.

Evail learned all men were cowards in prison. The tattoos were meaningless bravado, something akin to the tribalism of local sport teams. He stayed away from the W.A.R. boys and did his time. Most days, he ate with Mexicans, learned their language, how business worked south of the border. Otherwise, Evail kept to himself, reading Robert Jay Mathews, William Pierce, and Francis Yockey, along with the Bible. Most skinheads read Hitler's *Mein Kampf*, but Evail's head was shaved because of a book he'd read on Buddhist monks, and Hitler was an altar boy compared to the vengeful God of the Old Testament.

"How many times must I tell you," Evail said, "those W.A.R. goons have nothing to do with this."

Dime shrugged and looked over his shoulder. Evail followed his cousin's eyes to the bedroom window, slightly ajar behind the blinds.

"Did Father see you?"

"Nope," Dime said, grinning. "Came in through the window like we used to back in high school. Weren't nothing to it."

Evail nodded, considering his next words carefully. "From this point forward, I'll handle Guillermo. Hopefully, he's willing to work on a new arrangement. But you"—a small flicker caught and held in Dime's eyes—"*you* need to prove you're still worthy of the Cause."

"Shit," Dime said. "Name it."

"I want you to find an old friend of ours." Evail rotated toward his dead brother's bed then back at Dime. "I want you to bring me Lacey Brewer."

Dime's lips puckered, his face scrunching more than usual. "What you want with her?"

Evail had his reasons—the woman's history for starters, her blood—but he decided to tell his cousin only what he needed to know. "She's desperate, Dime. Always has been."

"So?"

"Desperation is a quality we can exploit."

"If Bunn gets wind of this, that'll be the end of it."

"The end of what?"

"You know, everything we been working on since high school."

"The movement has already begun," Evail said.

"*Shit*." Dime stared up at his cousin. "You got that girl out there already?"

"Bring me the mother, Dime. That is all I ask of you."

"Bunn's liable to kill both them bitches soon as he lays eyes on them." Dime paused, nose to the air, sniffing. "Damn that smells good. Think I might could get a plate for the road?"

"I will handle Father. And, Dime?" Evail said. "Please make sure you close the window on your way out."

"Half the reason you're so damn spoilt is this right here," Bunn said, hunched over the kitchen table, gnawing on a strip of bacon. "Thought maybe you'd grown out of sleeping the day away."

Evail checked the clock above the sink. "Apologies, Father. I had a late night."

"Momma's in here, still cooking breakfast and it's already past nine in the morning." Bunn spoke with half of the bacon strip in his mouth, the other half out, moving in time with his words. "Who eats breakfast with this much of the day gone?"

"Looks to me," Belladonna said, working the skillet, "like you do."

Bunn huffed and scarfed the rest.

"How many eggs you want, baby?"

Evail sighed, studying his mother. She was a large woman, wide in the hips, hair thick and straight, chopped off above her shoulders. She wore makeup every day. The same makeup. The same haircut. For as long as Evail could remember. Belladonna was consistent and strong, but had a weak spot for her boys something wicked.

"You know I can't eat eggs, Mother."

Before Belladonna could protest, Bunn interjected, "Son, I swear. It's one thing to stay out half the night, sleep the day away, but it's another thing entirely to deny your momma's cooking."

Evail's cell phone vibrated in his pocket. Bunn's eyes narrowed on the buzz. Evail looked at him as he answered the call, speaking in measured Spanish, then pausing, giving Guillermo space, room to be the boss and call the shots. Evail did not leave the kitchen. He nodded twice, and then he hung up.

"I'll take a bowl of oatmeal," Evail said, placing the phone on the table.

"Baby, we ain't got no—"

"Wait just one damn minute." Bunn's voice was skillet-hot, sizzling across the kitchen. "Were you just talking Mexican?"

"Spanish."

Bunn dropped his fork and stood. His thighs caught the lip of the table, rattling the plates and a glass of cold milk. "Talking Mexican, in my house? After all we done to rid them bastards from these hills?"

"Please, sit down."

"Ain't sitting for this."

"And let me explain how we're going to get back in business," Evail said.

"Us getting out the business was all part of the Lord's plan. Had bigger notions for the Ledfords than running crank. We doing God's work now."

"And we both know how that has worked out for us," Evail said. "Twenty drunkards and meth-heads gathered around a burning cross, hoping—*praying*—you have cold beer waiting for them, or some of that Ledford Lightning in the truck."

Bunn remained standing. "Takes time to see the Light."

"Do you remember how many men we had at our disposal when we were dealing?" Evail said. "How many toothless, maniacal hillbillies came out of their holes for those crystals?"

"Look at my face, son. Look what God done to me. He took my Rudnick. He set the greenhouse afire. Made it clear I's living a life of sin." Bunn's melted face tightened. "Besides, they done outlawed the cough medicine. Only place you can get it over the counter these days is—"

"—*Mexico*," Evail said, a thin smile slicing across his face.

Bunn sat down. He pushed his plate back and propped his elbows on the table, fingering a wad of skin at his cheek that still cracked and blistered each month. "You got the Mexicans bringing you cough medicine?"

Evail laughed. "The gentlemen from Juárez are definitely not bringing me pseudoephedrine. I could easily obtain a prescription for that."

Bunn's gnarly face twisted up in thought. "Evail, son, where the hell did you learn to talk like that?"

Evail took a deep breath, looked quickly to his mother

wringing her hands in the folds of her apron, and said: "Methamphetamine, pounds and pounds of it, already cooked. More than you could ever produce out in that little greenhouse."

"But—"

"Father," Evail said, a new heat rising in his voice. "How long do you expect Mother to keep working over at that school?"

"I's planning on getting up with the Highway Department come spring."

"But now you won't need to. When I was in prison I learned—"

Evail's voice fell away as he pushed the memories down, the open showers, all the men wet and hanging. So much had changed for Evail during his time behind bars. He came face to face with his worst fear. But Bunn was not the sort of man who believed in fear. So when Evail returned home, he never talked about it. He'd mentioned the subject to Belladonna but didn't tell her everything, just enough he hoped she could make sense of what was inside him, what had *always* been inside of him, the seed Rudnick planted on the long nights while they waited for the coyotes to howl.

"This deal," Evail continued, "will provide us much needed money, not to mention recruits."

"Recruits?"

"The white-blooded hatred you pine so hard for will come flowing down out of the hills to your porch. They'll be beating down that old door."

"But they'll be in it for the wrong reasons, Evail. Just chasing their next hit."

"Everyone is addicted to something, and sadly a righteous cause does not carry the weight it once did."

Bunn was silent now. Evail knew the old man had seen the numbers dwindling over the years. Not just at the rallies, but also in the hardwood pews of the Holy Redeemer Church. Bunn cocked the hairless eyebrow at his son.

"Let's say I agree with you. Say I could stomach doing business with Mexicans." The melted side of Bunn's face did not move as he spoke. "But what about the money? We got to pay them brownies, and I don't see no extra cash lying around."

Evail crossed his legs. "I have something that's worth more than money."

"Worth more than money?" Bunn said, eyeing his son's skinny thighs.

"I asked you before, and I'll ask you again: How much would you pay for a life, Father?"

"A life ain't something you pay for, Jesus done paid for it. A person's blood is holy, sacred in a way that's beyond this world."

"*All* blood is holy?"

Bunn paused, glancing over his shoulder at Belladonna. She stayed bent to the skillet, scrambling the eggs now with the bacon grease.

"*All* blood ain't holy. You know this, son. Don't tell me you already forgot the book of Genesis."

Evail breathed in deep through his nose. "Cain killed his brother Abel, and thus God cursed Cain, bestowing upon him and his people a visible mark. And if I remember correctly, that 'mark' is a darkening."

"Hot *damn*," Bunn said, his own mark—his scar—weeping and crinkling. "Can't remember the last time you stepped foot in the Holy Redeemer, but you sure learned your Scriptures." Bunn's smile melted as fast as it had emerged. "Still, knowing the Word and having money to pay off a bunch of Mexicans is two different things."

"I don't plan to pay them with money." Evail paused, looking from his father to his mother. "I have a girl."

A burning smell drifted across the kitchen. Smoke hovered in plumes at the ceiling. It wasn't until Belladonna dropped the skillet full of eggs on the table, black and crispy, that either man noticed the stench.

Evail looked down at the charred remains. "I told you, Mother. I cannot eat this."

"You get hungry enough," Belladonna said and turned back to the sink, "you'll eat anything."

Bunn said, "Damn straight," and pulled the plate of burnt eggs over his way. "Now tell me about this girl. She a Mexican?"

"No, Father," Evail said, watching the scars on Bunn's mangled face dance as he chewed. "She's worse."

19.

The gun felt small pressed against his neck. Jeremiah hadn't feared death for some time. He feared only dying, the process of it. He leaned back into the muzzle, testing the man who held it. Something told Jeremiah he wasn't dealing with a man. Not quite.

"Stop it, Mr. Fitzjurls. I just came to—"

Jeremiah finally recognized the voice.

"What the hell you pulling a gun on me for, boy?"

The pressure left his neck. Jeremiah turned. Colt's face was pale, almost green. The old sniper rifle lay on the seat beside him.

"I came to help."

Jeremiah watched him close, noticing how the gun quivered in his hand. "You call this helping?"

"I brought your rifle back. You left it beside the house. I didn't tell nobody."

"G-Ray see you in there?"

"Snuck in this morning, hunkered down behind the backseat. He never even opened the cab."

Jeremiah turned away, facing the windshield again,

pulling from the bottle of Jack. "What about Coach Turner? He ain't out looking for you?"

"Coach Turner lets me do what I want. All he's worried about is me scoring touchdowns on Friday."

"Y'all ain't got practice today?"

"Don't nobody practice football on Saturday. That'd be blasphemy."

"Where the hell you learn a word like *blasphemy*?"

"There's a lot about me you don't know."

Jeremiah grunted.

"But I know about you, Mr. Fitzjurls. Jo's told me all about her daddy and what happened that night."

The bottle hovered in front of Jeremiah's lips. "You don't know nothing," he said and took another long pull of the whiskey.

"You ain't even gonna say thanks for me bringing that rifle back?"

The drink burned hot all the way down, but Jeremiah liked the bite, liked feeling something inside him again. He exhaled slowly before saying, "And just what do you think I'm gonna do with this rifle?"

Jeremiah felt the heat of the boy's arm as it reached over the seat and pointed through the windshield. "I's thinking you'd do the Ledfords about like you done them dogs."

Shadows crept over the three dogs laid to rest out across the junkyard as the sun went down over the horizon.

"Shooting a dog and shooting a man two different things."

"Even if them men are Ledfords?"

Jeremiah jerked around and snatched the little six-shooter dangling from the boy's fingers. He held the gun steady despite the whiskey, a trained hand at both the bottle and the gun.

Colt looked back at Jeremiah without flinching, as if he'd stared down a barrel before. "Know about your nickname too. Know about 'The Judge.' Jo told me all about you being a sniper and—"

Jeremiah cocked the hammer back on the old Ruger. "You don't know nothing."

Colt closed his eyes, the gun six inches from his nose. "That's where you're wrong, Mr. Fitzjurls. You need me. I can guarantee that. If you ever want to see—"

Jeremiah pushed the muzzle into the boy's cheek, shutting him up quick. "Why in the hell you want to help me so bad?"

Colt kept his eyes squeezed shut and flared his nostrils. The look on his face said more than his mouth ever could. Jeremiah knew the answer. He imagined the boy's bed. Two teenagers plunging away at love. The whispers. The lies all boys told girls until it was over and they finally knew for themselves. Jeremiah jabbed the cold steel into Colt's cheek hard enough to feel his teeth. "Whatever you think you know about Jo," he snarled, "you're wrong."

"Know what I felt."

"Tell me about it then, boy."

"I'll tell you something better," Colt said and opened his eyes. "I'll tell you where she is."

20.

It was so dark Jo could have been dead. She'd tried to scream, but couldn't. Couldn't move either, the tape so tight and strong she couldn't curl herself into a ball, couldn't wipe the tears from her eyes. She lay in a straight gray line, the feed sack over her head going in and out with each breath.

If she could somehow rise up above herself and hover there like a ghost, she'd be afforded no more clarity. There was only darkness. A pit. A hole. A *cellar*. She imagined other bodies around her. The bodies didn't move. They were dead, just like the ghosts that haunted Jeremiah. Howls in the night, echoing off the thick concrete corridors in the junkyard. This was her lot in life. Jo saw that now. She was trapped.

Trapped inside her mother's skin. Trapped under the weight of her father's sins. Jeremiah had tried—God, how he'd tried—but in the end he'd only caged her like the rest. And now this: duct tape, a feed sack, and a pit so dark she could not see.

It reminded Jo of Christ *Zone*'s smoky sanctuary for

some reason, Brother Frank up on stage waving his hairy arms as he ushered his flock toward salvation. This wasn't much different. There was an emptiness to that place too. Sometimes, when Brother Frank made the altar call, Jo would close her eyes and enter the void. Her father was there instead of Cummins. Her mother smiled back at her through eyes that were her own.

Jo let her mind drift through the darkness to her parents, the two great mysteries of her life. She'd seen enough of her father to know what she'd gotten from him. He was built like an athlete, strong in the hips and thighs. He moved in an assured, confident manner despite the chains that held him. Jo knew the feeling. She knew, deep down, her father was the one who'd caged her more than all the others, but she still looked forward to seeing him.

Cummins Unit was a two-hour drive east.

When Jo first realized her father would spend the rest of his life inside those walls, she'd done some research: Cummins was bad nasty, the place carrying with it a history of violence like the men it held captive. Johnny Cash, a native Arkansan, had tried to help, strumming his guitar inside those walls, raising enough awareness and money to build a little prison chapel back in the seventies. A few years later, the warden took the rest of that money and had the prisoners install the state's first lethal electric fence.

Jo pictured her father in his orange jumpsuit behind the glass. She always liked that, liked how when she arrived— after she'd made it through the security checks, the lines, the buzzing doors and the guards—her father was always there, waiting for her.

Her mother was a different story, a whisper in the

Ozark hills. A ghost. She'd heard enough stories to know Lacey Brewer was a wild one. Jo felt the woman in her blood sometimes. She'd felt her back in Colt's bed as she'd shed the skin of her youth. No matter how hard Jeremiah had tried to raise her up right. No matter how hard he'd tried to protect her, Jo was still her mother's child.

She rolled again across the cellar floor. It was all she could do. There was no telling up from down, nothing. She banged into a wall, the breath going out of her, but she was glad for it, happy to have at least given some boundaries to her forsaken world.

Spinning back the other way now, Jo hoped maybe she could roll farther this time, just roll on out into the light and away from the darkness. But she was met with a bright infusion of pain, rainbow shards like broken glass.

Something poked hard at the gunshot wound on Jo's thigh. It felt like a yard rake, or maybe a hoe. Something sharp enough to stick.

On her back now, Jo tried to bend to her pain, touch the hole in her leg and afford herself some comfort, even if it was by her own hand. The tape crackled as she strained, adrenaline coursing through her veins. Jo remembered tales of mothers lifting cars off of their children. Fueled by the thought, she pushed harder, and the tape ripped free.

21.

The Judge looked like some ancient war rig thundering down the dirt road. The Ozarks took no heed of the truck, sturdy oaks and bristling pines standing tall and proud, watchmen without eyes, towers of wood and time. Colt had moved to the front seat, the M21 propped between his legs, like he and Jeremiah were heading out at the end of the day in search of deer scrapes and droppings of different sorts.

"You sure you're good to drive?"

The bottle between Jeremiah's thighs was empty. He drove with one hand on the wheel and one eye squinting, as if he were peering through the scope on that vintage rifle.

"I'm the one needs to be asking the questions," Jeremiah said.

"I already told you."

"Naw, boy, you ain't told me nothing. How the hell you know where the Ledfords live?"

Colt turned to the window, pouting like young boys do until they realize there's no good that comes from it. The truck drifted off the road and into a shallow ditch. Tree branches scraped the windows. Colt's forehead bounced off the glass.

"*Hey*," Colt said, hand to his head. "Watch the road."

"How about you answer my question."

"Everybody knows."

"That ain't an answer."

"The Ledfords are like a campfire story at Taggard High."

"You ain't even from Taggard."

"I know about the Ledfords."

"And that's it, huh? Your inside scoop's coming from a bunch of jugheads thumbing their nuts in the locker room?"

"I seen it, all right?"

"You've *seen* the Ledford place?"

Colt arched both eyebrows and folded his arms across his chest.

"*Boy.*"

The trees blurred together. The truck's tires churned.

"Before the season started, back around two-a-days, the guys took me out there late one night," Colt said, his voice steady in the truck's cab. "We crept up to the house. The porch light was on just like they said it'd be, and they told me if I wanted to be their quarterback, I better get up there and touch that light." He paused. "You know, like they was hazing me or something."

"You do it?"

"I'm the goddamn quarterback, ain't I?"

The empty bottle was back at Jeremiah's lips. "Watch your language."

"You're one to talk."

They rode on in silence. The sun was nearly down, cutting its way through the dense trees, leaves the color of fire. The light flickered across their faces as they came to a low-water bridge. Piney Creek covered the concrete slab in a rush of green and white. The Judge made short work of the current, plowing through the flow as if it were only a puddle, the water barely reaching the top of the truck's thick black tires.

As they crossed, Jeremiah looked down the creek and was taken back to when another boy was riding shotgun in his truck. He and Jake had fished these waters every summer, daylight till dark. Smallmouth bass loved the current. Waited for crawdads and minnows to come bouncing down through the fast water, then *wham*, a streak of brown muscle and red eyes. Jeremiah liked to fish the bottom. Tube jigs. That was the way to do it. Took patience. Had to think like one of those brownies. Had to make perfect casts upstream with no slack in the line. Had to keep it tight while the jig danced like dinner. Tip down, then up, setting the hook. Jeremiah liked to play the fish in, reeling slow. Liked to let them jump, watching those brownies glisten and shine, sparkling in the light reflecting up off the creek. The fish fought hard, but there was no escaping the hook. Eventually, they realized they were caught and would come slowly to the surface.

The Judge emerged on the far bank and Jeremiah thought of hooks. Who'd caught who? Fishing was sacred, holy in a way that other things of this world were not. You couldn't compare a situation like he was in now with fishing. No. This ordeal was better seen through the red eyes of those smallmouth bass. Jeremiah knew what it felt like to be hooked. He'd hooked himself many times. If the point went in past the barb, there was only one option. You had to push it all the way through.

"You hear me?"

Colt's voice brought the old man back.

"You're about to miss the turn."

"The turn?" Jeremiah said, looking up the long stretch of dirt road. "Don't see no turn."

"Right there. Past that rock."

The Judge slowed and Jeremiah narrowed his eyes. Beyond the rock there was a cut in the woods. Nothing more than a deer trail. "You sure about this?"

"I'm sure," Colt said.

The Judge bounced over the shallow ditch and they were in the thick of it now. No more low-hanging branches from the tall oaks and pines, but instead a mess of briars and vines, a sound like a thousand tiny fingernails scratching a dusty chalkboard.

Jeremiah took the wheel with both hands, leaned forward, and bared his teeth as the truck pushed deeper into the thicket.

"Cut the engine," Colt said.

"Huh?"

"Don't want them hearing us. We ain't far," Colt whispered. "We get through these pine trees and we're there. The grove makes the place real hard to see."

Jeremiah cut the engine and stepped out of the truck, Colt a few steps behind. Pine needles crunched as the old man and the boy crept their way through. Finally, the briar patch parted and Jeremiah saw the house.

He didn't know what he was expecting, but this wasn't

it. It was just a house, a white house. Looked something like a church. The sun was down now, but it wouldn't have mattered. The house sat in its own dusky cloud, a thick canopy of loblolly pines looming overhead. On the front porch a bare blub flickered against the coming night.

"That ain't it," Jeremiah said. "Ain't no way that's it."

"That's it."

"Got a mind to send your ass up there to knock on that door."

"That's it. I'm telling you."

Jeremiah turned, already making his way back to the truck, when Colt whispered, "*Look*."

In the light of the front porch a man stood talking on a cell phone.

"Damn," Jeremiah said. "That's—"

"—*Evail*."

Jeremiah's forehead scrunched. "Them boys in the locker room give you a full-on Ledford history lesson?"

"No, I just—"

Colt's words were cut short when a woman appeared, hobbling across the run of grass between the truck and the porch. She looked rough, like she'd spent her whole life bent to her work. She couldn't have been more than a hundred feet away, but she didn't see them, moving toward that porch light now like a moth to the zapper.

"Look like she just sprung up out the ground," Jeremiah said. "You see that? Where'd she come from?"

Colt didn't answer.

Jeremiah knew who the woman was. The sight of her took him all the way back to the courthouse. The way she'd wailed. *God.* The way she'd cried for her boy, and that judge just couldn't bring himself to have her removed. There were a right many people in Taggard who'd said Belladonna Ledford was a big reason the jury hadn't taken more time to deliberate. That sort of sorrow is hard on the ears.

"She ain't the one we have to worry about."

"Trust me, boy. I know."

Belladonna was nearly back to the house when she stopped. It was full dark now, the light from the porch casting her shadow in long runs across the yard.

"She looks," Colt whispered, "*scared*."

"Scared ain't the word."

Jeremiah watched as Belladonna stopped, turned back, and studied her tracks. His eyes were still on her when Evail stepped into the porch light. Another ghost from Jake's past. Evail had been a squirrely kid, a couple years younger than Jake, always toting a book around, titles Jeremiah had never read. Belladonna seemed startled by her son, talking fast, hands slapping at the night, pointing back the way she'd come.

Jeremiah raised the rifle to his shoulder.

"The hell?" Colt said.

Jeremiah leveled the gun out, peering through the scope back toward the darkness from which the woman had come. Things were brighter through the scope, lenses bent and curved at odd angles, catching all the light that remained.

"You can't just shoot them."

Jeremiah followed her tracks back to the hole. It looked like an animal's den, save for the rocks lining the entrance. There was an old iron door. Bolted and locked. Colt started whispering again beside him, tugging at his arm, but Jeremiah had already seen what he was looking for. He pulled his head back from the scope.

"What is it, Mr. Fitzjurls? What'd you see?"

Jeremiah exhaled, slowly, steadying himself like you were supposed to do before a shot. His heart thudded in his ears as he focused in and saw it again. He wasn't dreaming. It was there. A red rose—Hattie's rose—lay crumpled at the foot of the entrance, the pitiful safety pin glistening in what little light was left.

22.

Belladonna had spent the day worrying. The talk of Mexicans and a girl trapped out in her root cellar was too much. It hurt her to hear such things. Bunn had come a long way from his wild days. All of that was supposed to be behind them. She could stomach the Klan rallies, copying and printing all those tracts, even the history burned into her husband's melted face—but *this* was too much. Bunn and Evail had argued on into lunch. They'd quarreled at suppertime, bringing up the past, the one night that had defined every night that came after it. They were still going when Belladonna slipped out the back door and headed for the cellar.

She stood outside the great iron door and listened. No sounds came from within. For a moment, she allowed herself to hope.

Then she heard it: a cry she recognized from the early years of motherhood. The way an infant will just sit up and scream in the middle of the night, or right after they emerge from the womb, not ready to face the cruel, cold world that awaits them.

The beam across the iron door was heavy and rough to the touch. As Belladonna lifted it she thought of Mexicans, of what Bunn would do with *this* girl—the girl who carried such history, such pain—when the time finally came. The evil that would follow would erase the good years.

She opened the door without a sound.

There was only darkness and silence on the inside. Belladonna thought maybe her ears had deceived her. Maybe she had only imagined the cry, but then her eyes adjusted and slowly the girl came into focus. Belladonna saw the feed sack first, then the blue dress, mottled and torn, barely covering the child's upper half. Despite her bindings, the girl just kept writhing around, fighting against the long strips of silver tape wrapped tight around her body. Then—almost as if Belladonna had willed her hope into a reality—the tape crackled, *popped*, and began peeling off like snakeskin as the girl bucked across the limestone. Belladonna looked upon the pitiful creature for only a moment before shuffling back to the tree line and leaving the great door open.

Seconds trickled into minutes, the way time drags in moments of despair. When the girl finally emerged, Belladonna ducked behind a sappy pine, hidden from view. The girl took three steps on shaky legs like a colt just learning to walk. *Run*, thought Belladonna, but she just stood there on the giant slabs of rock leading into the cellar.

Then, as if some great current had shot through her, the girl bolted up and over the cellar, clawing her way through the brush, the briars, the sound of the dress ripping carrying through the night, and then she was gone.

Belladonna listened as twigs snapped and leaves crunched underfoot, a rush into the wild. The sounds lessened with time. Frogs croaked across the night, filling the void left by the girl. Belladonna stepped out from behind the trees. She knew a new darkness was coming. The woods, the steep cliffs and deep ravines—the Ozarks— would afford the running girl in her fancy dress little mercy. But at least she was free. Belladonna would not have to witness what was to come.

She was nearly back to the house, about to take the first step onto the porch and into the light, when a sound made her stop; the same cry as before. Belladonna looked back across the yard. The bloodhounds whined in their cage, pawing at the chain links. But there was nothing else, just a dark stretch of dirt and leaves that had been there forever. She was still looking that way when Evail stepped out from beyond the light and spoke her name.

"Lord have mercy, Evail. About scared me to death."

"What do you have to fear?"

Belladonna thought of the girl. Imagined her running through the briars and the thickets, tripping over downed logs, falling. Bruised knees. Scraped palms. Belladonna took hold of her apron, kneading it, and looked into her son's eyes. "Reckon you're right," she said. "There ain't nothing for us to be scared of. Not no more."

Evail grinned in the harsh porch light, his teeth crooked but white and clean.

"The guilty flee when no man pursueth."

"Don't go quoting the Scriptures at me," Belladonna snapped. "I ain't your daddy. Besides, what I got to feel guilty about?"

Evail peered off into the darkness, and Belladonna began to worry. She'd always fretted over her youngest son, but she knew something was seriously wrong when he'd stopped eating her bacon, even her eggs. Everything was different when he came back from prison.

"I doubt you have anything to worry about, Mother."

"You might be surprised." Belladonna took the first step onto the porch. It creaked beneath her weight. "All that talking you was doing with Bunn, that ain't good for a momma to hear."

"You're right," Evail said and lowered his head. "There are some things a mother should not have to bear."

Belladonna worked her way up the remaining steps, reaching out slowly for her son, taking him around the waist and pulling him into her. He tightened at her touch. Evail had always been afraid of the dark. She remembered rocking him to sleep, night after night, even with Rudnick right there in the bed beside them, even after he was much too old to be afraid of such things. There lived inside her youngest son a sin Belladonna could not name, but it had not stopped her from loving him.

Evail tensed all at once, the muscles in his back and arms going taut like those of some feral animal.

"What is it, baby?" she said, leaning back, looking into his eyes. They were tight and focused, peering out into the night that had scared him for so long.

"I believe we have company."

Evail lifted a single bony finger and pointed. Belladonna followed his aim. At the farthest reaches of the light, something stirred against the tree line. Belladonna's heart beat so thick and so fast she knew Evail could feel it.

"Expecting someone, Mother?"

"I already told you—"

"I know," Evail said. "I *know*, but I've always been inclined toward doubt."

Evail pulled himself free of her hold, and then he was gone. She heard the screen door rap hard against the frame. She hoped beyond hope that the girl had not retraced her steps. The door creaked open again behind her and Belladonna turned.

"No, baby," she whispered. "There ain't no need for that."

The pistol in Evail's hand glowed hot in the porch light.

"We'll see."

23.

Night descended in full and took with it their vision.
Even Jeremiah's scope was no match for the deep
black woods and the thick canopy of trees hovering overhead. The front of The Judge protruded slightly from the
thicket, the chrome grill grinning like a set of silver teeth.

"What're we gonna do?" Colt whispered.

Jeremiah let the question dance in the night before
answering, thinking of everything that had led to this
moment, thinking of war. He lifted the rifle again, peering
through the scope, but he could not find the rose. He'd
seen it, though. He knew it, and that meant Jo was still
alive.

Even though Jeremiah had never allowed his mind to
wander down the darkest path, secretly he'd feared the
worst. It was why he'd dragged his feet. Why he didn't go
straight out to find her. Jeremiah feared finding Jo's body,
her corpse, but that fear was gone from him now.

Jo had been right *there*. Hell, maybe she was still locked
inside the cellar. Maybe the old Ledford woman had
been sent out to feed Jo, bring her scraps from the table.

Jeremiah's blood rose in his veins as he snarled, "*We* ain't gonna do nothing."

"I can sneak over there. You can cover me."

"What're you gonna do when you get there?"

"I'm gonna save her."

Jeremiah shook his head at the boy's hope, his confidence. How many years did it take to scrape away such a thing? There was a heavy feeling in the old man's heart and it wasn't from the whiskey.

"There ain't no guaranteeing she's in there, Colt."

Colt's eyes stayed on the root cellar. "I know she is. I can feel it."

Jeremiah said nothing of what he'd seen, nothing of Hattie's rose. The boy was resolute and he could respect that. "All right," he said. "I'll cover you, but listen—"

The bloodhounds howled from their pen, a primal sound, deep and low, that took Jeremiah back to the junkyard. Made him think of the Royals.

"I'm listening," Colt said.

"I ain't promising I can help you. If the Ledfords come running, I'll be watching for Jo. Won't have time to watch you too."

Colt turned his eyes back on the bare bulb glowing from the porch. "But I've heard the stories. I know how you got that star hanging around your neck."

Lies and trickery, that's how you earned medals. Jeremiah felt silly, all done up like a scarecrow. "Shooting a man," he said and reached for the bottle but found it empty, "even these slimy bastards, takes more whiskey than what was in that bottle."

"Not even for Jo?"

Jeremiah groaned because the boy was right. Jo was reason enough to pull the trigger. She held a power stronger even than whiskey. Women like Jo were creatures for which wars had been fought forever. Jeremiah had read their stories in the books he stored in his vault. The Trojan War had Helen. The battle between Rama and Ravana fought over Sita. And the truth behind Jake's pain was much more than the townsfolk had ever known, more than a theft of scrap parts stolen in the dark of the night—that Ledford boy died because of a woman. A girl who, at the time, looked much like Jo.

"I'll cover you," Jeremiah said and turned to the boy. "But remember, I ain't had enough to drink."

The porch light and the whiskey did funny things to Jeremiah's vision. Made the world seem bigger, or smaller, than it really was.

Belladonna had vanished inside the house, but Evail remained. Jeremiah kept the rifle on the threadbare man, not smoking, not drinking, just standing there, holding the pistol tight in his bony hand. There was a look on his face like nothing at all. Jeremiah let the crosshairs settle on Evail's left eye.

There would be more hell to pay if he pulled the trigger. He'd come so far, and now he was close—close enough to see everything. That was the main advantage of being a sniper: distance. It was different than the boys on the front line, bayonets and bowie knives, the sound of flesh ripping and blood bubbling out. But then there was the boy, running in the dark, heel to toe, quiet, barely making a sound.

Colt crept up the tree line, passing beside the hounds.

He put a hand to the chain link, let the dogs lick his fingers, and moved on. The porch light only reached so far. Colt went in and out of Jeremiah's sight. The boy was nearly to the root cellar when Jeremiah noticed movement in the shadows across the lawn.

Evail had stepped down from the porch. More shadows now, more light. Headlights shined through the pines, three sets of them. *Another road?* Jeremiah thought. That made sense. There was no way this little cut in the woods was the only entrance to the Ledford property.

Jeremiah could barely make out Colt creeping along the tree line, not thirty feet from the hole. The headlights grew larger, brighter, lighting more of the property. Evail stood in the farthest reaches of the porch light. He took a short step toward the root cellar, then stopped as the lights tore the shadows from the trees.

Colt was in plain sight now. Jeremiah's heart thumped so hard he could not steady his aim. Maybe he couldn't do it? Maybe all those nights remembering every man he'd shot would keep him from taking another life. Maybe his hands would shake. *Maybe.*

Evail didn't move toward the three trucks as they rumbled into the front yard. He stood firm, caught between the porch, the cellar, and the approaching visitors. They were jagged vehicles with brush guards and mud tires and KC fog lights in rows above their cabs. The trucks looked like smaller, meaner versions of The Judge. Their lights clicked on and all was illuminated.

Colt stood frozen, left foot in front of his right, one arm raised as if he were about to run. Jeremiah knew if anyone looked the boy's way—and surely they would look, surely these men had come for what was in that cellar—they would see him and then Jeremiah wouldn't have a choice. He could talk of whiskey all he wanted but the truth about guns, the truth about death, was in the end neither left a choice.

Evail didn't move. His shadow reached all the way back, nearly touching the toes of Colt's dirty boots. Evail lifted a hand toward the trucks and spoke in a tongue Jeremiah did not understand.

More shadows now, long and skinny like tree branches, rifles appearing and dangling over the tops of the trucks. Men stood in the beds. Others sat in the cabs. Jeremiah counted five and whispered, "Shit."

He was at least twenty yards away, cloaked in the shadows, but that boy and Jo, they were right there in the thick of it. He tried to steady his breathing. He was sweating now, the scope fogging from his heat. "*Shit.*"

"Where is she, my friend?"

A man emerged from the lead truck. He was short, but carried himself with the swagger of a boss. Tattoos crawled up his neck, crept toward his cheeks, and chiseled his face to a point like a timber rattler. He held no gun, and that worried Jeremiah more than anything.

"You say you have her?" said the Mexican. "Then let me see her. See if she really worth the fifty pound."

Jeremiah couldn't keep the scope from fogging. Couldn't steady his hand or the crosshairs. The Bronze Star hung heavy around his neck. He lowered the rifle. In the harsh glow of the floodlights he saw Colt without the aid of the scope. He knew if he could see the boy, the other men could see him too. All it would take was one look.

"She is worth more than fifty pounds," Evail said.

"Ah, so you give us the deal?"

"Yes, to show you I'm serious. I'm in this for the long haul."

"You talk big, my friend," said the Mexican. "But I did not come here for talk."

Evail nodded, and Jeremiah knew what would come next. They would turn now to the root cellar, and whatever sinister deal these men had gathered for in the depths of the woods would transpire.

"*Evail?*" A new voice echoed through the trees. All heads and rifles and lights turned to the porch. Bunn Ledford stood with a shotgun leveled out at his waist, squinting.

Jeremiah took a deep breath and raised the rifle again. The gun finally settled in his hands, the crosshairs no longer bouncing or swaying, leveling out in the glow coming down from the porch. Jeremiah needed something to get these men moving, turning on each other before Evail led them to that root cellar. Jeremiah needed a distraction.

The porch light exploded over Bunn Ledford's head, catching the other men with arms at odd angles, frozen from the shock of the blast. Jeremiah worked the bolt, the action coming back to him. In a row of neat and clean shots, he cleared out the rest of the headlights and flood-lights, until all that was left was the night.

It was short lived.

The fire Jeremiah had feared erupted in flashes, white-hot streaks, whizzing and searing their way through the black. Jeremiah stumbled away from his truck, pulling up the hood of his ghillie suit as he started to run.

He limped through the open air, foregoing the cover of

the tree line for the speed of a direct route. Around him the woods were ablaze. Crackles and pops. *Gunfire.* Jeremiah kept his head down, tripping, stumbling, his breath a ragged wet wheeze. When he looked up, he was standing before the cellar. Jeremiah glanced once over his shoulder, then opened the hulking door. It came to with a soft gong. Black so thick he could feel it.

"Jo?" he whispered. "*Jo.*"

Something moved in the darkness. Instinctively, Jeremiah raised the rifle.

"Thought you said you weren't gonna pull that trigger?"

A light came on beneath Colt's chin. His cell phone.

"Where is she?"

"Don't know."

"But the flower," Jeremiah said.

"What?"

"The rose I gave her before the Homecoming game. It was out there. I saw it."

"Well, she ain't in here, Mr. Fitzjurls. I done checked."

There was something in the kid's countenance that seemed off. The gunfire had ceased, but they were still in the thick of it. Colt was just a boy, and though video games and the internet had shown him more than he should ever see, boys were still quick to scare. The old man knew that much from the war.

"You got something you ain't telling me?" Jeremiah said, still holding the rifle at his hip.

And then the light went off.

"*Boy,*" hissed Jeremiah.

"Shut the hell up." Colt's voice remained steady. "You hear that?"

"I don't hear—"

But then he did.

Low murmurs. Voices in the night growing louder. Their speech indistinguishable. Jeremiah didn't know which side had won the firefight, but it didn't matter. Neither would be pleased to find the two of them crouched there in the darkness where they expected to find Jo.

"*Shhh.*"

There was no hesitation, no tremors in the sound, just a low, steady stream of breath. Colt's confidence confused the old man. Jeremiah lay flat on the damp cellar floor. He shook his head and pushed the rifle to his shoulder, ready for what was to come.

The door opened.

A shadow filled the void. Colt's shadow. He glanced once over his shoulder to Jeremiah, eyes steady like his voice. Like he knew something the old man did not. The boy raised his hands in the signal of surrender as he turned to face the night and all that came with it.

24.

Jo couldn't feel her leg or the slap and scrape of the branches as she ran. The blue dress hung in pieces. She'd long since given up on trying to keep it in place. Her chest was streaked red, covered only by the strapless bra she'd had to sneak off and buy from JCPenney two days before Homecoming.

Jo heard the gunshots and stopped, hands on her knees, eyes wide and unblinking. The blasts sounded far off, muffled, and she was glad for it. Glad to have some distance between her and the hole from which she'd crawled.

More shots now.

A small war back there through the pines, and good riddance. She wished they'd burn the woods down, level them out and leave nothing but smoke and ash where evil once stood. But then a thought came to her, something maybe she should have realized before. She'd been running for so long, not thinking, just running. The thought came in the form of two words, a nickname, and she wasn't thinking of any courtroom or jungle or even the trucks. She thought only of her grandfather and the name men had given him back when nights like these were all there'd been.

The Judge.

Jo took two steps back the way she'd come, but even such a small retracing made her gut turn queasy, her feet go cold. The shooting had stopped now. Short lived for all its fury. She guessed it wouldn't take him much time, no shot wasted, not with Pop's level of expertise. But who knew how many there were? Who knew if he still had the power he'd once had. The nerve.

Though she imagined her grandfather as a man to end all wars—a true American hero—Jo was faced with the brutal question of survival. Go back to the man she loved above all others? Or run, as fast as she could in the opposite direction?

The older she'd grown, the more Jo had begun to see the chinks in his armor. The things he forgot, the missteps, the falls. Just two weeks ago he'd emerged from the bathroom with a bloody piece of toilet paper wrapped around his head. "Slipped in the shower," was all he'd said.

The branches slapped and scraped her again, the top of her dress falling down to her waist. She held her heaving chest, lowered her head, and plowed through the woods, deciding whatever lay before her was better than what was behind.

25.

Jeremiah pushed his face against the cool damp rock as the door swung shut behind the boy, muffling the voices on the other side. Jeremiah cocked an ear as if listening to a broadcast on some distant radio. The men spoke in plain English, and for that, at least, Jeremiah was thankful.

"Colt?"

This voice was calm and steady, just as the boy's had been, a coolness under fire. Jeremiah guessed it was either Evail's or Bunn's. But how did they know the kid's name? Jeremiah lifted his head from the cool rock and turned his ear.

"*Colt?*" the voice said again. "Were you the one who started the shooting?"

Jeremiah recognized the voice now. Evail had always had a funny accent, an inflection far removed from the Ozark hills.

"I, uh . . ." Colt said. "I's trying to help."

"You have already done your part."

"Now, y'all wait just one damn minute."

This voice carried the thunder from before. *Bunn*, thought Jeremiah.

"Easy, Father. Let young Colt explain himself."

"*Explain* himself?" Bunn roared. "Shit, Evail. He ain't the only one's got some explaining to do."

"I told you exactly what would happen tonight," Evail hissed. "The only thing I didn't foresee was Colt."

A pause, long enough Jeremiah imagined Evail and Bunn turning on the boy, curious looks in their cold black eyes.

"I's coming up the tree line, coming to see if you had her," Colt stammered, his steady swagger gone now. "And I guess one them Mexicans saw me and started shooting."

Colt sounded nothing like the boy who'd bravely walked out of the cellar a moment ago. In the silence, other voices emerged, machinegun vowels, passion brimming on the tip of the Mexicans' tongues. Jeremiah rose to one knee and shouldered the rifle.

"Colt. *Colt* . . ." Evail said. "I want to believe you, but there is too much riding on this transaction to simply rely on faith. There are two dead men back there, and my new friend Guillermo is very upset." Evail paused and Jeremiah tried to steady his breath. "Honestly, I think there's only one thing that will make him happy again."

"She ain't in there," Colt said. "I'm telling you. You just saw me come out."

"Someone shot out Mother's porch light, then pro- ceeded to shoot the truck lights. I thought maybe a ghost was among us—until you appeared."

"I said I's here to help. Shit, Evail."

Despite his training, Jeremiah stood in the depths of the cellar. It wasn't a tactical move. Far from it. Any good sniper knows it's best to keep your body as small as possible, especially in close quarters. But there were too many of them. It wouldn't matter if Jeremiah was crouching or kneeling or standing—he knew he couldn't take them all.

"What the hell's he talking about?" Bunn said, sounding as confused as Jeremiah.

"Nothing, Father."

"Manos a la obra."

"You're right, Guillermo," Evail said. "We are wasting valuable time."

Jeremiah heard more murmurs, and then came a rattling at the door. The whiskey had receded in his blood enough to tell him this was not the place to make his stand. As the door creaked open, Jeremiah lunged toward the depths of the cellar.

Colt watched as Evail shined a flashlight into the darkness and decay, the piles of emaciated squash, snap peas, and rotting leaves. It was almost Biblical: the rolling away of the stone, the empty tomb.

Colt's eyes flicked from Evail to the tattered hunk that lay in the farthest corner of the cellar. The ghillie suit rose and fell, invisible palpitations to the unknowing eye. Colt exhaled because he knew the old man was hidden under there.

The little Mexican clicked his teeth. "No bueno."

"I'll find her," Evail said.

"American women," Guillermo said, shaking his head as he exited the cellar, "are muy impredecible."

Colt stayed back, watching as Evail paced, kicking at the different piles of rubbish. He'd nearly stepped on Jeremiah twice but each time turned to a different pile, sending leaves cascading down across the damp floor.

"Colt, son," Bunn said, backlit from what little moonlight shone through the open door. "How in the hell'd you get wrapped up in this mess?"

Colt said, "I been wrapped up in it," watching as Evail kicked one last pile of rubbish and then exited the root cellar, trotting to catch up with Guillermo.

Bunn shook his head and spat, the way old men do when they don't want to hear any more. A moment later, he followed Evail out through the iron door. Colt was the last to exit, glancing a final time over his shoulder to the mass of dead leaves on the cellar floor. Once outside, the first thing Colt heard was the boss Mexican say, "Veinticuatro." He thought maybe it sounded like a number, but he wasn't sure. In fact, Colt wasn't sure about that man at all.

Guillermo was different. The tattoos on his neck and face came alive in the light of the moon, slithering in long black runs: pumas, dragons, a cartoon woman wearing a cowboy hat and nothing more. Twenty feet behind him, two of his kind lay sprawled in the dirt dyed red from their blood. If the loss bothered Guillermo, he didn't let it show.

The firefight had finally ended when Colt emerged from the cellar and witnessed Belladonna turning on a string of Christmas lights dangling in the trees. Evail was the first to raise his gun above his head, then Bunn, and finally the remaining Mexicans. Small sounds like a child playing cowboys and Indians drifted through the night and found the men with hearts still beating through to their ears. In unison they had turned, and there stood Guillermo, hands at his waists, fingers curled to form pistols, firing away. "Is it over?" he'd said. "But *Ma*, I want to stay out and play." He'd raised his fingers, blown smoke from the imaginary barrels, and holstered the guns into nothing.

Guillermo stood before Colt now, and though he'd yet to lay a hand on a single weapon, he struck a fear in the boy he had not felt before. And Colt knew evil. He'd been brought up in it, but this Mexican—he was different.

"Veinticuatro," Guillermo said again, all the flare gone from his voice, jaw set, fending off the shadows that crawled up his neck.

"Twenty-four?" Evail said. "Twenty-four what?"

"Hours."

"To find the girl?"

"You a quick one, cowboy."

Colt's eyes darted between Evail and Bunn, their faces so different, yet much the same. There was a hardness that resided in both of them, a look you couldn't fake.

"Or what?" Evail tried.

Guillermo groaned and bobbed his head like a strutting rooster. His teeth were completely gold, diminished in the darkness, almost as if they weren't there, like the gun the man never carried.

"We could take the boy?" Guillermo jeered, nodding back toward his men. They grinned and swayed in the night. "Chicos bring more than chicas these days. This more your speed, no?"

Evail straightened and glanced sideways at his father.

Guillermo grinned. "Sí, Papi, and we fuck your woman, too."

Bunn lunged forward, a look in his eyes Colt had never seen before, but Evail caught him by the shoulders.

Then Colt took hold of his arms. Bunn was stronger than expected, a deep-rooted oak against the storm, the strength of age and time. Guillermo continued his strut then stopped suddenly, taking a Blow Pop from his breast pocket and sticking it into his mouth. He walked up close to Bunn, the old man still jerking and fighting against his boys.

"Veinticuatro," said Guillermo and crunched the sucker with his teeth before he turned to walk away.

Bunn jerked free, straightening his shirt and mumbling as the Mexicans disappeared into their vehicles. The trucks came to life and started through the trees. In a matter of seconds, they were gone.

Evail threw up both arms and stomped around the edge of the house until his slender frame was swallowed by shadows. A few minutes later, the bloodhounds howled and an engine's roar thundered out from the tree line. Two headlights appeared in the distance, growing brighter as the ATV pulled up alongside Colt and Bunn. Evail sat behind the wheel, the dogs free of their cage and following close behind.

"You saw her enter the motel?" Evail spoke into a satellite phone cradled in the crook of his neck. "And you're sure it was her?"

Bunn stepped forward. "Where the hell you get a phone like that?"

"Good, cousin," Evail said, ignoring his father. "Now bring her to me."

"*Cousin?*" Bunn barked.

Evail smiled at his father but spoke into the phone. "Call this number when you have her, Dime. I look forward to hearing her voice."

The cell phone's light died and Evail's face went dark.

"You sent *Dime* after somebody?" Bunn said. "All them books you read and you ain't any smarter than that?"

"Don't worry about Dime, Father." Evail's eyes drifted back to the dead Mexicans in the yard. "We need to find the girl."

Colt followed Bunn's gaze, fearing what was to come. If what Jo had told him was true, Jeremiah could start, and end, this war with that old rifle. Colt knew the history too. He'd known it all along, but that was before tonight. Before Jo had opened herself up to him and let him inside. Colt could still feel her warmth. He remembered the taste of her lips, a sweetness like nothing he'd ever known. All of that would be gone if Bunn got ahold of her. He'd skin the girl alive. And what Evail had planned for her wasn't much better. There was only one person Colt could think of who might be able to stop them.

"What about Momma?" Colt said.

"What about her?" Evail snapped.

"Colt's right," Bunn said, sucking his teeth. "With everything swirling around out here tonight, who knows what might happen. Somebody's got to stay back with Belladonna and keep watch over the house. Might as well be me."

"*No*," Colt said then caught himself. "I mean . . . You need to go with Evail. He'll need you to work the dogs."

"Work the dogs?"

"Besides," Colt said, "I bet Momma don't want you around right now, anyway."

"And why's that?"

"I figure she's the one let the girl out."

Bunn's molten face tightened.

Evail made a sharp, whistling sound with his teeth.

Colt added fuel to the fire. "She probably heard y'all talking about it. Momma's all the time listening. Y'all know that as well as I do," Colt said, talking fast. "And I bet she's pissed after all that shooting. Them beaners blew her porch light out."

Evail's eyes moved from the downed Mexicans to the tree line, carrying with them a look of death. Bunn bent to a dog, rubbing his hand over its snout. Colt watched the two men, studying their moves, but he could not read them.

"Fine," Bunn said, grunting as he plopped down in the ATV. "I'll work the dogs."

Colt exhaled, already turning for the cellar, but then Evail's voice stopped him.

"And Colt will tend to the dead."

The boy squeezed his eyes shut. He knew exactly what Evail was telling him to do. He didn't want to see it, though. Not up close like that.

"Do what?" Colt said, rotating slowly back to face them, the roar of the ATV's engine adding to his fear. But they were already gone, leaving him alone with their mess. In the distance, the hounds howled and the two red tail-lights glowed like tiny devils.

26.

Jo saw the moon in Piney Creek, only a sliver, but it was there and that was something. The Piney ran through downtown Taggard, meandering its way under bridges, behind worn out factories, and eventually emptying into Lake Dardanelle, where the old nuclear cooling tower remained tall and pointless. Jo stood by the water. She lifted the dress, stepped off the bank, and let herself cry, adding saltwater to the clear, cool stream.

The water rose up over the wound in her thigh. It felt good and clean. Dogs howled in the distance. Redbones. *Bloodhounds*. Jo remembered the stories her grandfather had told of such dogs. How they were sometimes used to hunt wild boar, even bear. The dogs howled again, closer now, and Jo started to run.

The water turned cold as it rose under the dress she had hoisted in both hands. The creek would help with her scent. She thought briefly about stopping and letting the current push her all the way back home. But she knew it was too slow. She emerged on the other side and saw two headlights breaking through the brush.

Jo ducked into the woods on the other side and prayed as she ran. She spoke to God aloud, her voice rasping out between breaths, asking Him questions that had come in the night, the bone-hard man's voice echoing in her ears. Jo asked the Lord if she was any different than Brynn Barker. She wasn't Queen, that was for damn sure, but there was more to it than that. More to the past, bleeding into the present now, the sky gray ahead of her, a thin fog hanging low over the creek as Jo sliced her way through.

She prayed harder, asking for forgiveness as the memory of Colt's bed swam to the surface. Could that have led to this? She thought so. Not just because of the panties she'd left back on the highway somewhere, but because of this night. She knew, somehow, it would stay with her.

All the basketball practices over the summer in the steamy Bulldog Gym served Jo well. She ran far enough she couldn't hear the men behind her anymore, the wound in her thigh throbbing with every stride. She slowed to a walk and cocked an ear. She heard nothing. Jo took a deep breath, her muscles relaxing for the first time in what seemed like forever, and then a dog whimpered behind her.

It looked nothing like the dogs in her grandfather's junkyard. Nothing like the Royals. Jo crouched and pawed at the water's edge. She hefted a fist-sized rock from the bank, but the dog just stood there, droopy ears, sad eyes, tail wagging slightly, side to side.

This bloodhound didn't seem anything like the stories she'd heard. Jo squeezed the rock in her hand and suddenly it made sense—dogs didn't hunt people. Not even bloodhounds. And whatever scent this one had gathered from the cellar she'd already washed off in the creek. She was just a person out in the woods, and this was just a dog.

Jo knew dogs.

She squatted down and motioned for the hound with bent fingers, trying to lessen the threat. The dog came to her, head down, showing no signs of aggression. His shoulder blades alternated slowly as he crept forward, long tail slapping lazy at his haunches. Finally, his muzzle was in her hand. Jo ran her thumb along the ridge of his nose. For a moment, she forgot about the chase. Dogs had always carried that power for her. She'd worked at the Humane Society since she was twelve. Every once in a while, after a new litter was born into the junkyard, she'd sneak a puppy out of the cage and across the street with hopes of a better life. Her mind was back there, back in the shelter with the puppies and the gigantic bags of dry dog food, when the redbone howled.

The rock connected flush with the hound's eye socket, a hollow pop, and then nothing. Jo stood, rock clenched in both hands. It was only when the dog slowly closed its eyes that she realized what she had done and why she'd done it. A silent whistle sounded in the night somewhere. The dogs bayed. Jo took off again through the woods.

When she made it to the creek bank, the rock fell from her hands. As she bounded back into the cold waters, the rock remained, stained red, a mark that made it different from all the others.

27.

The mass of leaves and tangled debris turned to man as Jeremiah rose to his feet in the cellar. The door was closed. No light. He'd waited a good while. How long, he wasn't certain. He'd heard the boy talking. Heard an engine and dogs. Add all those things up, and he knew the sum was not good for Jo.

Jeremiah pushed open the great iron door. The dead Mexicans stank already. The Viet Cong had been the same, quick to stink. Something about their diet. Too much soy sauce or some shit. Jeremiah shook his head. They'd told him so many lies about the Vietnamese. Gave them a silly name like "gooks," something less than human. Problem was, they bled red like any other man.

Jeremiah kept close to the tree line, creeping his way back toward the truck.

As he approached, The Judge looked different, diminished somehow. It wasn't until he went to open the door and pull himself into the cab that he realized what had happened.

Jeremiah stepped back, surveying the damage from the wild spray of the Mexicans' automatic rifles. The Judge looked like an amputee, its great mud tires nothing but deflated bags now. He reared back to kick at them but heard a crunch from behind and paused.

In a motion so fast it defied time and age and drunkenness, Jeremiah spun and leveled the rifle on the boy. "Give me one good reason not to shoot your ass."

Colt's hands were up, just as they had been when he exited the cellar. "I can explain."

"You got about five seconds."

"Not here," Colt said. "We got to move."

"*We?*"

"Jo's out there, Mr. Fitzjurls, and them hills ain't forgiving."

Jeremiah clicked the rifle's safety off. "Might say the same about me."

"Belladonna let her out. Couldn't stand the thought of what Evail was gonna do with her, what Bunn might've done if he got close enough. You know, considering the history."

"History?"

"Got a lot I need to tell you."

"Them five seconds about up."

"You shoot me and they'll hear it. You want another firefight?"

Jeremiah started backing away, the rifle still aimed on the boy.

"You don't know these woods like I do," Colt tried.

"And why do you know these woods so damn well, Colt Dillard?"

Colt looked down and kicked at the dirt. "My last name ain't Dillard."

The sight of the boy down the length of the barrel brought pain to the old man. Jeremiah saw his final victim again. The girl was as close now as she'd been all those years before in the jungle of Khe Sanh. She'd never left him. Through the scope, he could see all the details he'd never be able to forget. She was young, half the age of Jo now, and there was a birthmark below her left eye shaped like a broken heart. The girl stepped into the bamboo hut's open-air window after the trigger had been pulled five times already. He saw the tears in the girl's eyes, the way she wasn't looking down at the bodies beneath her feet. She wasn't screaming for the loss of her family. She just stepped into the window, like she knew where the shots had come from, like she knew there was one more out there waiting for her.

"What are you then, boy?" Jeremiah said, shaking himself free of the past.

Colt's eyes rose, looking almost cross-eyed down the long run of blue barrel. "I'm still here."

The gun lowered, moving from the boy's head to his heart.

"And that should mean something," Colt said. "I could've snitched. Could've told them you was in that cellar, but I didn't."

"They would've strung you up just for bringing me on the property."

"But I came back. Why the hell would I come back to you if I wasn't honest about trying to find Jo?"

Jeremiah lowered the barrel to his waist.

Colt looked past the old man and into the woods beyond. "She's out there. Don't you get that?"

"Yeah," Jeremiah said. "And that's why I'm done

talking." He turned his back on the boy, walking past the truck down the little trail that had led them there.

"Well, you're going the wrong way."

Jeremiah kept walking.

"Jo wouldn't have gone to the road. She's looking for water."

"Water?" Jeremiah said, stopping now.

"The Piney runs all the way back into town."

"How the hell you expect Jo to know something like that?"

"I taught her."

Jeremiah needed a drink. These were the nights whiskey was made for, cold dark nights when the fire needed to burn from the inside out.

"We got two problems," Jeremiah said.

"We got more problems than that."

Jeremiah pointed. "What we gonna do when they find my truck? Everybody in Taggard knows The Judge belongs to me."

Colt said nothing, looking only at the wasted tires then back to the field and the dead Mexicans.

"Second, if you're coming with me," Jeremiah said, "I need your cell phone and I need to see what else you got in your pockets."

"You're wasting time."

"If you're coming with me," Jeremiah said, propping the rifle up over his shoulder, eyeing the boy, "those are the rules."

Colt stood a good distance away. He looked back toward the woods, back in the direction he said Jo had gone, and then he turned to Jeremiah.

"Fine," Colt said. "But just remember: if we find Jo dead out there—or if *they* find her first—you were the one back there making all these damn rules."

Jeremiah nodded, knowing what was at stake. "I hear you, kid." He paused and spat. "Now go get me some gasoline."

They didn't hear the boom until they were deep into the woods, a low, chest-pounding thud—The Judge going up in flames. The hope was that the explosion would provide a distraction, something to pull Bunn and Evail off the hunt long enough for them to gain some ground. Jeremiah prayed when they got there his beautiful truck would be burnt beyond recognition. Prayed the dead Mexicans Colt had dragged over would burn, the boy pulling them along by their pointy boots and lifting them into the bed without much trouble. Jeremiah could only hope the explosion would work like he'd planned. Any good sniper knows he needs surprise on his side, all the way up until the bullet hits the brain.

They hurried through the woods, following a trail the boy seemed to know well. Colt's wrists were bound with a zip tie Jeremiah had salvaged from the truck's bed. The boy trotted along, hands at his groin, cursing the old man for hindering him even further.

"This really necessary?" Colt asked between footfalls.

Jeremiah grunted in return.

"You already crushed my cell phone. Took everything I had in my pockets."

"I'm still not convinced you ain't leading me straight to them," Jeremiah said. "What the hell makes you think Jo would come this way?"

"Told you, I showed her these trails."

"You're telling me you brought Jo out here? Brought her right up close to Bunn Ledford, the man who hates her most in this world?"

"Didn't take her to the house, just brought her out to the woods. Went hiking and stuff. She said her whole life was spent going from the junkyard to the high school and then over to the Humane Society in the afternoons. What kinda life is that?"

"A safe one."

They ducked along the trail, but there were no signs of Jo. No blood, no pieces of her dress, nothing. Jeremiah had already begun to worry, not just about the trail, but everything else.

"What was Bunn getting at back there?" Jeremiah rasped. "What's your history with the Ledfords?"

"Belladonna," Colt said. "She's where my story starts."

Jeremiah studied the boy stomping along beside him. In the darkness, the old man could've almost mistaken Colt for Jake. He carried himself like a quarterback. Kept his chin up, his chest puffed out, accentuating his broad shoulders and trim waist. The only thing that didn't fit was Colt's hair. An unruly mess of chewed-off curls. Thick and mangy. Like the boy had to use hedge clippers twice a week to keep it all under control.

"She's the only reason I'm standing here today," Colt said, and Jeremiah turned back to the trail. "Belladonna's got a big heart. Same reason she let Jo out that cellar's the same reason she took me in. Didn't care what Bunn said."

"Took you in?"

"Found me on that porch under the light you shot out.

Weren't wrapped up or nothing, just sitting out there on my ass in the middle of December."

"Bunn Ledford took a baby boy in?"

"Told you it weren't Bunn that made the decision. Belladonna was itching to fill the hole Rudnick left, and that's just what she did. Taught me to read and write, taught me everything until I was about ten, then Bunn took over."

"What'd he teach you? How to burn a goddamn cross?"

"Tried, but it didn't take. Kinda hard to listen to lies when you're living one yourself. Never knew nothing about my blood kin."

Jeremiah's mind drifted back to the drunken, hazy mornings spent half asleep in those rigid Methodist pews. Even after he laid the bottle down, even sitting in Christ *Zone* with the other toothless sinners, he'd never been able to shake his past—sins so dark no god worth a shit would forgive him. That was always how he'd reasoned it. Figured maybe if Jo grew up all right, if she married a good man, had a whole bunch of kids, and lived a half-decent life, maybe then—and it was still a big maybe—he could rest in peace.

Up ahead, Jeremiah heard the current. "You think she's just gonna be sitting in the creek waiting for us?"

"If she's half as smart as I think she is, she'll be heading downstream, back toward town."

Jeremiah huffed and carried on, the water a distant rumble but growing closer with every step. "So Belladonna took a shine to you, huh? How'd that go over at them KKK rallies?"

"She wouldn't let me go. Kept me locked up at the house. Shut off from the rest of the world. I never thought much about the rallies. Seemed like church or something to me, everybody dressed up in white robes, prancing around out in some field. Hard to hate what you can't see, or maybe it works the other way around. I don't know. But I do know I didn't like it. Didn't buy their shit for a minute."

Jeremiah said nothing. He was starting to realize why the boy and Jo had found each other. Their worlds weren't that different, a lifetime spent trying to hide who they really were.

"But then Evail got out of prison and started coming around. Said I turned out different than what he's expecting."

Jeremiah nodded.

"Always going on about the same damn thing. Football. Said I had it in my blood. Said I could be great, and if I's great I could make it out of these hills and back into the real world. Always talked about Harrison like it was some sort of Promised Land."

"*Harrison?*"

"Home of the White Arkansas Resistance. You heard of them?"

"Yeah," Jeremiah said. "I've heard of the W.A.R. boys."

They were closer to the water now, a peaceful sound in the still of the night. Jeremiah listened as Colt spoke faster, like he wanted—*needed*—the old man to hear his story.

"Took me a while to realize it weren't football Evail was worried about. That was just an excuse to spend time with me, take me out in the yard, teach me how to hold a ball, how to throw one. Tackled me for years and years, until one day I got tired of it and ran his skinny ass over."

Jeremiah remembered teaching Jake the same lessons.

"But it was all just a cover. What he really wanted was for me to grow up and be the hotshot quarterback at some high school. Didn't matter which one. Evail thought if I's the quarterback, I'd get all the girls."

"The girls?"

"While he's in prison, Evail heard about these big factories south of the border where they cooked meth, more meth than any American could ever dream of because Mexico's laws are so shitty."

Jeremiah picked up the pace, hustling over the fallen logs and rotting leaves.

"Said these Mexicans were ready to start dealing over in the States. But they weren't looking for money. They wanted girls. American girls. The prettier the better."

"Naw." Jeremiah didn't want to hear the rest.

"So Evail got to thinking, and he had that chip on his shoulder from your boy killing Rudnick, and he knew Jo was about my age, and the rest—well—you can probably figure out the rest."

"Then why'd he send you to Harrison?"

"That was Bunn's doing. Figured if he sent me out of Craven County maybe it would make things easier. Something like that. Only spent one year there, freshman year. Then Evail came for me."

"And brought you back to Taggard?"

"Took me down to the courthouse. Had Belladonna there to sign some paper that changed my last name. Then he took me over to the high school. Signed the transfer papers himself."

"But he ain't your daddy."

"After Coach Turner saw what I could do on that field,

it didn't matter if my daddy was dead or alive—Dale Turner was gonna make sure I played ball for the Bulldogs."

They reached the top of a small berm and the creek sprawled out, hissing in the darkness, weaving its way back toward the glowing lights of Taggard. There was no bank beneath them, only a sharp fall to the cold waters below. On the other side, a rocky beach ran the length of the creek, easy walking.

"You gonna make me cross that water," Colt said, lifting his wrists, "with my hands tied up like this?"

Jeremiah turned to the boy, flicked open the blade of a lock-back tactical knife he kept in his boot, and cut the zip ties loose. As the small bits of plastic fell free of his wrists, Colt lifted both hands and whispered, "You see that?"

Jeremiah didn't move.

"On the far bank," Colt said, his voice rising. "Something's over there."

When Jeremiah finally turned, he heard a splash and realized the boy had jumped.

The old man raised the rifle.

Colt slipped and fell, plowing his way through the thigh-high current, each step quicker, more frantic than the last. The curved trigger was cool to the touch. Jeremiah leveled the crosshairs on the boy's left leg.

"Forgive us our trespasses," Jeremiah began, but before he could finish his prayer the boy lifted both hands and motioned to the bank. He shouted against the rush and churn of the water. Jeremiah couldn't make out what he said, not at first, but then the boy yelled out again, and this time the word rang true: "*Jo!*"

The gun moved fast, following the tip of Colt's finger. It was dark, too dark. Jeremiah couldn't make out exactly what was lying at the back edge of the bank, right where the underbrush and trees began.

"*Jo!*" shouted Colt again.

The blurry image came into focus. First a paw, then a bloody snout. *A goddamn dog*, Jeremiah thought.

Colt was already to the other bank, running, stumbling across the rocks. Jeremiah held steady, hoping the boy would see the dog and realize he needed to keep his damn mouth shut, when a pair of lights cut through the tree line, followed by howls.

Jeremiah turned in time to see the ATV tearing along through the thickets, the dogs out front, noses to the ground. His foot slipped from the high bank. The creek came next. Colder than expected. The lights grew brighter, the dogs louder, and then he sank fast beneath dark waters.

28.

They were close. How close, Jo didn't know. The howls
did funny things in the night, echoing down the
stream, bouncing off the limestone bluffs that ran alongside the water. Jo scrambled over the rocks, keeping near
the tree line, hoping the darkness afforded her some cover.

The dogs' howls gathered and grew in strength like they
had something treed. Jo ran. She knew the creek. Colt had
taught her well. They'd floated it back in the summer after
he'd just arrived. It was too early for them to do what
they'd done the night before. Jo hadn't even thought of it,
and Colt didn't bring it up. He didn't push too hard. The
sun hung hot and heavy in the sky, so different from this
night in early October.

She'd kissed him then, or let him kiss her, a forceful
embrace full of passion and tongue. They'd taken a picture in the late afternoon heat, the cicadas buzzing, heads
pressed together at the temples, smiling in the red canoe
they'd rented from the hippies who lived down by the
water. The creek was green, almost translucent. Colt took
the picture, a selfie, his toned arm extended as far as it

would go, veins running from wrist to elbow. She remembered him trying to push the button when they came upon fast water and how he'd almost dropped her—

Cell phone.

Jo pawed at the depths of her tattered bra, hoping beyond hope that somehow the phone remained. Her fingers found its hard edge tucked safely down where her dress clung tight to her ribs.

Jo stopped and backed slowly into the cover of the woods, praying the phone still worked. It was soaked, but the light came on. Her own face greeted her from the lock screen, a reflection of sorts. Colt was there, too. The picture from the canoe trip, from this very creek.

With trembling fingers she tapped the screen, entering her passcode. Somehow, it worked. She dialed 911, then cancelled the call and opted for Mona's cell.

"Mona, please," whispered Jo, the phone pressed tight to her ear. "Pick up."

But there was nothing, no rings, no dial tone, nothing. She pulled the phone back from her face. Two words answered the riddle, tiny and glowing in the upper left-hand corner of the screen: NO SERVICE.

Jo hissed one of her Pop's favorite words, remembering how Colt had explained the bluffs worked like a big shield for cell towers. He seemed proud of it, happy he'd taken her to a place where they were truly alone. Jo crammed the phone back into her dress and continued on. She feared what lay ahead because she knew what was coming, remembered the sound and the rush of it, water splashing, and that big rock waiting right out in the middle.

Big Mother.

That's what Colt had called it, saying, "Big Mother's the scariest whitewater in all of Arkansas, a class five rapid. On the weekends people pull off on the bank just to watch the canoes tump over. It's awesome."

She heard the rapid now, imagining she'd somehow awakened it, a low growl like a den full of sleepy-eyed bears. Colt had also said there was no getting around Big Mother. You had to go through her if you wanted to reach Twin Bridges—the creek's only downstream access point—and get back to your car and cell service.

The narrow rock bank forced all that green water down a channel that led to the rock for which the rapid was named. The rock was the size of a truck, something like The Judge laid to rest in the creek. The problem with Big Mother was she pulled you to her. She was concave beneath the surface, and that strange shape caused one hell of an undertow. Colt said he'd seen a good many canoes go under, come out on the other side bent in half like a fortune cookie.

Jo stood before the beast now. Even the water seemed afraid, billowing out on either side of the rock's face, creating a boat-sized wake. There were no banks, only limestone bluffs this far downstream. She dipped her toe in the water. It was cold. She thought of the cell phone. How it was working now, but after the water and Big Mother there was no telling how it would come out—much less how *she* would come out—on the other side.

There was a ledge, skinny, but wide enough at least for her toes. It was higher than she would have liked, but it was there. The gunshot wound sent a wave of nausea up from her thigh. She gritted her teeth and took two steps toward the ledge, knowing that it would be a slow go, but it would be better than Big Mother. Then the dogs howled again.

The howls pushed Jo back into the creek. The ice-cold water stole her breath. She pulled the cell phone from her dress and held it high above her head like she'd seen a few drunks do with beer cans when they'd ventured down a rapid on their backsides. That's what she was doing now, feeling for the bottom, legs out in front of her, riding it down.

Then there was no bottom.

Jo suspended, floating. The water deep and strong. The bluffs flew past above her, a rush of green and stone. She tried to paddle with one arm, the other still fighting to hold the phone above her head. Big Mother expanded, growing bigger, more menacing than even The Judge. In the lichen and the shadows clinging to the rock, Jo thought she saw a face, gnarly and misshapen. Was it her mother? Was this what had become of the woman who remained only in faded pictures? Like all girls raised by men, Jo pined for soft hands, the flowery smell of shampoo, a woman to tell her what not to wear and the right way to fix her hair.

She was thinking of her mother when the current took her under, her face scraping roughly across the submerged rock. The cell phone fell from her fingers, drifting to the bottom like the maple seedpods she'd played with as a child. The last thing Jo saw before she closed her eyes was the dim glow of her cell phone screen. The picture. Her face and Colt's pressed together, smiling back through the green creek water, now and forever more.

29.

Jeremiah opened his eyes under the dark swirl and saw Jo. Back in the junkyard, back to the night he'd found her. Hattie alive, the roses nothing but small sprigs of green. Jake still awaiting trial. Three knocks. Nobody knocked that time of night, not in the junkyard. Jeremiah had just cracked the door and there she was: a beautiful baby girl wrapped in a bath towel. She didn't cry. She never cried. And whoever had left her was gone.

Under the water he saw Jo as a child again, wrapped in that towel, smiling, not even one year old. He held her tight as a bullet whizzed past, streaking the water in a line of bubbles. Then another. Jo dissolved and the creek bottom replaced her. Bullets everywhere now.

Jeremiah fought to stay submerged. He took hold of a sunken rock and pulled it to his chest like he'd done his granddaughter all those years before. The current was strong, dragging him downstream as the bullets cut lines through the water. He closed his eyes, expecting this to be the end, but then he felt something sweep up against his leg, a hard, familiar shape poking into his thigh.

The old rifle had found him.

With the rifle in his hands, Jeremiah came alive. He stood, the water only reaching his hips. Hands working quickly, pulling the bolt, drying the bullet, the hammer, and then a crisp snap as he re-chambered and put the gun to his shoulder.

He expected hellfire, either by the hands of the Ledfords or the hands of God, but what he found was only the quiet flow of the creek. Voices carried quick down the water. Jeremiah followed them with the gun. Bunn and Evail were bent over the high bank, talking with Colt down below. Jeremiah chose Evail over Bunn. That bald bastard was the one to take first.

Safety off. Slight pressure on the trigger. Jeremiah began to pray, but then Colt started splashing along the bank, pointing upstream.

"She went that way," the boy shouted, his voice carrying with the current.

"Then what the hell was all that splashing around down there?" Bunn yelled back, holding the shotgun level at his waist.

"Just the dogs," Colt said. "The bloodhounds. You was shooting at your own damn dogs."

Jeremiah felt the water beneath him, cool and clean, unaware of the violence men had brought down upon it. Jeremiah could end it all in less time than it took to breathe, but the water was so oblivious, so innocent. And that boy was saving his ass again.

Bunn's and Evail's heads turned quick, following Colt's finger, and Jeremiah ducked back beneath the surface, swallowing all the air his lungs would hold. Jo wasn't there this time, but she'd been there. There was no way to explain it other than an awareness of blood. He could feel her in the water. She was on up ahead of him somewhere. He was sure of that now. The water washing away the memory of those soiled panties and their implications, the worries the old man had been pushing down since he'd first heard the news in the holding cell. The creek had carried Jo downstream just as it had done him, and maybe she was safe.

At the end of the breath, Jeremiah rose again, squinting as he watched the red taillights of the ATV bounce around the next bend. He stayed crouched like that for some time, letting the water rush around him, wash him clean. It felt like baptism but without a preacher, without being dunked. Just a good clean flow. A hollowed-out feeling like heroin, or whiskey, the bottom of the bottle but before you come down.

He let the water carry him. Each minute putting more distance between him and the Ledfords—all three of them—bringing him closer and closer to Jo.

The bluffs grew steeper after a while. The jungle and the junkyard were with him in the river, the towers he built on the shattered remains of other people's lives. The bluffs were like the towers. There was no reason for him to be thinking of the junkyard, no reason he wasn't up and out of the water, rushing down the bank to find his granddaughter, yet there he was.

Jeremiah could've ended it all back there. No questions asked. Just three dead shitheads washed out into Lake Dardanelle. With any luck they would have gotten sucked up under a rapid, stayed there a while, and when somebody finally found the bodies, the creek would have done them just as it'd done the rocks beneath him, round stones washed smooth and clean. Jeremiah was almost proud. He'd known for a long time it took more guts to keep from violence than to fall victim to it. He'd lived that life, enough of it already, and now he floated in the waters and was washed anew.

It took him a while to float down to Big Mother, a critical amount of time given the circumstance. He knew of the gnarly rapid, had wrapped many a canoe around it as a boy. But even as he grew closer—already the flow picking up—he did nothing. He just let the water take him.

Jeremiah bounced absently off Big Mother, pivoting there against the rock, drifting down the left side, the less treacherous side, as he floated along unharmed like a drunk driver stumbling away from a mangled wreck.

The big rock seemed to grin as he went by, growing smaller as Jeremiah drifted beneath the bridge's underbelly of iron and swallows' nests. Looking back, he thought he saw a blue light shimmering up from under that rock. Maybe he saw something dangling there, wavering in the water. Jo's dress was blue. He remembered that. But Jo was on up ahead of him. That's how it worked. One generation led to the next, so on and so forth, on through to the end.

30.

When Dime kicked in the motel room door, Lacey Brewer was face deep in the lower fold of a fat man. The air smelled of cheap wine and cigarettes.

Dime almost laughed, but then remembered he was holding a gun, his Sig Sauer P320. Instead, he walked forward, the fatty's eyes growing wider and whiter as Lacey practiced her craft, seemingly deaf from the depths of the fold. Dime recognized the man. George Barker Junior. The banker with the skinny wife. The even skinnier daughter. Dime touched the Sig to fat Georgie's nose.

"*Disgusting*," Dime said. "That's what this is."

Lacey jerked back from the crease. "What the fu—"

Dime hit her so hard in the back of the head she shot forward and racked George Junior in the balls. He doubled over, hitching at his starched khakis and looking up at Dime with red watering eyes like he'd been shot.

"Go on," Dime said and jerked his thumb over his shoulder. "*Get*. Ain't telling you again."

George Junior, the banker whose daughter had just been named Homecoming Queen, waddled out the motel room door, grumbling like he was pissed his postgame festivities had been cut short.

Dime turned to Lacey, a small line of blood trickling out from her nose, and said, "You know why I'm here?"

"Never had a guy itching so bad for a blowjob."

The gun barrel dangled inches from her busted mouth.

"Shit," Dime said, then spat on the floor. "Bet George tastes like ass."

"They all do, but it's easier than working at Walmart. Pays better too."

Dime looked as if he were going to spit again, but instead swallowed. "You know why I'm here?"

"Starting to think it ain't got nothing to do with a blowjob."

Dime placed the gun's muzzle on Lacey's cheek, her sunbaked skin going a shade lighter where the tip dug in. "Evail's got your little girl out at the Ledford place."

"Ain't got no little girl."

"That right?"

"Last time I checked."

"Then you don't care he's gonna trade her to some Mexicans?"

"*Trade* her?" Lacey said, rubbing her cheek up against the barrel. "What's that supposed to mean?"

"You know," Dime said, fidgeting. "For sex and stuff."

Lacey's eyes crawled over the length of the gun then back up at Dime. "So?"

"*So?* I'm here to get you, take you back out there so you can see her before she gets what's coming."

"What for?"

"Evail told me to." Dime pressed the muzzle in deeper.

"Evail, huh?" Lacey said. "Been a while since I seen his skinny ass."

"Just go on and stand up. Don't make this harder than it's got to be."

Lacey smiled, doe eyes looking up at him, then turned and took the barrel into her mouth, gagging when her lips touched the trigger guard. Dime let out a small whimper, but didn't move the gun. Lacey slurped away at the piece until eventually Dime could stand it no longer.

She worked him like a professional, pulling out all the stops for Dime Ray Belly. His sweatpants were down around his ankles, eyes closed, lips curled, when she snatched the gun from his hand and leveled it out on his short, thick member.

Dime let out a little yip as a thin white line drizzled from his tip. Lacey's brows arched, her eyes going from the dribble to the man as her finger found the trigger.

"Know some guys like it rough," Lacey said, "but damn, Dime."

He made a move for her, a quick jerk of his shoulders, but Lacey cocked the hammer back and said, "You so much as touch me, man, and I'll blow your nasty turd dick off. Don't give a shit about you, or whatever you came here to tell me. I'm getting the fuck out of here." Lacey shook the gun at him and took a step back. "We clear, man?"

Dime put both hands to his crotch and nodded.

She took another step back, keeping the gun on Dime, his sweatpants still bunched around his ankles, dick hanging shriveled and drained. Lacey grabbed her purse and an overstuffed sequined backpack. When she made it through the door, she turned and ran for the busted Impala Dime had driven since high school.

Lacey had to hotwire the Impala. No way she was going back in for Dime's keys. She was almost a mile away from the motel—going in the opposite direction of the Ledford place, as far away from the creek as she could get—when she heard a dog bark. Sounded like it was coming from inside the car. Then she saw the lights, felt the vibration, and realized it was Dime's cell.

The two fuzzy purple dice dangling from the rearview mirror swayed, side to side, as Lacey read the name glowing on the screen. She thought about pitching the phone out the window. She picked it up instead.

"You really think your dumbass cousin could bring me in, Evail?" The car slowed as Lacey pulled off on the shoulder. "Twin Bridges? The hell you want me to meet you at the creek for?"

She dug at her jeans until she found a crumpled cigarette and placed it in her lips.

"And if I do, what's in it for me?" she said. "How much?"

Lacey ran her tongue along the front of her teeth, tasting both men. She spat out the window. The Impala's tires crunched as she pulled a U-turn on the dark highway. They squealed when she hit the gas.

Jo was caught beneath the great rock. Dark like cave dark. Black like the cellar had been, but different. The water churned around her, the slow pulse of the creek thudding out a heartbeat's rhythm. Jo writhed inside Big Mother's watery womb, slapping at the boulder's mossy underbelly. She could feel the dread rising from her heart to her head. She had to keep her wits about her. Had to think it all through. Had others been down to these depths? Was that why the rock had been given such a name? Those questions gave her hope, hope that others had survived to tell of the bottom.

Jo found hold against her captor, the rock cold and slick on her bare feet. She pushed and the current took over, ripping her loose of Big Mother's clutches.

She broke the surface, inhaling the night as she punched at the water. The air tasted of honeysuckles and new life. She dog paddled until she could stand. Water dripped from the tattered remains of the blue dress. The strapless bra gone, swept away in the undertow. Jo was exposed but unaware. She floated on. Big Mother seemed smaller now, like all hardships overcome. Jo lay back in the water and it was no longer cold.

The sky was chock-full of spermy clouds. A few dots of light shone through. Jo floated on her back, eyes to the stars. Jeremiah had told her once that looking into the night sky was like looking back in time, snapshots of the cosmos from long before. He'd explained how it took millions of years for starlight to reach our eyes. How that single ray had been traveling through space just for her, and once she saw it, it was a part of her. *You're made of the same stuff as them stars*, he'd said. *Stardust.* She'd liked that. Her grandfather always found a way to make her feel special, even after everyone else was gone. If she'd only listened to him, gone back to the junkyard after the game, climbed up Babel to do just what she was doing now—none of this would have happened.

She could almost smell his Stetson cologne, feel the little whiskey bottle in his coat pocket pressing against her. She'd never seen him take a drink. Not a drop. Why he kept that bottle so close she didn't know. But she knew it was a hard way to live.

Jo floated along and felt her grandfather in the water. Soon the underbelly of Twin Bridges replaced the stars. A swallow darted out, zigzagging through the night as Jo stood from the water. She couldn't shake the thought of her Pop. She felt him in this place.

Exiting the creek, Jo looked back over her shoulder to Big Mother, smaller now in the distance. When she made it up the trail leading to the highway, she stood for a moment, still thinking of Jeremiah. He would come for her. She knew it. Jo looked over the bridge's railing. The creek was empty, the water cooing like an infant.

Lights appeared on the highway. Jo squinted, feeling a sudden rush of warmth. Again, she hoped for her Pop. It was only when she stepped onto the asphalt that she realized how exposed she really was: bare feet, dress in shards, no panties, her bra washed away in the stream. Warm blood leaked from her thigh and forehead, gathering in beads like liquid fever.

She fought to cover herself, but there was no hiding her current state. Jo simply let her arms fall to her sides, watching as the headlights grew brighter, almost blinding, and then the car was beside her, the headlights shining on down the road.

The window made a sad creaking sound as it came down. Jo's eyes were still adjusting, the driver's head only a faint silhouette, a cigarette dangling from thin lips. The tiny orange glow turned red, and in the soft light a woman's face shone through.

31.

"Why did you leave the property? We explicitly told you to stay with Mother."

Colt barely heard Evail. His mind was back downstream with Jo and Jeremiah, hoping beyond hope that somehow they had found their way, hoping they had found each other.

"And that explosion," Evail said. "We circled back and found a truck. A burning truck."

"Told me to get rid of them Mexicans," Colt said, keeping his eyes on the creek. "So I got rid of the Mexicans."

Evail stared down on Colt, the muscles in his jaws pulsing as he said, "I don't remember there being a truck over that far from the house."

"The way all that shit went down, might be a whole lot you don't remember."

Evail narrowed his eyes. "I want to know why you left the house."

The night had grown cold. A chill ran up Colt's neck, fanning out behind his ears like a spiderweb. He shuddered against it and shoved his hands in his pockets.

"Answer your brother," Bunn said, riding shotgun in the ATV with the shotgun laid across his lap, the bloodhounds sniffing the bank beside him.

"I saw her running back through the woods. What'd you expect me to do?"

"Why would she have come back to the house?" Evail said.

"Same reason her dumb ass went upstream," Colt said and swallowed. "Stupid's in her blood."

Evail clicked his tongue as the ATV's tires crunched over the rocky creek bank. They had continued upstream maybe a mile or more, Colt guiding them farther and farther away, offering up small bits of evidence to keep them going. He was good at lying. It had consumed most of his life. Lying about his blood, his kin, lying when he got to school and the boys asked him where he'd come from. "Back over in Yell County," he'd say. Or sometimes Colt named towns like Memphis or New Orleans, cities he'd never seen, only heard of.

"She might be stupid," Evail said, "but she seems to be skilled at evading us."

"These woods big, son," Bunn said. "She could be any-where. We better go on up a little farther."

The ATV's engine roared, sending pebbles flying from beneath its tires. Colt watched them disappear around the next bend. He paused there, alone, and bent to the water, touching it with his palm. For a moment he thought he could feel Jo, like he had the night before, but the feeling was erased by the sound of the ATV already coming back down the creek. Colt stood, steadying himself as the two men approached.

"Belladonna probably about to have a stroke," Bunn said, restless now in the front seat. "Let's get on home."

"We don't want Mother to worry," added Evail.

"What about the Mexicans?" Colt said.

Evail looked out through the ATV's roll bars. "I have not forgotten Guillermo."

"Then what? Why're we giving up the hunt?"

The ATV growled on idle. The creek made its way around the thick-ribbed tires and on downstream. Evail smiled in the glow of the console lights. "Don't you remember the first rule of hunting?"

Hunting with Evail was not hunting; shooting, killing—those words better described the time Colt had spent in the woods with his brother.

Colt flexed his jaw, fighting to keep his cool.

"Our little trips?" Evail prodded. "Those were special times."

Colt remembered the stereo blaring out the predator call, the slinky creatures creeping through the night, the way Evail had done nothing with them, just shot them and left them in the fields to rot.

"I remember how you done them coyotes."

"That's right," Evail said. "It's not smart to try and sneak up on a scavenger. They'll see you, smell you, long before you ever get close enough to shoot." Evail's eyes scanned the tree line. "Just like Father said, these woods are big—the girl could be anywhere."

"You think you can lure her here with some sort of distress call? That's what you're saying?"

"I have something better." Evail's eyes glowed in the night. "I have someone she would like to meet."

Colt bit down on his bottom lip.

"This whole mess started because of a girl," Evail said. "Not the girl you're thinking. Oh, no. She was just a product of the debauchery."

Bunn shifted his weight in the passenger seat.

"Look at the old man," Evail said, nodding to his father. "He knows."

"Swear to God," Bunn said. "If I ever get my hands on that bitch, I'll put an end to her ass real quick."

"Not yet," Evail said. "We need her."

Bunn grumbled, gripping the shotgun's synthetic stock.

Colt's mind swam like the current.

"I'm speaking of the girl's mother, Colt." Evail's voice echoed up from the water as if he were inside the boy's head.

"Jo don't even know her momma. She's *never* known her. Besides, how the hell's that woman gonna find us out here?"

"I gave Dime a call when we went upstream a moment ago." Evail paused and turned his eyes on Colt.

"My ass. No service on the creek."

Evail lifted his satellite phone from a dry bag in the back of the ATV. "When the call finally went through, it wasn't Dime who answered. Can you guess who answered my call, little brother?"

The look in Evail's eyes, Colt couldn't read it. All the years he'd spent under the same roof with him, and still he couldn't read him.

"Lacey Brewer." Evail leveled his gaze back out on the water, ignoring the way Bunn was bristling beside him. "Apparently, she got the best of cousin Dime. So I asked her to pick the girl up for me at Twin Bridges. It's the only possible exit point downstream."

"If all that's true and this woman really is Jo's mom, then why the hell would she bring her to you?" Colt said, staring straight back at his brother now.

"She's desperate. There's no telling what she might do."

Colt clenched his fists and tried to think of another way.

"I know what you're doing out here, Colt. I know why you didn't follow the plan. Why you didn't answer my call. And I don't blame you. Every man is subject to his own vices. But please, tell me this," Evail said, licking his lips. "Was your little romp worth it?"

Colt's fingernails dug into his palms as he remembered the bed and Jo and how she'd shown him the way. It wasn't just the one night, though, it was everything that led to it: the creek, the canoe, all the days he spent chasing her, courting her, a glimpse of a life that was so different from the one he'd known.

"Could you feel it when you came together?" Evail said.

A shadowy image of Jo beneath the covers flashed through Colt's mind. He pushed it down, calling up a memory of her reclining in the red canoe instead. The way it moved when she moved. How he'd felt like they were connected in a way that ran deeper than the creek.

"Could you feel it in your—"

"*Enough*," Bunn said, loud enough to silence Evail. "Stop messing with the boy. Let's go."

"Blood is thicker than water," Evail said, laughing as he jerked the ATV into gear. "But for a woman like Lacey, the crystal rules supreme."

The hounds moaned, restless, finding no scent of the girl this far upstream.

"And, Colt?" Evail waited for the boy to look at him. "Please just stay out of my way from now on."

When the ATV rounded the bend, as soon as it was out of sight, Colt ran, Evail's words rattling through his brain. *"Blood is thicker than water."* There was nothing in this world stronger than blood. Colt knew that now. It was a truth he could hold on to. The woods flew past in shadows and blurs as he ran back toward the house and Belladonna, the only blood he'd ever known.

32.

A single ray of fractured sunlight slipped in through the open window, and Mona knew her twenty-four hours were up. She'd done everything by the book, but the book only got her as far as the Ledford property, not past the gate. Not up on that crumbling porch where the bare bulb burned. She didn't even try knocking on the door. Without a warrant, the Ledfords would've laughed her all the way back to the Sheriff's office.

Mona had done the paperwork as soon as Jerry left the holding cell. It didn't help matters that she'd put the application in late on Friday night. Prosecutors and judges were on call during the weekends. They'd have to review her application, pass it along, and there still wasn't any guaranteeing Mona would be granted access to the Ledfords' land. A twenty-year-old murder case was a longshot for probable cause. So Mona kept going, kept searching, all up and down Highway 7. She'd called every single one of Jo's girlfriends. No one had seen her, nobody except Colt.

There were reasons why Mona had put off talking with Colt Dillard, namely the fact that she'd helped the two get hooked up after the game. If anybody in town got wind of that, it wouldn't look good.

Still, Mona should've been out there looking for Jo. She should've spent the night in her office. She should've stayed there all the way through to the morning, going over the evidence, putting the pieces together. Instead, she was sprawled out on a scruffy love seat in the dingy trailer her daddy had left her, smoking what was left of a king-sized joint.

Mona took a long drag and held it down, trying not to think of the girl, hoping maybe the answer would come to her in this place that had once belonged to her father. The trailer sat beside Blue Hole Pond, smack dab in the center of one hundred and fifty acres on the outskirts of Taggard, a place called Gum Log. Most nights Mona slept in the office, but Gum Log was where she went when she needed to clear her head.

Everything was mixed up and backwards. Mona felt a connection to her father. She finally understood why, maybe, he'd made the mistakes he'd made back when Jake Fitzjurls was the talk of the town. People made mistakes. Everywhere you looked, people made them. But sheriffs' mistakes are like surgeons' mistakes; they're magnified. Nobody blamed Chuck McNabb, not back then, at least not to Mona's face, but then they didn't reelect him, and then Chuck died.

It'd been raining the night Rudnick Ledford was shot in the back, twice. A tornado tore through the east side of Taggard. To this day, there's still a line cut through the woods where those pines never grew back.

Chuck McNabb's biggest mistake had been running his

mouth. He'd run it to Jeremiah, assuring him there was nothing to worry about. Then, when they found Rudnick crunched up in the trunk of that Buick, the chrome bumper slicked red with blood, public opinion shifted. Chuck ran his mouth all over *The Courier*, saying how he was going to catch the killer—come hell or high water—he'd bring justice to Taggard.

Mona had a damn good guess about what had happened to Jo, but she wasn't running her mouth about it. She wasn't doing anything, either, which was better than doing the wrong thing. The weed she'd snatched from the evidence locker hadn't quite settled her down yet, but Mona could feel a warmth growing in the pit of her stomach.

Made her think of men for some reason. How most men couldn't get past the fact that she was a sheriff. Didn't help that most of them had had run-ins with Chuck McNabb back in the day, her daddy always showing off his shotgun, always talking big. The boys kept their distance, kept far enough away Mona never had a chance to find a boyfriend, much less a husband.

She'd enjoyed having Jo around. Looked at her more like a kid sister than a daughter. Mona placed her hand on her stomach, imagining what it would feel like to have a baby growing in there. Would it feel like this? Like getting high? That's what she was thinking when her cell phone buzzed across the coffee table.

It was funny, the way it moved: vibrating then stopping, vibrating again. Mona giggled then put her hand to her mouth, feeling the dope now, good and strong. It'd been a long time. And this was probably some high-grade Mexican stuff.

Mona slapped for the phone, thinking maybe this was the call she'd been waiting for. Maybe her search warrant application had been approved. Mona reached for the phone again, but her hand fell heavy and missed. She blinked hard and finally took hold of the device, eyebrows arching as she read the text from Officer Jenkins.

She was out the door, swerving down Highway 7 toward the junkyard before she had time to remember she was high. The road flew by in melting globs. Stoplights smiled back at her with red mouths, white teeth, the world glowing in a purple haze. Mona clicked at her phone, bringing up a picture of Jo at one of her basketball games. It cleared her out, made the lines on the road go straight.

Problem was, Taggard was at least a twenty-minute drive in from Gum Log. Mona pushed the cruiser on up past ninety to a hundred.

Jeremiah's tongue was swollen and dry, the last of the whiskey sweated out somewhere back along Highway 7. When he'd arrived at Twin Bridges, Jo wasn't there. He could feel her, though, in his bones. She was on up ahead of him. He just had to make it back home.

The sun painted the same scene on a new day. The junkyard hid the daylight behind the towers, long streaks of red breaking through.

Jeremiah looked upon his kingdom as he approached. There was a hole in the fence. It'd been there for years. Mangled chain link cut by a rushed hand, an opening just big enough to crawl through.

Jeremiah ducked into the hole.

He'd never patched it. Even after the police took away

the yellow tape. After a year had gone by. After Hattie died and Jake went to Cummins. Even after some other atrocity became the talk of the town—still—Jeremiah left the hole un-mended.

It was the hole that led to everything else, and if anything, it had grown wider over the years. Gaping now. Drawing him in.

He'd been drunk the night it happened. Jake's voice cutting through the haze, saying, "We need to crunch that car," wired and scratchy.

It was four in the morning. The car looked like any other car, an old Buick that had been sitting on the lot for at least a year. Jeremiah knew what he needed to do. Had known for some time. Things were getting tense with Jake and the Ledford boy.

Jake was the quarterback—Rudnick the running back—on the best team the Bulldogs had had in years. Even Brother Frank could feel the tension. Jeremiah remembered the old coach calling two days before the storm. Saying something about the boys fighting in the locker room. Thought it had to do with a girl named Lacey. Thought she was caught in the middle, in the worst way possible. She'd already had the baby by then. Wouldn't even bring her around. And everybody in town just knew that baby girl was Jake's. But Jeremiah couldn't get a sniff of his granddaughter, not at first, not until everything went to shit.

When Jeremiah crunched the Buick, he could feel the boy inside. He didn't see him, though. Didn't even open the trunk, telling himself it was just another dog that had wandered over from the Humane Society. Still, he felt the weight of what he was doing. Heard the odd squish the

Buick made in the crusher. He'd flattened enough cars—enough strays—to know better. And then, two days later, long enough for the stink of what had been done to fill the junkyard, up walked Bunn and Belladonna. Dumbass Sheriff Chuck McNabb grinning right alongside them, telling Jeremiah he didn't have nothing to worry about, but then he did. Belladonna down on all fours when she found the blood trickling out of the crunched-up Buick's trunk, crying like she was the one who'd been shot.

One more day.

Jeremiah never could get over that. How if they'd waited one more day the big truck would have come and taken away all the crunched cars for recycle. It'd all been planned, and that's what got Jake in the end. The jury saw how meticulous he'd been. He'd waited for three hours sitting atop Babel, waited like any good hunter knows to do. He left the scrap parts out for them, all the hubcaps and stereos the Ledford boys had been gathering and placing back next to the hole they'd cut in the chain-link fence. He baited them, waited for them to show, but somehow, after all that planning, Jake forgot about the cameras.

Only reason Jeremiah got the cameras was because Jake kept bitching about people stealing from the junkyard. Saying it wasn't right for Jeremiah to be out there busting his ass, and then let some degenerates come in and steal from him. So Jeremiah bought cameras. And if the premeditation, the shots in the back—if all that didn't lock Jake up for good—the cameras did.

Couldn't really see him do it on the little grainy video. Just saw Jake walk out there beneath the towers. Two flashes. Could have been lightning in a storm like that. And then Jake walks back, almost stumbling, like he'd run a mile, or shot a man. Looking tired. Bone tired.

Didn't matter how many members of that good ol' Arkansas jury had their concealed carry permits, Rudnick Ledford had been shot twice—in the back—and there was no getting around that.

But Jake let the other one get away, that one with the wild name. *Evail.* And Jeremiah knew, even then, there would be hell to pay.

After the case was over, those three knocks came at his door and Jo entered his life. He'd wondered about that baby girl for months. She was just young enough to not remember anything. Jeremiah moved his girls into the junkyard for good. Sold the house outside of town, the five acres that went along with it, so he could buy more cameras, more locks, more guns. He barricaded them into that place where everything went to die. Concrete walls so thick you couldn't tell if it was raining or snowing or a tornado was blowing up outside.

It'd been too much for Hattie.

She was Jeremiah's first, and only, love. Eyelashes an inch long, standing in the afternoon sun the day before he was shipped off to Saigon. They were already married, and she waited for him to return. Faithful in a way that's hard to find these days. Problem was, the man who came home was different from the one who'd left. Jeremiah had seen death up close, gotten a taste for it, mowed down an entire family in a bamboo hut and they gave him a medal. A damn star. It was that star that put Hattie in the body bag. It shouldn't have been like that, but it was. Mona found her on the back steps of their old house, the place he'd sold to buy more guns, more cameras, trying to stop what had already started.

Jeremiah hadn't heard Hattie get up in the night. She couldn't sleep in the junkyard. Said it felt wrong. By then Jeremiah was sober, and that was hard on Hattie too, trying to sleep with this new man in her bed. Jeremiah was so consumed with the baby, with Jo, he didn't even notice. He took to the girl like he took to drinking, an all-consuming desire. Jo filled the hole the bottle had left and there was no longer any room for a wife.

Jeremiah studied the hole in the fence. It was small, but so much pain had come through it. He took hold of the chain link, remembering the phone ringing in the dead of the night. Mona McNabb, freshly elected despite her father's mistakes. First female sheriff in Taggard's history, working her ass off, doing the best she could for the town. Her voice was too young. Jeremiah remembered that, how she sounded like a girl, telling him he needed to come identify the body at the morgue.

"What body?" he'd said.

Mona had no answer, asking him only to please come to the morgue, and identify the body. He went. Took Jo with him because she was a baby and you couldn't leave a baby alone in a house, even if she was sleeping. Jo slept through the entire thing. Slept as he parked his truck downtown. Slept as Mona unzipped the bag. Slept when he finally saw Hattie and the red hole she'd planted in her forehead, blossoming like her roses had yet to do. Jo slept through it all, but she was awake now and in trouble. Jeremiah couldn't wrap his mind around what would come next.

He thought, maybe, if Jo were up there, waiting for him when he got inside the office, maybe then he'd come back and fix that hole in the goddamn fence. Maybe this would be the end.

A Dodge Charger, all souped-up and clean with *Sheriff* and *Craven County* emblazoned on the side, sat in front of his office. Jeremiah let himself hope, imagining Jo cupping a mug of hot cocoa, steam rising and warming her cheeks.

But there was only Mona, waiting in her squad car, alone.

"Holy shit," she said and popped the door. "Got a text from Officer Jenkins. Said he saw you walking up the road with that—"

"You found her yet?"

"I's just about to ask you the same thing."

Jeremiah looked back to the hole in the fence. The history ran deep in these blood-soaked, hallowed grounds. He clutched the rifle and made up his mind, wishing suddenly for another shot at those bastards. Sometimes, that was the only answer.

"What the hell are you wearing?"

Jeremiah had forgotten about the ghillie suit. He looked down at himself. "My sense of fashion was compromised by the United States Marine Corps."

"Tell me you didn't go out there."

"Where've you been?"

"I've been right here," Mona said, stepping out of the cruiser, "doing my damn job."

"Your job, huh?"

"What's that supposed to mean?"

"Means I wouldn't put it past a McNabb to sit on her hands," Jeremiah said, walking past her toward the office, "especially while the shit's going down."

"What was 'going down,' Jerry? You're telling me you went out there? To the Ledford place?"

"Yeah," he said and walked through the office door, "I did. And just as soon as I get loaded up, I'm going back out there."

Mona stepped into the office as Jeremiah disappeared behind the vault's steel door. She said, "*Loaded up?* What's that even mean?"

Jeremiah emerged again, holding a tattered cardboard box. He took a single bullet and raised it to the light coming through the door.

"This is a three-oh-eight, full metal jacket," he said, spinning the bullet between two fingers. "Barely see these anymore. Everybody's going for hollow points now. But I can hit a target the size of a baseball from eight hundred yards with this. Don't have to worry with ballistics when you can shoot—and I can still shoot."

He emptied the box into a pocket on his ghillie suit. Jeremiah stared hard into Mona's eyes, daring her to say something, anything. "*This* is what I call 'loaded up.'"

The home phone rang out across the living room. They both turned to it, then back to each other, the bullets jingling in Jeremiah's pockets.

"Expecting a call?" Mona said, going for the phone.

"Let the machine pick it up."

"God, Jerry, you're probably the only person left in America with a landline and an answering machine."

Jeremiah watched as Mona lifted the receiver to her ear. Her mouth fell open but no words came out.

"Who is it?" he said.

"It's . . ." Mona shook her head, both hands trembling as she pushed the phone his way. "It's for you."

33.

Lacey dropped the little pill in the glass of water and sat it atop the Gideons Bible on the nightstand. She stirred the drink with her index finger. The water remained clear and cool.

Lacey had gone back to the Motel 6 just outside of Taggard, the same room where she'd done Dime dirty. Checkout wasn't until eleven and she didn't have anywhere else to go. Evail's snaky voice played on repeat inside her head. He'd mentioned a shit-ton of money, more than ten years' worth of blowjobs. Said he'd pay Lacey all of it if she'd just bring him the girl.

Jo was on the bed, legs at odd angles, snoring softly. She wore one of Lacey's old T-shirts. The shirt was too big, but good for sleeping, *This Is My Happy Face* plastered across the front in loud black letters.

Lacey had stripped Jo from the remains of her Homecoming dress. It was painful. She remembered how her daughter had looked all those years before, every inch of her skin soft and warm, carrying with it the scent of cookie dough, a little salty but sweet.

Everything was different now.

Short dark hairs rose amidst razor bumps in places that had once been smooth. The girl was big, long arms and legs, a healthy weight. She wasn't wearing panties or a bra, and that worried Lacey, thinking maybe her daughter had followed in her footsteps, but then she saw the bruises already rising beneath her ribs, the scrape on her forehead and the wound still seeping on her thigh, almost every inch of Jo's skin clawed red. Lacey hoped it wasn't like it looked. It didn't matter. Not anymore. What was done was done, and Lacey was sure of one thing and one thing only: Jo was no longer a girl—she was all woman now.

Lacey smoked with the windows closed. Thick clouds hung near the ceiling. She sat, legs curled beneath her, and watched her daughter sleep, trying to decide if she could really do what she'd been asked to do. Evail had said nothing of a motel room. He wouldn't be happy about that, but he could get over it. This was some heavy shit, and she needed time to sit and think. She needed a smoke.

Jo stirred, stretching with her arms out, fists balled, and then she jerked upright, eyes wide and unblinking.

Lacey said, "Easy, sister."

"Who the hell are you?"

Lacey laughed. Jo had fallen asleep in the car as soon as she sat down. Just passed straight out and slept on through till morning, till now.

"You don't see the resemblance?"

Lacey watched her daughter watch her. There was a mirror across from the bed. Lacey always liked that when she would bring the men to these dingy motels. She liked to watch, imagining it wasn't really her beneath the hairy guy or the well-hung skinny dude. No. It was only a reflection.

"I don't know you."

"Guess that's right," Lacey said, still looking in the mirror. The face that looked back at her was no longer her own. In her mind, she looked like Jo—cheeks clear and clean, no wrinkles, no sadness, breasts still grape-skin tight.

Jo was up now, scrambling across the room, peeking out through the peephole and into the parking lot.

"They ain't out there, Jo."

The girl turned at the sound of her name, crinkling her nose at the withered remains of the woman perched and smoking on the bed.

"You gonna make me spell it out for you?" Lacey said, shrugging. "I'm your—"

"No," Jo snapped. "I've seen pictures of my mom. She was beautiful."

"Women get a tough run at life. All that makeup only covers so much."

Jo's hand went to her thigh.

Lacey nodded, pulling from her cigarette. "Looks like you already got a good start there."

"I'm fine."

"Keep telling yourself that." Lacey reached for the glass sitting on the Bible. "Here. Get some water in you."

Jo eyed the glass. "Tell me why you're here. Why the hell now?"

"You're mine, all right."

"I've tried calling you, for years," Jo said, looking anywhere but Lacey's eyes. "Jake wouldn't ever tell me anything about you, and Pop wouldn't even let me say your name."

"Jeremiah?"

Jo nodded.

"Old bastard probably—"

"Don't," Jo said. "You don't get to talk about him like that."

"Fair enough. You smoke?"

Jo shook her head.

"Good."

The oversized T-shirt consumed Jo, making her look even younger than she was. Lacey had the wall unit set on high heat. The smoke churned on the ceiling. Warm air filled the room.

"First thing I need you to know is that I'm sorry," Lacey said.

"No shit."

"But there's more to it. That's why I brought you here. Whatever comes of all this, I wanted us to at least get a chance to talk."

Jo seemed to be counting Lacey's words, measuring them. "I'm listening," she said, taking a seat on the far end of the opposite bed.

"I loved your daddy, still do, and from that love came you."

"How old were you when you had me?"

"Sixteen. Younger than you are now. You imagine that?"

Jo folded her hands together in her lap.

"Best advice I got is keep that pussy locked up. Don't no good come from it, none that'll last anyway."

"So you had me, but then you left me? That don't make sense."

"Not now, but back then it was the only option I had, especially after Jake got sent away."

"So that's your excuse? Couldn't handle being a single mom?"

"Jake was a senior. I's just a sophomore. And he was going to school, playing ball, and working extra at the junkyard, just trying to provide for you." Lacey paused, lifting the glass of water again, offering it to Jo. "We had this little trailer out near the lake. Your grandma didn't like that none, and Jeremiah was too drunk to care."

"He don't drink no more," Jo said, reaching across the bed toward her mother, motioning for the glass of water. She took the glass and drank it down in one gulp.

Lacey sucked hard on her cigarette, nodding. "I's just looking for an escape from all the nights of you crying and me not sleeping, the breastfeeding, the worrying. I'd a done just about anything for a Saturday night. Just a couple hours where me and Jake could go out, have some fun like we used to." Lacey stopped and exhaled. "Sixteen years old."

"You said that already."

"Nothing seems real when you're sixteen. But I'm here to tell you, all those choices you make, every little dumbass thing you do, follows you on through to the end."

Lacey watched her daughter through the line of smoke rising from her cigarette. The girl seemed suddenly tired, face sinking, losing some of its color. Lacey talked faster.

"Evail's the one got me started, but God, he was so

skinny, so weird. There weren't no way I's gonna go with him. Then I met Rudnick—"

"Got you started?" Jo said, her voice weaker now. "Started on what?"

"Drugs, hon."

"What kind of drugs?"

"Just weed at first, nothing crazy. Evail was growing it out back behind their house, up the hills a ways, selling it at school. He always had an eye for business. Guess it ran in the family. It was nice. Not much of a hangover, made the long nights a little shorter."

Jo's eyes lolled. She blinked them back into focus.

"Then came the other stuff. Pills, needles, and finally just meth. Meth was strong enough to make me forget all of it, even Jake, even *you*. And Rudnick was better looking than Evail, and I didn't have nobody like Jeremiah. All my family's back in Marion. You ever been to the Delta?"

"Been over to Cummins," Jo mumbled. "When I go see Jake."

"They got it rough over there, nothing but flat-ass farmland, rice, and soybeans for days."

Jo's head moved up and down. "I've seen it."

"There's a difference between seeing it and living it, hon." Lacey waited for her daughter to give her lip, but she didn't. "My momma sent me to my granny's house. Sent me up to these hills when I's thirteen, after I got my period and a attitude. Granny died about three months before you were born. Think the idea of me and a baby at sixteen just did her in. Then it was only me, out in that trailer, night after night, while Jake was working himself to death trying to give us a better life."

"So you started doing meth and running with Rudnick Ledford?"

"Sounds stupid now, don't it?"

Jo stood, wobbly on her feet.

"You all right, hon?"

"Trying to stomach all your bullshit."

"You sure? I had to clean you up when we first got here. Had to change you out that dress. That hole in your leg looked nasty."

"What happened with Rudnick?"

"Same thing happened with Jake."

Jo was back down again, breathing in shallow gasps on the bed.

"Condoms just made it hurt, and most the time I was so high I weren't worried about nothing. So out pops another baby. Rudnick went to work trying to provide for me just like what Jake was doing."

Lacey paused, the ash dangling from the tip of her cigarette a quarter inch long. She flicked the embers onto the Bible on the nightstand and continued. "Problem was, Rudnick didn't know how to work. Don't get me wrong, he and Evail had been hustling since they was boys, but the Ledford family business was even dirtier than the junkyard."

Jo looked up, her eyes red and watery. "The Ledfords were drug dealers?"

"Hell yeah. Cooked it and sold it. Had more money than anybody in Craven County back then. Problem was, Rudnick wanted to go straight, or I guess *straighter* than the drugs."

Jo groaned.

"Sound like you already figuring out what come next."

"The junkyard," Jo said. "Jake out there waiting for them."

"Yeah. Rudnick started stealing those scrap parts, pawning them off, selling them. That was his big plan. How he's gonna provide for me and his baby that was on the way."

Jo's eyelids began to droop. Lacey leaned forward, waving the cigarette's red tip in front of her daughter, close enough to get her attention, close enough to feel the heat.

"And then Rudnick tells me he's got a big haul." Lacey took a short drag from the cigarette, head cocked to one side. "He's been working late nights in the junkyard, gathering up good stuff—stereos, hubcaps, and chrome bumpers. He left that night and never came back." Lacey paused, took a drag from the cigarette. "Then, a year or so later, Jake was gone and I had me two kids, no man, and was hooked bad on crank. And honey, you can curse my name for the rest of your life, but that shit was hard." Lacey looked down at her cigarette, then back up at Jo. "Hell, come to think of it—I done you a favor."

"A *favor*?" The word came out hot and fast, a fire burning again in Jo's eyes. Lacey noticed the wobble in her daughter's knees as she pushed up from the bed, the wispy smoke cloud swirling around her, and then the fire burned out.

Jo fell sideways, eyes rolling back in her head. The bed groaned under her weight. She bounced, jiggled, and then was finally still. Soft snores fought against the churn of the wall unit, the room no longer warm, just hot.

Lacey smoked the rest of the cigarette and reached into

her purse for another pill. She went to pop it from the silver package, but stopped and looked again at her daughter.

"Got a granddaddy that care for you, even bought you that fancy blue dress for Homecoming," Lacey said, still struggling to get the second pill free. "Hell yeah, I did you a favor. Can't quite decide if I got another one in me."

34.

The kitchen still smelled of breakfast. The pots and pans already clean, drying on the rack by the sink. Belladonna sat at the table, toying with her apron, waiting. They'd been out all night. Why she'd made breakfast she didn't know. Needed something to do with her hands. Thinking if she scrambled the eggs, fried the bacon, then maybe she could call her boys back home.

But the kitchen stood empty.

It felt too much like the night she lost Rudnick, kneeling by his bed, hands clasped, the flickering bulb on the porch calling for him. The light was gone now. She knew it. Heard the bulb get blown to bits when the shots rang out and that Mexican started whooping and hollering, pointing his dirty brown fingers at the shadows with his teeth bared, shining dull like the moon.

The sun fought its way inside and ticked across Belladonna's face. The front door opened. She didn't turn to it, fearing which of her boys had returned, and which had not.

"Still got some breakfast?"

"Yeah, baby," Belladonna said and stood, already

moving about the kitchen, pulling the bacon and the eggs and two biscuits from the oven. She had the whole spread on a plate with a glass of cold milk when she finally turned and whispered, "*Colt,*" the plate loosening in her hand, almost falling. Belladonna caught it, steadied herself, and set it down before him. "Eat."

"I'm all right."

"Don't look it."

"You let her out. Didn't you?"

Belladonna closed her eyes and saw it all again. The way the girl had run from that cellar, darting back through the trees, not caring if the branches took hold of her, not caring what was in front of her, only behind.

"Yeah, I did."

"You know Evail's gonna go full psycho when he figures that out." Colt crunched into a strip of bacon, chewing absently. "Surprised he let me go."

Belladonna opened her eyes. "What you done, Colt?"

"Nothing worse than you."

Another round of flashes in Belladonna's brain, memories of her boys and the greenhouse out back, all the drug-heads drifting around, how bad it had gotten. "Evail ain't the one you got to worry about," she said. "Thought maybe you would've figured that out by now."

"You talking about Bunn?"

Belladonna surveyed her kitchen, searching for a chore to occupy her mind. The pots and pans were still drying. The counters already scrubbed clean. There wasn't a thing left for Belladonna to do except talk to the boy. "Be glad you only got to know him after the fire, after he saw the light of God, like he always put it."

"The light of God?"

"I'll never forget that night," Belladonna said. "Evail running back through the woods, bounding up on that porch out there. And I's glad for it, happy to see him. He'd just started to tell me what had happened in that junkyard, when a great boom echoed out across the hills."

"God," Colt said. "The greenhouse?"

"The flame's nearly white it was so hot. No red or orange. Didn't even look like a fire. And Bunn just walked out of there, hands down by his sides, not screaming or nothing. Didn't even drop and roll. Just walked out from that fire, his skin melting, hair aflame, and watched it burn."

"Didn't even holler?" Colt's face tightened, revealing two dimples in his cheeks.

"Bunn always gave credit to God. Said there weren't no reason to scream. It was a good fire, the white heat of it. Said it was Holy like the burning bush."

"How the hell that man gonna see God," Colt said, "then turn himself over to the KKK?"

"The Klan came before. Long before. Bunn was a mechanic at the old nuke plant. Worked hard to keep that tower standing, keep power running all across the state." Belladonna closed her eyes, tracing over old scars in her mind. "But then the plant went under, and Bunn never could find another job that suited him. Said there weren't no jobs. Not with all the illegals flooding in, wave after wave."

"So he started cooking?"

Belladonna nodded, measuring her words before she said, "Worst part was he had our boys out there selling that stuff. Called it 'Ledford Lightning.'" She made a sound like a laugh but did not smile. "Always thought the name sounded silly, like some dragster over at the dirt track in Centerville, but there weren't nothing funny about it. Fought Bunn as long as I could, but damn, we needed the money. Needed it in a bad way. Should've known better, though. Everything comes at a cost."

Silence hung thick across the kitchen, a long run of it. Belladonna's eyes drifted to a family picture tacked above the table, the two boys' faces screwed up tight, trying hard to match their father's solemn expression. Belladonna was the only one smiling. They'd taken the photo for the church directory decades ago. Belladonna remembered liking the way she looked, a momma bear with her cubs in tow, but Lord, she hated that picture now. Couldn't look at it for more than a few seconds without wanting to rip it from the wall.

"It was the Lightning that led to the junkyard," Belladonna said, her voice barely louder than a whisper. "They say all sins equal in the eyes of God. But I don't believe it. Not no more."

"Always thought Rudnick got caught stealing scrap parts? Thought that's what got him killed?"

"That secret gonna have to die with him. Don't want things getting bad again."

"It's already bad," Colt said. "And it's only gonna get worse."

"I don't blame you for helping that girl."

"She's still out there, Momma. Jo's running through the hills as we speak, running from whatever hell Evail's got planned for her."

"Done all I can do."

"Naw, you ain't," Colt said, picking around the food on his plate. "Need you to tell me something."

The kitchen was aglow in the morning sun, specks of dust floating through the slanting rays. Belladonna's momma had told her dust was just bits of dried skin, might even be some of the old Ledfords, the ones that built this house, Grandpa Moses and all his brothers, still floating around in the kitchen. What would they think? What would those bygone moonshiners have to say about what had become of their world?

"What you need to know, Colt?"

"Evail figured out pretty quick I's covering for Jo. He called me on it, then said it didn't matter. Said he called somebody that was gonna come get her. Said it was a woman."

"*Lord.*" Belladonna let out a long rush of air. "He knows better."

"That's what he said. Like he was getting at something that—"

Belladonna raised a hand, stopping him. "This girl, she the one that stays with Jeremiah?"

"I ain't talking about Jo."

"I am," Belladonna said. "Why you taken to protecting her so much, Colt? Just cause it's the right thing to do?"

"It's maybe a little more than that."

"*Maybe?*"

Colt looked at her now, his cheeks flushed red, young eyes full of something she couldn't name, not until Colt named it for her. "It's serious, Momma. The way I feel about her, it feels funny. Feels like love."

The kitchen turned hot in the morning sun. A new worry filled Belladonna, an ancient, almost biblical kind of fear.

"What kind of love you talking about, Colt?"

He looked away then right back at her, quick. "All of it."

Belladonna jerked up straight.

"What?" Colt said, eyeing her.

"You ever thought about that girl's story?" Colt opened his mouth to speak, but Belladonna cut him off. "Ever thought about why we kept you out here in the woods all these years?"

"Naw, I guess—"

"There were reasons, Colt. Commandments written in blood, and it weren't just your daddy's blood, or even the blood Evail's out chasing now."

She watched it coming together in Colt's eyes, a look of revelation spreading across his face. "This woman Evail called," Belladonna said, "she's where this story starts, where it'll probably end. She's the biggest damn crank-head in all of Craven County, our best customer for years. Bad news, through and through, and we've done our best to keep you from her. Keep her from you."

Colt blinked, slow at first then faster as he stood. The chair fell behind him, rattling loud across the kitchen. A dust cloud rose up from the floor and flickered in the morning light, the ghosts of the dead Ledfords dancing again.

"Call him," Colt said.

"Who?"

"Evail. Call his ass and make him tell you where that woman's taking her. Where they're gonna meet up."

"What makes you think he's gonna tell me? You and me, Colt, we're in the same boat when it comes to Evail."

Colt clenched his fists, rage welling up, a hot burn like whiskey. Belladonna knew the look. All the Ledford men carried it down deep inside of them. "What're you gonna do if he tells me?"

"Call him," Colt said again, taking the rotary phone off the hook and passing it to her.

Belladonna knew he wouldn't quit, not with that old Ledford fire burning in him. There was only one way she could get Evail to talk to her, only one other card she had left to play.

Evail answered after the first ring.

"Tell me where that bitch is taking her." Belladonna hadn't planned on cursing, the word just came hot out of her mouth, leaving a taste like blood. "No, you listen, Evail. You answer me and I won't tell nobody how you changed when you came back from prison. Tell me now, son, and that secret dies with me. Won't nobody have to know what you really are."

Belladonna could hear him breathing on the other line. She could almost see Evail's eyes going to Bunn, wondering if she'd ever told the old man, wondering if that was why his father never looked his only surviving son in the eyes. It wasn't. She'd never told a soul about Evail's tastes, and if Evail wanted to keep it that way, he better get to talking, fast.

"Yeah, I know, Evail. Colt's standing right here." Belladonna extended the phone toward the boy, arching her eyebrows at him. "Say something."

Colt said, "Hey."

The phone was pressed tight into Belladonna's cheek again, thick hair spooling around the coiled cable as she fought to stand her ground. She'd sat back and watched her boys make every wrong turn in the book, and she was tired of it. So damn tired her knees shook and her lips trembled, listening as Evail finally told her what she wanted to know. Belladonna said, "All right," and then she hung up the phone.

"They're meeting the Mexicans at the nuclear plant. The tower. Evail said Lacey was gonna bring the girl to them and he was gonna pay her for it." Belladonna stopped, like even having to speak it was too much. "That what you wanted to hear?"

Colt said nothing. All the fury, all the fire from before—gone—replaced now with a new fear, hollow eyes staring back at a woman he knew was no longer his mother. The dust twinkled in the sunlight, gathering in his ears and nose, seeping into his pores. He yanked the phone back from the wall, spinning the rotary dial quick, clinking out the numbers.

"Evail ain't got nothing else to say to you," Belladonna said. "Hell, he may not talk to me after all this."

Colt kept his back to her, standing there in the dusty sunlight, the remains of all that had come before him floating in the air.

"Yeah," Colt said, nodding like whomever he was talking to now was standing right beside him. "I need to speak with Jeremiah."

35.

The phone hung in Mona's hand between them. Jeremiah looked at her as if she were holding a live snake by the tail. She extended the phone out even farther and shook it.

The receiver was warm against Jeremiah's ear, still carrying Mona's heat. The boy's words were shaky, uneven, but the old man heard what he needed to hear. Jeremiah registered the location and reached into his pocket, running his fingers over one of the long sharp bullets, cold to the touch.

"So they're headed up toward Denton?" Jeremiah said. "That's where they're taking her?"

On the other line, Colt asked the old man if he was deaf.

"Appreciate this, Colt. Stay put. You hear me?" Jeremiah pressed the phone tight to his ear, trying to muffle the boy's shouts. "All right, *Denton*. I'm on my way."

He brushed past Mona and slammed the phone down on the receiver. She took hold of his arm, her grip stronger than expected.

"What?"

"You're not going to Denton. Me and Officer Jenkins can beat them there, get Jo back, and all this'll be done."

"Same way your daddy took care of everything?" Jeremiah said, fighting her because he had to. That's what Mona expected.

"Don't."

"Already tried it that way, Sheriff. Ain't sitting back and letting this happen again." There was truth in Jeremiah's words. Even though he was lying about the location, even though he'd heard Colt say the nuclear plant—the cooling tower—there was truth in his indignation.

"And you expect me to just sit here," Mona said, "listen to you say all this, and then what? What happens when you shoot them? Or they shoot you?"

"I reckon you'll do the same thing your daddy did."

"Damn it, Jerry."

He looked at her now, standing there in the doorway, backlit, shadows on her face, blond curls glowing. Mona was a good woman. A woman like he wanted Jo to grow up and be.

"I'm begging you," she said.

"You really expect me to just sit tight?"

"I can't make you do nothing. I'm just asking you to let me do my job."

"You know what's waiting for you out there?"

"I know about Bunn and Evail."

"There's more than that, Mona. We're dealing with Mexicans now, a guy named Guillermo, and he's got a whole crew of bad hombres with him. You and Randy ready for all that?"

Mona's eyes darted side to side, doing the math. "It won't

just be me and Randy. I can have a whole brigade ready, if you'll just promise me you're gonna stay right here. You promise me that, and I'm gone." Her eyes lingered on him. She didn't blink. "I ain't leaving until you promise, and you're wasting time—*Jo's* time."

Jeremiah put his hand on the back of the sofa where Jo loved to curl up and do her homework. In just a few months, she'd be away at college. Her whole life ahead of her. Mona was still staring at him. He looked away, not wanting to lie straight to her face.

"Fine," he said. "I'll stay put. But when all this is said and done, you promise me you'll do it *right*. Don't let Randy dick up the crime scene, don't let a single one of them get away. Whoever's out there pulling the trigger, you make sure you lock their asses up. Lock them up for good."

Jeremiah leaned back and kicked the door to his vault shut. A hollow gong echoed off the concrete walls.

"I promise," Mona said. "We'll lock them up. Every last one of them."

Jeremiah moved toward her, reaching out his hand, wanting to seal the deal, knowing what he planned to do and still hoping that Mona would hold up her end of the bargain. She bypassed his hand, slipping both arms around his waist and squeezing him tight. Her hair smelled like Jo's, fresh fruit in the summer, a dash of lavender.

"And that gun," Jeremiah said without looking at her. "You'll use it if you got to?"

Mona leaned back. "You asking me or telling me, Jeremiah?"

"There won't be no time for a choice. I know that much. You got to make up your mind now."

The lines around Mona's eyes tightened. She gave him a quick nod.

"All right," Jeremiah said and waited, trying to burn the moment into her memory. "Go do your damn job."

There were tears in Mona's eyes when she turned from him, trotting out the door for her patrol car. Jeremiah watched the Charger—blue lights already flashing but no siren, not yet—pull onto the highway through the monitors in the office. She turned north, in the direction of Denton, and the old man sighed.

Before he left, Jeremiah took a half-pint bottle of Maker's Mark from way in the back of a top row cabinet. The good stuff, or at least as good as Jeremiah'd ever had. The whiskey burned all the way down. "Do your job, Sheriff," he whispered, pulling from the bottle again. "And by the time you get back, this'll all be done."

Jeremiah slammed the office door shut behind him and hobbled for Jo's car. A moment later, the Ford Fiesta tore out of the junkyard, heading west, toward the nuclear plant—the tower—the best position in the whole of Craven County for a sniper to set up an ambush.

Inmate: 06-2140
Cummins Unit
P.O. Box 500
Highway 65
Grady, AR, 71644

The other day I's driving up through the hills around Mount ███████. Didn't really have no place to be. No place to go. So I just took off and got high. I weren't smoking nothing, if that's what you're wondering. I's just flying across them blue highways.

Zipping around the switchback curves in my shitty Ford ███████ *like I's driving a Porsche or something. That four-cylinder engine groaning, damn near about to fall out every time I banked a curve. When I made it to the top, the engine caught up and leveled out, but the hills just kept rolling.*

Always surprises me when I see pastures up that high. It ain't natural. But there's still these big green fields up on top of them hills. Somebody, way back when, had to cut all them trees down. Wanted to try and grow something in that hard-packed hillside dirt.

There ain't no crops growing up there these days, I can tell you that much. But there are a bunch of cows. Skinny Herefords with a few Limousins thrown in. Look like oversized goats. That's what I's thinking when I came over a little rise in the road and saw this momma cow standing over a newborn calf.

I pulled over and watched her lick that little calf's withers.

Lick the ears and nose. She'd even bend down and nuzzle its tiny body with her head. Kinda give it a shove and make it move some. But that calf weren't moving. And that momma knew it.

She'd raise her head up and make this low, sad sound. Jesus. And then she'd go right back to licking again, moving that stillborn calf around with her snout, not ready to give up just yet.

I sat there a while, watching that same sad cycle on repeat, long enough for the turkey vultures to catch wind of new death on the mountain.

Them buzzards pissed that momma off good. Made her eyes bulge red. She stood her ground, though. Stood right there over her baby, swinging her head side to side like she was crazy. The vultures fanned their wings and hissed. They weren't going nowhere.

I's almost out the car, ready to do something, when I saw a blue truck with a bed stuffed full of hay come chugging up the far side of the hill. All the other cows went running for it. Like that momma cow weren't still over there snorting and staring down them vultures with her crazy cow eyes.

Couple seconds later, the whole herd stood gathered around that truck, mooing and chewing at the same time. Guess that was too much for the momma cow. She took one teetering step back, still kinda swaying her head, like maybe she wasn't sure about what she was doing. But then she took another, and another, and then she was gone, trotting over to that blue truck, ready to put something good in her belly again.

I pulled away as the vultures closed in.

Jo

36.

When Jo opened her eyes, the woman was gone. She blinked, trying to recall what had happened. Why was she on the floor instead of the bed? She recalled the pain, the stories that woman—her *mother*—had told her. Nothing made sense.

Smoke hung eye level in the motel room. Jo scanned the nightstand for more water, but the glass was filled with cigarette butts now, tomato-red lipstick staining the filters. Jo blinked again, the toilet flushed, and Lacey Brewer stepped back into the room.

"Feel better?"

"Not really."

"Let's go get you something to eat. How's that sound?"

Jo's stomach grumbled. "You go get it."

The woman walked between the beds, still carrying beauty in her legs, strong thighs like Jo's, jeans melted onto every curve. "Checkout's at eleven. Besides, we need to get out of here and get you some fresh air."

"What about—" Jo cut her words short, not wanting

to speak their names. The cellar, the escape, the creek and Big Mother; all of it was still too close for comfort.

"You ain't got nothing to worry about," Lacey said. "Momma's got you now."

Lacey was sitting out in Dime's Impala, waiting on the girl, but Jo had said she wasn't leaving. Said, "No damn way," and as much as Lacey liked her grit, she knew they needed to get going. Time was ticking.

Night had turned to day outside the Motel 6, the morning burning away and bringing with it a strange new heat. Made Lacey consider what she'd done, what she was doing. She kept the ketamine pills on her always, thinking it was ironic, the way those men thought they were the ones screwing her. Then they'd wake up with a sore dick and an empty wallet and what could they say? Who could they tell?

When the pill set in and Jo crashed, Lacey had simply sat and watched her daughter sleep, trying to figure out what she should do next. Didn't help when Dime's cell rang again, Evail on the other line telling her the plan had changed and where to make the drop, promising her enough money to turn red blood green.

Lacey sucked from the cigarettes as if the answer awaited her at the end of the pack. Her mind drifted like the smoke, back before she'd moved to the Ozarks, back to when her momma made her mow the yard in the heat of a Delta summer. Her daddy damn sure wasn't around to do it, and Momma Brewer wasn't about to be caught dead out pushing a mower. Lacey remembered the chug of the small engine, the smell of gasoline. All the trucks honking as she mowed that grass, calling out to her in those jean shorts cut up too high for a twelve-year-old girl. But what she remembered most were the lines she left in the lawn. She liked finishing the job, looking back and seeing nice straight rows, crisp and clean. Problem was, if she got off, even just a little, it messed the whole yard up, and before she realized where she'd gone wrong—every row was crooked. Lacey learned quick there was only one way to fix it: she had to start over.

Across the parking lot, the motel room door cracked open and Lacey shouted, "Come on, girl," waving her arms. "Ain't nobody out here."

Finally, the door opened all the way and Jo emerged, limping across the parking lot. Her feet slapped to a stop on the concrete a few steps out from the Impala, her eyes crawling all over the vehicle. "This is your car? It don't look nothing like you."

"Lordy mercy," Lacey said and slapped the wheel. "Just get the hell in."

It wasn't until they were driving, the cool breeze drifting in easy through the rolled-down windows, that Lacey realized Jo was only wearing the baggy T-shirt. Motherhood, like anything else, she guessed, took time and practice. Two things Lacey'd never had a knack for.

She reached over and kicked on the heat. Didn't take the car long to warm. Felt good. Real good. That cool breeze lifting their thick hair, dancing with it. The heat blew out from the floorboards, warming them from the toes on up.

"See," Lacey said. "This ain't so bad."

Jo said nothing.

"Where you wanna eat?"

"Taco Bell." Like the girl didn't even have to think about it, like she was about to get a free meal and was damn sure going to get what she wanted.

Lacey grinned. "Sounds good to me."

They ordered, and when they pulled up to the drive-thru window, a greasy-faced boy was already making eyes at them.

"Fourteen dollars and seven cents," he said, trying to wink.

"All I got's a ten," Lacey said. "You make that work?"

The boy looked over his shoulder. Not many customers in a Taco Bell at ten in the morning despite the allure of the breakfast burrito. When he turned their way again, he was all smiles, teeth like nacho cheese. "Hell, for the two of you, I can make it free."

"Appreciate that, hon," Lacey said and stuffed the wadded ten back in her bra.

The boy left the window to go bag up their food. Lacey felt Jo eyeing her. "You learning anything?"

"Yeah. How to be a slut."

Lacey let it ride. She'd been called worse. "There's a difference between a slut and a woman that gets free tacos."

"And what's that?"

"A slut gives it away for nothing. Your momma's always got a price. That's the way the world works. You scratch my back, I scratch yours. You heard that one before?"

"What'd you get when you gave it away to Jake?"

"Got you."

The girl brought her legs to her chest and wrapped her arms around her knees. "What'd you get when you gave it up to that Ledford boy?"

"You want me to spell it out for you?"

"I know how it works."

"Thinking you know better than you're letting on."

"What's his name?"

"Who?"

"My brother. You give him away too?"

The name was on the tip of Lacey's tongue when the greasy boy slid open the drive-thru window. Lacey didn't turn right off, just sat there, staring at her daughter.

"Shit, lady," the boy said. "Don't leave me hanging. I'm breaking the law here."

Lacey turned, eyeing the bag dangling between them, wet at the bottom from the beef juice and pools of nacho cheese.

"Thanks, baby," she said and snatched the bag, already rolling up the window.

"That's it?" barked the boy. "Give you fourteen bucks' worth of tacos and all I get is a lousy *thanks*?"

The window was only a crack now, but Lacey couldn't keep her mouth shut. "What you expecting?"

"Thought maybe your sister there would show me some leg," he said and grinned. "Fourteen bucks' worth."

Lacey turned to Jo. The girl's mouth hung wide open, eyebrows raised. "You wanna show the boy your appreciation, *sis*?"

Jo's mouth snapped shut. She looked from her mother to the boy, fingers curling around the hem of the oversized T-shirt. The boy's eyes burned hot on her legs. When she finally lifted the shirttail, revealing the deep purple bruising and busted meat of her thigh—the wound looking something like the innards of a lukewarm soft taco—the boy sucked air and slammed the drive-thru window. Lacey laughed loud and free. The tires screeched as they drove away.

They didn't make it far. Jo kept watching the woman trying to eat and drive, and finally, after they'd swerved twice onto the rumble strip, Jo'd had enough.

"God, just pull over."

"What? Why?"

"For one thing, I don't want to die because you're trying to drive and shove that taco in your mouth. And for another," Jo said, staring at Lacey with the look all teenage girls give their mothers at some point, "you're not even going the right way."

They sat and ate in the gravel parking lot where there once stood a gas station, two holes bored down in the pavement where the pumps had been. The October breeze swirled across the blacktop. They left the heat on while they ate.

"Not too bad, huh?"

Jo swallowed the last of her four tacos but didn't say anything.

"Remember when I could eat like that. Enjoy it."

"Why don't you cut it with all the 'Mom' shit," Jo said. "Just take me back to Pop."

"That's the plan, hon, but you think he's gonna wanna see you in a T-shirt with nothing on underneath? You think that might raise his suspicions a little? Make him start wondering what you been doing since he seen you last?"

Colt's bed came back to Jo in waves, how it was bad then good then bad again. How it had led to this. Jo was sure of that now, confident God was punishing her. This was what Brother Frank had been talking about behind the pulpit in Christ *Zone* for all those years. This was hell, plain and simple. The only way it could get any worse was if Jeremiah found out. Jo decided then and there she'd do whatever she could to keep it from him.

"I don't got no more clothes."

"Maybe I could help you out."

"You got clothes?"

"I got a backpack in the trunk. Look like we might be about the same size."

"Fine."

They exited the vehicle. Jo watched as Lacey popped the trunk, lifted a sequined backpack, and dumped its contents amidst the jumble of beer bottles, electrical wires, and other things Jo didn't think were legal.

"Gross. Have you been living in this car or something?"

"Or something," Lacey said, dropping a pleated thong into the trunk. "Go on. Pick you out whatever you're gonna wear for your big return."

Jo rolled her eyes. She could count the times she'd rolled her eyes—and gotten away with it—on one hand back in the junkyard. Jeremiah wouldn't stand for such a thing, but it was like this woman deserved such treatment, like she was begging for it.

"Looks like a bunch of shit, you ask me. Stinks too." Jo lifted dirty blouse after dirty blouse, halter tops with spaghetti straps, red bras, pink panties, and shoes with six-inch heels.

Jo was holding a spiky stiletto, trying to think up some underhanded hooker joke, when she was hit from behind.

It was a hard blow, sending her reeling headfirst into the trunk. The lid slammed, a sharp sound like gunfire, but Jo did not hear it. The seedy undergarments, the jagged shoes—her mother's world—condensed around her.

37.

Jeremiah had taken the back roads, driven up on the far side of the plant, and parked about a half mile out from the tower. It loomed above him now. A convex cylinder shaped something like an old blunderbuss. Jeremiah remembered the steam rising from it back in Taggard's glory days, back when the town was booming. How Jake had always called it the "Cloud Maker" when he was a boy. Now the sky was silky blue, barely a cloud in sight.

He trotted against his limp past the crumbling reactors lining the lakeshore, rifle in one hand, bottle in the other, pulling from it as he went. The stairs were rusted and spiraled around the tower. With each pass Jeremiah looked down on the fractured parking lot, fissures where water had settled and frozen, expanding and creating a tangled web of cracks. By the time he climbed to the top, Jeremiah was so high he could barely see anything.

The blue sky turned suddenly black and Jeremiah felt his heart darken with it. He was back in the jungle again, crouched on a ridge, the M21 aimed directly through the window of a bamboo hut. He glanced over his shoulder, wanting to ask Carlos something about wind direction, but found only the rusted exhaust pipes zigzagging across the top of the tower. Jeremiah blinked, half remembering the Bouncing Betty that had taken Carlos's left leg, and eventually his life. Jeremiah had carried his spotter through the jungle, holding out hope he could somehow get Carlos all the way back to Houston, but barely made it a mile before he came to the ridge and that little bamboo hut that would haunt his dreams forever.

Down below the tower, the first vehicle pulled into the plant parking lot, but Jeremiah did not see it. He was lost in the memory now, stepping into the hut after he'd pulled the trigger, wondering if what he'd done had had anything to do with war, or was it just a way to make up for Carlos, for losing him? Each member of the family was lying face down with red stains budding out of their backs. Jeremiah had taken the shots center mass. The jungle was dense. A twig could alter a bullet's flight enough to cause a miss, but if he was aiming for the torso, there was a good chance missing the heart meant hitting the lungs. Either way, a kill was a kill.

Blood dripped through the cracks in the bamboo floors. Jeremiah moved toward the bodies, putting his fingers to their necks, checking for a pulse. One kill. Two kills. Three kills. Four. They added up, each body a little different than the last. Some warmer than the others. Some cold.

The girl with the broken-heart birthmark lay curled on her side under the open-air window where she'd looked through the scope at Jeremiah and smiled. His training told him he had to check her pulse and confirm his kill—there was a Bronze Star waiting for him.

The girl was still beneath his feet. He could feel her, but somehow he knew the girl wasn't the same anymore. The old man, the young man—every man that Jeremiah had ever been or would ever be—leaned forward and pushed the girl's shoulder until her face was revealed. There was no birthmark. Not anymore.

There was only Jo.

A rose grew out from her open mouth where her tongue should've been. The petals widened, the stem extended, taller, longer, the thorns dimpling her pale pink lips. Then, without warning, the petals wilted, going brown at the tips. Jeremiah caught the flower before it touched the blood-soaked floor, but he could still feel it dying. He jerked, trying to save what he could. He jerked again, harder this time, and Jo's eyes opened, darting down to the prickly stem then back up at Jeremiah. She shook her head, her eyes telling him, *No*.

But Jeremiah could not stop.

Not then.

Not now.

He shook himself loose of the past, gave his heart time to steady, and brought the rifle to his shoulder, peering through the scope as the tower creaked in the mounting wind. The blue sky was gone, replaced with a line of swirling dark clouds. From this far up Jeremiah couldn't tell the two men apart, just shapes where head and shoulders—hearts—should be. But he knew it was them. The vehicle was too small to be a car, and there were two of them. The Ledfords. Jeremiah could just make out Evail's shaved head and Bunn's hulking figure. The boy wasn't with them.

Then the other vehicles rolled in, two trucks driving fast. The Mexicans. The rifle barrel moved and again Jeremiah could only make out faint shapes. No telling them apart from this high. The wind kicked up and brought with it a chill. Jeremiah could feel the storm coming in his bones. He imagined taking the shot. The creek, those calm dark waters far behind him now. If it came to it, he would pull the trigger, and though there would be no little trinket for the government to bestow upon him—no parade when he returned to the junkyard—he'd have Jo. She was all that mattered.

It would be a long shot, maybe farther even than eight hundred yards, but he could make it. In a way, Jeremiah was thankful for the distance. He wouldn't have to see it up close. There was no blood with a shot this far. Only bodies falling, the echo of the rifle's blast reaching dead ears long after the bullet entered the brain. He calculated for the wind and adjusted the crosshairs. Through the scope, the little cross hovered three inches above the man's head. The downward angle would make the bullet rise, but this much wind would also push it down. Three inches seemed about right. Jeremiah clicked the safety off and exhaled.

"Forgive us our trespasses," he breathed, "as we forgive those who . . ."

Evail felt something. A pressure on the back of his neck, a heat, like when you're alone and you glance back over your shoulder. Nerves. The whole deal had dissolved into a clusterfuck. Even the weather had turned to shit. Heavy clouds hung low in the sky, casting swirling shadows across the parking lot as Guillermo and his goons stepped out of their trucks. Evail knew he didn't have what they'd come for. He didn't have shit. Just a phone call to a crank-head bitch who was anything but reliable.

"Where is she, my friend?"

"She's coming."

"But time is up. You not remember our little deal?"

"I remember."

Guillermo cocked his head at Bunn. "So you bring the melty-face man?"

"You didn't say anything about me coming alone."

"No, all I say was you better have the girl." Guillermo flashed his gold teeth. "But I don't see her."

"She'll be here."

Guillermo clicked his tongue, cocking his fingers and pointing them at Evail. "*No bueno*. And that is too bad. I think we could have been good friends."

The sound of tires on the pavement made all heads turn but Guillermo's. Evail looked over the Mexican's slick black hair to the vehicle barreling straight for them. Evail gritted his teeth as the tires of Dime's Impala skidded across the cracked pavement and a woman's face took shape behind the wheel.

Guillermo turned, smirking. "You make her drive her-self? Maybe I underestimate you, my friend."

Jeremiah exhaled and glanced over the scope, spotting the car tearing across the lot. He didn't recognize it, but then a girl stepped out. Despite the distance, he could tell that much.

A girl had exited the vehicle.

Eye to the scope again, he saw what he feared: the

girl was wearing a blue dress, ripped and tattered, barely anything left. She looked bad, worse than he'd imagined. Like all the girl had gone out of her, pure woman now, but there she was.

His hope.

His salvation.

Jo.

38.

Evail knew Lacey was a dumb bitch, stupid enough to spark this whole nasty ordeal, but he never expected her to come waltzing into the middle of the swap wearing her daughter's blue dress. He almost felt sorry for Dime, realizing Lacey must have gotten the best of him in a bad way. Bad enough to jack his beloved Impala.

Lacey stared back at Evail, her eyes deep and black, all pupils, like right after a good drug hits the vein. She had to be high. Who knew what she'd done with Jo. Probably traded her off to some trucker at the closest gas station. She was that desperate. Always had been.

"You think *this* worth fifty pound?" Guillermo pranced around Lacey, crotch pushed forward, appraising her. "Look at this dress. *Come* on."

"She's been running," Evail said. "She will clean up."

"I smell bad pussy, my friend. This one have something that won't wash off."

Evail felt his father bristle beside him. Bunn recognized her, and that wasn't good, his mangled face quivering at the sight of the woman who had started it all. Bunn's fingers flexed around the black plastic stock of the shotgun resting across his lap.

"I could show you a thing or two, José." Lacey's voice sounded like she'd smoked three packs on the drive out.

"*Listen* to her!" Guillermo jeered, fidgety in a way he hadn't been when the guns were blazing back at the house, a look on his face like maybe he'd seen enough.

"Trust me," Evail said. "The men in Juárez will love her, Mr. Torres. She's worth the fifty pounds."

"Veinte."

"Twenty what?"

"Pounds, ese. No way I give you more than twenty."

Evail saw the man's ruse now. All of it an act; get them out here, talk shit, lower the price. Evail remembered the time he'd spent in prison, how it didn't matter if they were bartering over imitation sunglasses, cigarettes, or romps in the showers—Mexicans loved to haggle.

"I'm starting to think I could have brought you the best-looking woman in America, and we still would've had the same problem."

"This dirty chica not worth *ten* pounds."

"Ten pounds?"

"The longer you wait, the less you get, my friend."

Bunn stood from the ATV now. Evail watched in horror, knowing the one thing Guillermo wouldn't relinquish was control. He'd made that point crystal clear right from the start.

"Whoa, John Wayne," Guillermo said. "You want to be the hero?"

"Far from it, my *friend*." Bunn's voice was as ragged

as his face. "I got something to say, and I want this bitch to hear it."

"*Father*," whispered Evail.

"Setting them straight, son." Bunn didn't turn to Evail as he spoke, still staring holes into Lacey. "That ain't no girl, and she ain't what you think."

Guillermo grinned. "I think she a dirty puta."

"That'd be a start."

"*Bunn*."

"Lost my Rudnick cause this little whore couldn't keep her legs shut."

"Sí, sí!" Guillermo said, bouncing on his toes. "She not even worth ten pounds."

"Naw, she ain't worth nothing. Matter of fact, I'd like to take this girl with me. If that's all right with you, Mr. Torres."

Guillermo and Evail both stared at Bunn, the muscles around his eyes tense, rippling under the molten scars. Before Evail could try and stop his father, Guillermo said, "Por qué?"

"You want to know *why*?" Bunn said.

Evail's mouth fell open.

"Sí," Guillermo said. "Why I let you take what I have come here for?"

"You said it yourself. *This* ain't what you're after."

Guillermo forced a laugh, turning back to the other men. He spoke to Bunn without looking at him. "You drive a hard bargain, ugly man. I like you. We give you twenty pound for the whore."

"Told you already, son. I'm taking this one."

"Listen, I give you a deal—"

"*You* listen," Bunn snarled, pointing back to the Impala, and that's when it finally registered with Evail. "I'd put good money that the deal—the *girl*—you came for is still hunkered down over in that car."

Guillermo's eyes shone now. "You are certain?"

"This woman here, she's the momma, and I get the feeling like maybe she's trying to do one good thing before her time's up." Bunn leaned forward and spat. "But it's too late."

Lacey jerked as one of the Mexicans grabbed her from behind.

"Yes," Evail said. "He's right. Check the—"

"How much?" Guillermo yipped and clapped his hands together like a child.

"I told you," Bunn said. "She ain't worth nothing."

"No, how much you willing to bet the girl inside this car? You say you put 'good money' on it. How much?"

"Well, I—"

"Would you bet your life, Papi?"

The Mexicans' assault rifles rattled as they took aim on Bunn and Evail.

Guillermo said, "Sound like a deal to me," and started skipping toward the Impala.

38.

Mona was driving fast, afraid of what she'd find when she came face to face with her past. What had her father felt when he'd found the blood dripping from the trunk of that crunched up Buick? Mona didn't know, but she felt the cycle, the pull of it, another page in the annals of backwoods history; small crumbling towns like Taggard all across the Ozarks where people scraped and clawed, just fighting to survive.

And then it started to rain.

Splattering against the cruiser's windshield in sideways gusts. A tornado siren wailed in the distance. The cruiser swerved down Highway 7, the rain running in slicks across the asphalt, flooding the ditches on either side of the road.

Mona fought against the guilt, just like her father had for so long. She should've done more. She should've gone straight to the Ledford place and kicked the damn door down. Instead she'd spent the night out in her crappy trailer, smoking a joint.

The buzz was gone now. Mona saw clearly the white and yellow lines of the road and jammed the gas pedal down to the floor. The engine whined. She was nearly to Denton, home of the Pirates, when her radio crackled:

"Sheriff?"

"What is it, Randy?"

"Got a call from one Lacey Brewer. She said, 'Shit's about to go down at the nuke plant.'" A pause. "Them her words, not mine."

It registered then, what Jeremiah had done.

Mona whispered, "*Shit*," and whipped the cruiser around without losing much speed. "That sounds like Lacey."

"Yeah, I'm pretty sure it was her. You know we went to high school together and—"

"Radio the others, Randy. Everybody. Tell them to meet me at the plant."

"Wanna be more specific, Sheriff? Plant's a big place."

"The tower," Mona said, already seeing how it would unfold, realizing Jeremiah's plan all along. "They'll be at the cooling tower. Not a doubt in my mind."

The only thing keeping Jeremiah from shooting the bastards was Jo. He couldn't imagine why she had driven herself out there, what sort of secrets she held that would lead her to this place, but still, she didn't need to see it done. She was too close. She'd remember it forever.

He'd always thought it would get easier—the killing—but it didn't. The veil was lifted at some point. He remembered the realization washing over him in the jungle, sitting in his position for days on end, barely moving, barely breathing, the elephant grass dripping wet, and him all the time thinking. Too much thinking was never a good thing; it led to answers.

Once he'd seen the truth, Jeremiah knew he'd never be the same. How they gave him time off, put him on rest and relaxation, always with other snipers, or the other deep cover boys like the Rangers or the Seals, soldiers with blood on their hands. The officers patting him on the back, telling him, "Good job, son. Damn proud of you." It was all a trick, a reconditioning of the mind to get him to go out and do what they wouldn't. It wasn't natural to kill. The medals, the parades, the condescending nicknames—it only suppressed the pain for so long.

Sitting atop the tower, Jeremiah didn't want to pull the trigger. Not again. But it was raining now, each drop washing away the years until he was back in the junkyard, the place where all of this started. Beneath him, the men were moving like ants, forming a tiny line as they marched toward the car, the one Jo had driven to this place.

Jeremiah looked down the rifle and through the scope.

A Mexican smelling of hair gel pushed a gun into Lacey's back. She watched as the men approached the Impala slowly. Watched as Guillermo pressed his face to the driver-side window, his breath fogging the tinted glass.

"Is empty." Guillermo turned from the window and frowned.

"She ain't gonna be sitting in the front seat," Bunn said. "Check the floorboards. The trunk."

Lacey's toes went cold. "I'll go with you!" she shouted. "I'll do whatever you want, *whenever* you want it."

The butt of Bunn's shotgun connected flush with Lacey's

cheek. A wet sucking sound followed. Lacey's vision blurred. She'd been hit before. She fought to keep her eyes open.

"Before we get to arguing," Bunn said, calm, cool, "just go on and check the trunk, Mr. Torres. If the girl ain't in there, then we can talk."

"If the trunk is empty, the time for talking is over."

Lacey was about to shout again but a hand that tasted of dirt covered her mouth. She squirmed as the first tear sliced down her cheek and across the man's scaly knuckles, blending in with the rain.

Guillermo eyed her as he slinked around the car, reached in through the driver-side door, and popped the trunk. He moved toward the rear of the vehicle, walking on his toes, taking his time. Guillermo stuck his head in then leaned back, a sad look on his pointy face as he waved a skinny finger, each movement getting faster, more frantic.

"You fuck me? That's what this is? Get the beaner out in the sticks and try to fuck him?"

Evail opened his mouth, but Guillermo cut him off, shaking his head as he slammed the trunk lid shut. "The *one* thing I told you. That day in Texas? I told you not to fuck me. I told you *I* was the boss."

Lacey's eyes darted between Guillermo and Evail. Evail's mouth hung partway open, like he couldn't believe what was happening. Lacey could believe it, though. She knew guys like Guillermo. She knew he didn't play fair. Guillermo had some sort of score to settle, his own personal bone to pick, and a bunch of cronies with assault rifles.

"*Me* pay *you* money for a girl? It was silly to even think this. Maybe you didn't. Maybe this is why you have not deliver."

Bunn's fingers tightened around the shotgun's stock.

"The girl for your lives. That's a good deal, no?" Guillermo snapped and his men pointed their rifles at the Ledfords. "Maybe you don't like it, but it's the only deal you have left, my friends."

"Wait," Evail said, turning on Lacey. "Where the hell is she?"

Lacey closed her eyes. She wasn't sure what was happening, but she remembered how she'd hit her daughter in the back of the head with that tire iron. The way Jo fell hurt her mother, made her insides go tight and burn. Evail was closer now, but Lacey couldn't see him. She was lost in the darkness behind her eyes, remembering how she'd called 911 on the drive in, giving them the location and the details of what she'd done, what she was doing, but not giving them everything. A life of crime had taught Lacey not to trust the cops. She knew the Craven County Deputies and whatever other broke-dick officers Mona McNabb could summon wouldn't be enough to stop the Ledfords. She knew if she wanted to save Jo, she had to give herself up. She had to start over.

When Lacey opened her eyes, the muzzle of Evail's handgun was pressed to her forehead, so close she couldn't see the dark hole or the tip of the bullet hiding deep inside there. She could just feel it, the weight of all she'd ever done, leading her to this moment.

Headlights twinkled in the distance.

Lacey blinked, making sure she wasn't imagining things. She blinked again and the lights were still there, a faint flicker of hope in the swirling storm, growing brighter and brighter. Lacey shouted, "The *po*—" her voice muffled behind the Mexican's hand. She jerked free, screaming louder as she pointed back toward the road. "The *police*! It's a setup!"

Guillermo sprang back from the Impala like a cat, both hands raised in the shape of his imaginary pistols. The approaching vehicle was hidden behind a line of brush edging the lake. All eyes watched as the headlights glinted against the rain, headed their way.

Bunn already knew what he was going to do; he'd simply been waiting for his opportunity. He didn't care if the Mexicans had turned on Evail and all their guns were pointed at them. He didn't care who was coming down that road. He'd preached about God's fury for years—shining the white light of Jesus upon the world and burning the darkness away. The moment was upon him now.

They weren't looking when Bunn pulled the trigger, startling like a flock of birds at the sound. Lacey fell funny, her body slamming against the car, hitting the concrete hard, ass up, the blue dress in tatters, revealing what so many men had seen before.

Guillermo's head jerked between Lacey's mangled body and the road and Bunn's smoking shotgun, a look on the little Mexican's eyes like what had happened was beyond him.

"*There*," Bunn said. "Now y'all best turn them guns around and—"

The good side of Bunn's face fell away before he could finish the sentence. There was no sound, no report, just a whizzing in Evail's right ear, warm blood on his cheek, the crunch of the bullet burrowing into the concrete. Evail went down next, pinned to the pavement beside what remained of his father. The Mexicans were firing toward the truck turning into the lot when the sound of gunfire finally reached them, delayed like thunder by the distance, a few beats behind the rising body count. One by one the Mexicans fell, some with fingers still wrenched tight around their triggers, the shots popping small and pointless in the sky.

The last man standing was Guillermo.

He stared back at the truck that had stopped a hundred yards out, eyes full of wonder. There was no gun. No rifle barrel dangling from a rolled-down window. No gun anywhere. There were only the dead, surrounding Guillermo, filling his heart with dread, the same kind of fear he'd struck inside so many during his reign as baddest of them all.

Bunn's ratty Ford Ranger sat motionless, the engine chugging on idle. Colt gripped the steering wheel white-knuckle tight. So tight, he couldn't breathe. Ahead, all were dead but Guillermo. The little man had his gun out now, a gold-plated Glock, pointing back toward the truck, up in the sky, anywhere and everywhere. Colt ducked down in the seat, exhaled, and when he peeked back over the dash, Guillermo was dead.

Colt didn't hear the shot until he opened the door and started running, a reverberation that rattled down from the tower and filled the parking lot that had stood empty for so long.

Puddles of blood seeped across the pavement as the boy maneuvered around the bodies, looking down at Evail and Bunn, men he'd called brother, father. Then the blue dress caught his eye. Colt blinked and saw it crumpled at the foot of his bed only two nights before, Jo warm under the covers, both of them unaware of the blood they shared.

Everything was different now. The dress tattered like a flag left out in the storm. For a moment, nothing made sense. Colt knew where the shots had come from. He knew they'd rained down from on high, but why would the old man have shot—

It wasn't her.

This woman was older, thinner in places where Jo had been thick. Belladonna's words came back to him from the kitchen, rising like a dismal tide and seeping out through his eyes. Colt fell to his knees, taking the hand of his mother for the first and final time, knowing in his heart why Jeremiah had done what he'd done.

Jo.

The old man would have torched the earth to save her, and from the looks of it, he had.

Lacey's fingertips were still warm, the last of her heat running up Colt's arm and into his heart. Tears dripped from the boy's nose onto his mother's face. He stood, pocketing the gun Guillermo had dropped, and turned to the tower where he knew the old man was watching him. The churning dark clouds were all he could see.

Sirens wailed in the distance.

A chill clamped down around the boy's heart like fingers folding into a fist. Colt knew they couldn't help him. Even if Mona McNabb rolled up with every officer this side of the Mississippi, she couldn't save him now. Colt was the last Ledford standing. He was the one who'd taken Jo away. He was the reason she was gone, and Jeremiah knew it. The only thing Colt didn't know was what the old man was waiting for. Why hadn't he pulled the trigger already?

Colt took one step back toward the Impala, and then he started to run.

39.

The crosshairs traced the boy as he raced through the storm. Jeremiah wanted blood, more blood, enough to fill the hole in his heart where Jo had been.

"Forgive us our trespasses . . ."

He'd only whispered that line of the prayer when he'd pulled the trigger on the other men. What Bunn had done, shooting her in cold blood—shooting Jo in the *back*—was reason enough for all of it.

Far below the tower, Colt stopped running and turned, staring up at the old man like he knew. The rain came down harder, blurring the boy's face, distorting it just enough to take Jeremiah back to where it all began. He blinked, expecting the girl to surface again. Except there was no girl. There was no birthmark. Not this time. That ghost had haunted him long enough. The face that wormed its way into Jeremiah's brain was the one he'd forced down for so many years.

That bamboo hut just outside of Khe Sanh was washed away in the storm, replaced by the crumbling towers of the junkyard, pillars the old man had built himself. It was all the same trick, and Jeremiah had learned from the best. The government had taught him well. The only way to keep killing was to forget, and that's just what he'd done.

Until now.

Jeremiah blinked against the scope and saw Colt running again, darting across the parking lot, headed straight for the nearest vehicle. Finger on the trigger, steady crosshairs three inches above the boy's heart, Jeremiah was ready for the end.

A pressure on the back of his head stopped him, though, the quivering prick of cold steel in an unsteady hand. Jeremiah didn't have to turn to know who was behind him. It was the way Mona's hand shook, holding tight to the gun she'd never fired, trying to convince the old man she was finally ready to use it.

The exposed wires were the first thing Colt saw when he slid in behind the wheel of the Impala. Red and yellow wires dangling out from under the steering column. There wasn't a key in the ignition, either. Colt was still coming to the realization the vehicle had been hotwired when he saw the fuzzy dice hanging above the dash.

Colt didn't question why—or how—his mother had stolen this car from Uncle Dime. There were no questions in the boy's head. Only fear.

Even as he'd run across the parking lot, zigzagging through the rain, Colt could feel the old man looking down on him. Just like he'd done the first time they met out on the football field. It was almost like Jeremiah knew, right then, who Colt really was.

Lightning popped in the distance, illuminating the hump

of a rolling Ozark hill. When the thunder rolled down from the heavens, Colt shuddered and gripped the wheel. He didn't know how much the old man knew—or if he was safe inside the car—but Colt knew better than to try and make a move.

Through the rain-slicked windshield, the bodies reminded Colt of the coyotes Evail slaughtered without reason, the sharp pop of the rifle still ringing in the boy's ear. Belladonna had warned him of this. She'd told him not to leave the kitchen, but he had. The keys had still been in Bunn's Ford when he made it out to the truck. Colt took it as a sign. A signal that maybe he could still save them— Lacey and Jo—the only real family he had left.

Any hope Colt had was shattered when he'd turned the truck into the plant parking lot. The storm had only just begun but the shots were already raining down, bolts of fire from a clouded sky.

Each echoing report brought the pain of what Colt had done to the surface. He was back in the bed again, Jo beside him, smiling as he told her his secret. Then she was under him. Colt regretted that part. He'd moved too fast. Pushed too hard. And then it was over, and now she was gone.

The rain thumped against the window, a steady churn swirling across the parking lot, rising like the guilt inside the boy. There was no longer any doubt in Colt's mind that he was the reason everything had happened. He was the reason Jo was gone.

Colt slapped the steering wheel so hard the car shook. He waited a moment, his fingers curling, forming fists, and then he began punching the center of the wheel, the horn yipping every time his knuckles smacked the vinyl. When all the fire was gone from him, Colt leaned forward and rested his forehead on the wheel.

The rain wasn't as strong now, the steady fall giving way to a soft patter. Colt's heartbeat thumped in his ears, loud enough he almost didn't hear it. A soft whimper that took him back to his bed again. A helpless sound he recognized, coming from the trunk.

Jeremiah shook his head and almost smiled, proud of the sheriff for putting the pieces of his puzzle together. Mona was thinking like him now, thinking like a marksman. A killer. The girl he'd known before would've pulled into the parking lot with blue lights blazing, the cruiser's siren announcing her arrival. Instead, Mona had gone to the highest vantage point possible. The tower. Maybe she'd lost her baby teeth. *Maybe*, Jeremiah thought, *she was finally ready to do her damn job.*

"How long you been standing back there?"

"Long enough," Mona said.

"Long enough you could've done something about it?"

"Way I see it, you just made my job a hell of a lot easier."

"Keep telling yourself that." Jeremiah spoke out the side of his mouth. "But you and me both know you ain't never gonna pull that trigger."

Mona waited a moment before she said, "You keep pointing that rifle at Colt and you won't leave me no choice."

Jeremiah stared down the rifle at the boy hiding inside the car like that could save him. The full metal jacket could tear through the roof of that car and into his skull like a pencil poking through paper.

"You hear me?"

Jeremiah said, "I hear you," and adjusted his cheek on the rifle's stock.

"You told me to do my job. Made me promise once the shooting was done I'd do it right." Mona's voice grew stronger. "The shooting's over, Jeremiah. I'm sorry, real damn sorry, but that boy down there don't got no say in this."

The crosshairs swayed absently over the roof of the car. Jeremiah told himself he'd pull the trigger as soon as the headlights flashed on. Didn't matter that all he could see were the boy's hands. The old man knew his heart. Just like he'd known the moment Jake's heart had turned black.

Mona tapped the back of his head with her pistol. "You see them blue lights coming down the highway?"

"Don't see nothing but that boy."

"That *boy*," Mona snapped. "Jesus, Jeremiah. He ain't—"

"Should've killed both them boys back when I had the chance."

Mona made a quick, sharp sound with her mouth but said nothing.

"Didn't think the little one was a threat. He's just a kid. Probably not even sixteen years old. And squirrelly. Evail's always been squirrelly."

Mona whispered, "*Evail?*"

"Like he had a corncob shoved way up his ass or something. Sure as hell didn't think he'd be the one to come back and take . . ."

Jeremiah sat up and wiped the rain from his eyes with the back of his hand. He wasn't speaking to Mona. He wasn't trying to tell her anything, he was just trying to get it right in his head, this story that had haunted him for so long.

"What are you saying, Jeremiah?"

The old man leaned forward and pressed his eye to the scope again. "I'm saying I let a boy get away before, and I don't aim to do it again."

"You—*you* . . ." Mona stammered. "What about Jake?"

Jeremiah could feel his son's heat in the swirl of the storm clouds. Jake staggering through the junkyard office, asking his father why he's carrying that old rifle out in the rain. Didn't he know it'd get all rusty? Jeremiah knew, and Jake never saw it coming. The boy didn't have a clue why his father told him to take the rifle and go check the yard. The old man had his reasons. That's why he turned the cameras back on. Had them ready to record his only son walking through the storm with the murder weapon in his hands.

It wouldn't have mattered what Jeremiah did that night, though, Jake was too far gone. Hooked so bad on the worst stuff possible he never would get the story straight. Couldn't even remember if he'd pulled the damn trigger or not. That was reason enough for Jeremiah to let his boy take the fall. He'd seen so many soldiers' lives drained by the needle, drop by drop. Jeremiah knew how hard it was to come back down from that sort of high. Hell, the bottle was bad enough. Jake didn't have it in him. Night after night, Jeremiah had watched his son sneak out into the junkyard and give his hard-earned money to those mangy boys in exchange for some Ledford Lightning. Jake was hooked bad, so bad a beautiful baby girl wasn't even enough to save him.

There was only one way to put an end to the whole mess and give that child a chance. And that's just what Jeremiah had tried to do. What he'd spent the last eighteen years of his life fighting for, but now Jo was facedown on the pavement, raindrops battering her blue dress like machine-gun fire. And there was only one person Jeremiah could think to blame.

"Daddy had the tapes," Mona said, her voice bringing the old man back. "He had—"

"Your daddy didn't have shit."

"And the body. Belladonna found Rudnick's body in the trunk. The day before the recycle truck was supposed to come."

Jeremiah grunted and rubbed his bad knee, remembering how he'd slipped climbing down from Babel after he'd taken the shots. A twenty-foot drop, and he was already old, even back then.

"Slowed me down," Jeremiah said and wondered for the thousandth time if the fall had been God's punishment. One more day and Jake could've stayed out of Cummins. Nobody would've had to know.

He waited for Mona to ask another question. When she didn't, his finger traced the trigger, sliding along the curved steel. With a weight set to exactly three pounds, it wouldn't take much and all of this would be over. The boy was still sitting in the front seat, punching the steering wheel like he knew what was coming. Like he knew what he'd done and wanted to pay his penance. In the jungle,

Jeremiah had convinced himself of the same lie, fighting hard to believe what he did was somehow justified. He even tried explaining it to the other snipers, tried telling them the truth he saw through the refracted lenses of his high-powered scope, but they just laughed it off and started calling him—

"Jeremiah."

Mona's voice tore through the jungle and found the old man lost within the clouds.

"You hear me? I can't let you do this, Jeremiah. I can't . . ."

Jeremiah was gone. *The Judge* sat alone atop the tower, plotting his final execution as he watched the boy through the scope. The conversation with Brother Frank came back to him from on high. Jeremiah felt the Lord's pain now. Jesus's pain. It couldn't be easy, watching the people you love turn from you every chance they got. All that killing. All that evil. Jeremiah realized he'd been wrong, though. Jesus would take no joy on his day of reckoning. But still there'd come the fiery sword, the eyes aflame.

Colt jerked his head up from the steering wheel and cocked his ear toward the trunk, waiting to hear the whimpering again. But there was only the rain, nothing more than a sprinkle now.

Without thinking, Colt slid his left hand down past the exposed wires and took hold of the trunk-release lever. He still wasn't thinking when he gave it a pull and felt the lid pop open at the back of the car. He waited, his mind darting to the bed again, to the moment after he and Jo had done what was now unbelievable. *Unforgivable.* Colt could feel her in his blood, the blood they shared, a hot flash of shame coursing through him. His fingers found the door handle. He yanked it open.

A single ray of light tore down from the billowing clouds, but Colt did not see it. His eyes were trained on the trunk lid, bouncing a little on its hinges as it dangled there, wide open. With every step he took toward the back of the car, Colt felt the old man, the crosshairs, the history of violence that had led them all to this place. There was no undoing what they'd done.

Colt was two steps away from the trunk when he stopped and slid his hand into the waistband of his jeans. He'd almost forgotten the gun was there. Forgotten he'd pocketed it as he'd knelt beside his mother and felt the warmth leaving her hand. Colt was fully aware of the gun now, the weight of it. Guillermo's pistol was heavier than expected, like all the power in the world was packed down tight in the depths of that golden barrel.

What little rain was left stopped. A new silence hung thick in the air.

Colt took the final step and closed his eyes, leveling the gun out on the dark depths of the trunk. Whatever was waiting for him in there—whatever he was about to do—he didn't want to see it. His finger slid in around the trigger, sending a shock wave up his wrist, into his heart. Then he heard the report.

A single shot. A soft pop in the distance. A flash of lightning gone wrong.

The gun fell from Colt's hand and hit the pavement without a sound.

40.

The rifle lay beside the old man, a pool of red leaking out from under him. Mona stepped over his body and took the gun before the blood touched the barrel. She wanted to see what he'd seen. What made him jerk like that? The sudden movement that had left Mona no choice.

Through the scope the parking lot took shape. All those bodies littering the ground like sandbags. The Impala right in the middle of the mess, but where was the boy?

Running.

Headed east toward what was left of the crumbling nuclear plant as the blue lights washed over the cracked concrete.

Mona exhaled and started to pull away from the scope when a movement from the back of the Impala caught her eye. The trunk was open. The sheriff saw that now, and then she saw what Jeremiah had not.

A shadow.

Rising from the rubble, the glow from the approaching cruisers' headlights burning the darkness away, revealing the scene in vivid detail. It was a girl. Mona could tell that much now. A girl rose up from the Impala's trunk, the cords in her neck pulling tight as she ripped a silver strip of duct tape from her lips and screamed.

The old man stirred beneath Mona's feet, both hands going to his bad knee and the hole the sheriff's service pistol had planted there. He swallowed before he said, "Mona?"

The sheriff peeled her eye from the scope again and took the rifle in her hands, considering the weight of a weapon that had taken so much from so many. It was a solid tool, well-built and sturdy, but it had served its time. Just like Jeremiah.

Mona didn't say anything before she pitched the rifle over the inner edge of the tower. She just stood there, listening to the gun clank and thump off the walls, and then it was gone.

The girl's voice reached the top of the tower again, another scream, a cry against the blood that surrounded her. Jeremiah's eyes burned wild and feverish in the hazy light, staring back at Mona as she leaned forward and took him by the arm.

"Is it her?" the old man wheezed, ignoring the click of the handcuffs as they tightened around his wrist. "Answer me, goddammit. Is it—"

Mona shook her head and whispered, "You have the right to remain silent," as she bent down and lifted the old man by his elbow. She could feel his body tighten at her grip, the pain coursing through his shattered knee as he struggled to stand, but he didn't make a sound. Jeremiah didn't say a word. He didn't have to. It was like he could feel the girl down there, sitting in the trunk with a silver thermal blanket draped over her shoulders, all of it playing out in flashes of red and blue, blood and time.

Mona gave his elbow a gentle tug, prodding him toward the spiral steps. Jeremiah leaned into her shoulder, using her body as a crutch, and together they took the first step down.

Inmate: 06-2140
Cummins Unit
P.O. Box 500
Highway 65
Grady, AR, 71644

The Royals still howl in the night, Pop. I hear them and I think of you. Think of you now more than ever. Try to remember what you was like back before the tower.

Before the war.

Sometimes, late at night, I can feel Colt through these concrete walls, sniffing around in the junkyard. Gets me so worked up I can't sleep. That's what started me writing these letters.

Got to tell somebody how I can still feel Colt out there. Felt him just a couple nights ago. No way I could hear him through all that concrete. I felt him. Took that little pink hand cannon you bought me, walked straight out into the yard, but he was already gone. Nothing out there but shadows, all them ghosts that haunted you for so long. Mona tried explaining everything to me one night but I made her stop. Felt like if I knew the whole story, that might be the end of it.

Found a litter of brindle pups a couple weeks back in a cardboard box up past ███████ along Highway ██. Damn near a hundred degrees in the shade and there them pups were, sitting right next to that hot black asphalt, baking in the heat with their eyes closed, crawling over each other, scratching for a momma they'd never know.

What kinda person does that? Leaves them pups to die? Them pups opened their eyes this morning. Got them

some nice comfy beds too. And collars. Blue for the boys.
Pink for the girls. All my dogs got collars and big round
bellies. Got me twenty-three dogs, not counting the Royals.

The Royals something different altogether. Wild at
heart. Crazy as shit.

Ozark dogs.

Tried letting them out their cage the other day and lost
two pups. Didn't make that mistake twice. Learned real
quick there's some dogs you got to keep locked up.

Wild dogs howl for blood. I learned that much.

Almost midnight but I can still hear the Royals out there
in that pen, trampling each other and their empty food
bowls. They don't know no better. They been forgotten.
Left to fend for themselves in that little-ass cage. I can feel
their pain now, even through all this concrete, these walls
you built around me, I can still feel them.

And I can feel you too.

Love,
Jo

AUTHOR'S NOTE

Ozark Dogs is a novel. The people found inside this book are products of my imagination. They are no more real than the Boy Who Cried Wolf or any other character found in children's fables. Every event in this novel has been fabricated, stretched to the farthest reaches possible, all in hopes that maybe some truth can be found in the spaces between.

Truth about what drives us, what we hold most dear, and what we're willing to do to protect it.

Of course, any work of fiction comes from an author's experience: the world he encounters, the stories he reads/hears/watches, and the marks those stories leave on him.

The inspiration for this novel came from a story that happened in my hometown. I'm not the first—or last—crime novelist to draw inspiration from local headlines, but this story changed me in ways I wasn't expecting.

For much of my life, I believed there existed a list of things I simply would not do. Lines I wouldn't cross, no matter what. I'd never cook meth or cheat on my wife, and I definitely wouldn't murder anyone.

The older I've gotten, though, the more I've realized the choices we make are relative. Relative to our circumstances. No one can say for sure what he/she will or will not do. Life is much too complicated for such certainty.

Fiction, on the other hand, is the perfect place to explore such complexities.

Any good novel sheds light on the gray area. The space between right and wrong. Or, as Greg Brownderville, "The Poet from Pumpkin Bend," once wrote, "Everything that shatters, everything that scatters, everything that *matters* is a mystery."

By the time I finished writing this manuscript, I knew one thing for certain—this story matters.

It matters to the people in my neck of the woods. It matters to people in New York City and LA It matters because, although none of these characters are real, they could be any one of us.

Eli Cranor
London, Arkansas
2022

ACKNOWLEDGMENTS

For whatever reason, I thought the "Acknowledgments" section of my second novel would be shorter than the first. I was wrong. Dead wrong. The further I go into this magical mystery ride, the more people I have to thank. Here goes nothing . . .

There's a good chance Johnny Wink holds the record for most times mentioned in an author's acknowledgments/ dedication. There's a reason for that. Johnny loves words. He loves writers. He's constantly reading other people's work, underlining his favorite passages and counting absolute phrases. When I was at my lowest, I asked him if I'd make it; did he think I'd ever sell my first book? And he said, "Well, Eli. You either will or you won't." Thank you, Wife.

I call Johnny "Wife" because of a short story written by a dear friend and flat-out killer writer by the name of Alex Taylor. Me and Tay went fishing for smallies a couple summers straight. I learned a lot about writing on those trips. I learned a lot about life. "Write what you write and let the devil take the hindmost." Thanks, pard.

Mike Sutton is the brother I never had. He's my fiercest champion, my closest reader, and the guy I'm going to call if I have ten minutes. He lived the stories I write. Came up from nothing and clawed his way to the very tiptop. I haven't met many people out there who work harder than me, but Brother Mike is one of them. Love you, man.

None of this would be possible without Peter Lovesey. Thank you, Peter, for everything, but especially for hooking me up with the great folks at Soho. Juliet Grames, you're the editor I always dreamed of and one hell of a writer. I don't know how you do all that you do. Paul Oliver, you're officially the smartest dude I've ever had the pleasure of drinking fancy whiskey with. Thanks for putting up with my endless ideas. Bronwen Hruska, thanks for keeping this whole thing going. And thanks to all the other amazing people at Soho: Taz, Steven, Rachel, Sheri, and others I'm probably missing.

Thanks to David Hale Smith, agent and angler extraordinaire. Business is one thing, friendship is another, and you, my friend, are a master of both. So damn grateful you gave me another shot. Let's wet a line sometime soon.

Thanks to Naomi Eisenbeiss for keeping DHS straight, and for taking the time to read my work and offer such valuable insights.

Thanks to my early readers, Robin Kirby, Josh Wilson, John Post, Travis Simpson, and Brandi Easterling Collins. Your notes and time are always appreciated.

Thanks to Ace Atkins for braving a Memphis snowstorm last March to help launch my debut. Thanks to William Boyle for the movie recommendations and getting my foot in the door. Thanks to S.A. Cosby for sending so many readers my way and for being such a genuine guy. Thanks to Michael Koryta for the long talks about the industry and for teaching me to ring the damn bell. Thanks to John Vercher for getting out of bed to answer my call. Thanks to Alex Segura for the love and support. Thanks to Dwyer Murphy for giving me the opportunity to talk shop with my heroes. Thanks to Michael Farris Smith for offering such straight up advice at that bar in Nashville. Thanks to Greg Brownderville for "grape-skin tight" and for writing a poem called "Mystery," which is where I got that final line in the Author's Note. Thanks to James Kestrel for connecting so deeply with my work. One day, I'm either coming to the island or you're coming to the lake—fingers crossed for both. Thanks to all the authors I cut my teeth on: Larry Brown, Flannery O'Connor, Jim Thompson, Elmore Leonard, Toni Morrison, Harry Crews, and too many others to count.

Thanks to Christy Cranor (aka "Minky") for your never-ending faith in me. I hope I grow up to be the man you already think I am.

Thanks to Finley Cranor (aka D) for reading this book back when it was almost twice the size it is now. You recorded every hour it took you to read it and said I had to pay it back somehow. The best I could do was dedicate this book to you.

Thanks to Emmy, my baby girl, for inspiring me to write this story. You're the smartest kid I know. I'm holding out hope that you'll be penning books of your own one day (but if not, that's cool too).

Thanks to Fin, my boy, for showing me the best this world has to offer every single day. You're rough as a corncob, but sweet as molasses. A winning combo if there ever was.

Thanks to Mal, the yin to my yang, my rock against every storm. You're my first reader, my best friend, and the absolute best thing that ever happened to me.

And finally, thanks to you, faithful reader, without whom none of this is possible.